M000201444

THE
BLACK
TONGUE

THE
BLACK
TONGUE

MARKO
HAUTALA

TRANSLATED BY JENNI SALMI

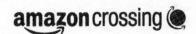

This is a work of fiction. Names, characters, organizations, places, events, and incidents are either products of the author's imagination or are used fictitiously.

Text copyright © 2014 Marko Hautala

Translation copyright © 2015 Jenni Salmi

All rights reserved.

No part of this book may be reproduced, or stored in a retrieval system, or transmitted in any form or by any means, electronic, mechanical, photocopying, recording, or otherwise, without express written permission of the publisher.

Previously published as *Kuokkamummo* by Tammi Publishers in Finland in 2014. Translated from Finnish by Jenni Salmi. First published in English by AmazonCrossing in 2015.

Published by AmazonCrossing, Seattle

www.apub.com

Amazon, the Amazon logo, and AmazonCrossing are trademarks of Amazon.com, Inc., or its affiliates.

ISBN-13: 9781503945845
ISBN-10: 1503945847

Cover design by Scott Barrie

Printed in the United States of America

As long as a working capital of accumulated hatred and suspicion exists at the center of the community, it will continue to increase no matter what men do.

—René Girard, *Violence and the Sacred*

THE GRANNY AND HER HATCHET

You're all sitting here wondering what Granny Hatchet does. Granny Hatchet kills children.

She's as old as the oceans and the sky. She lurks along the seashore, shuffling her feet between large rocks and behind fallen trees. She minces like a mink on her bare, slim toes. And everyone who happens upon her yard without permission either dies or goes insane. She waits until some foul-mouthed girl or boy drops behind the rest of the group, either to take a piss or to text a friend or to look at a butterfly or to save a little baby bird. She waits until you turn your back on her. Then she whacks you right between your shoulder blades with her hatchet and all the air is knocked out of your lungs and your legs go numb.

She turns you over.

She sticks her black tongue out at you.

She has a wispy old-lady mustache.

And then you're done.

You just want to crawl into a hole where you wait to die.

Sometimes she eats your heart. She digs it out of your chest with that hatchet of hers, even if you're still alive. She plants these hearts among her potatoes and waits until they've turned almost black. Then she chews on the hearts with her toothless mouth. She thinks wearing dentures is demeaning. And this chewing can take up to an hour. She closes her eyes and remembers the good old days and how everything used to be right in the world.

She sees everything in the Suvikylä woods. She knows who you are just by the way you smell. When she takes a whiff of the wind, she looks like a fox sniffing gasoline, nostrils flared, alert.

She sneaks around in the shadows and stares at all the apartment buildings with their lights turned on and TV screens flashing and people's shadows moving behind curtains, and she mutters nasty things at those shadows.

She's invisible to most, unless she wants to be seen. She can stand so still that you will look past her although she's standing right in front of you. She's been on Earth for so long that you can't tell her apart from a knotty burl growing on a tree. So if you're walking along a forest path and suddenly the air around you smells like potatoes in a damp root cellar, you'd better run. Don't stop and look around. You'd better haul ass.

She lived in Suvikylä before the apartment buildings and town houses and rich folks' homes at the end of Patteriniemi Road, and she loathes them all. The buildings are too straight and square, and their walls echo everything back at her. She trudges across yards, but only when it's dark, moving slowly and hunched over as if all her muscles were wracked by uncontrollable spasms.

But in the woods she can hold her breath for an hour. Sometimes she lies down so still that moss spreads across her shoulders and maggots squirm their way into her mouth, thinking, *This ripe carcass here is a real treat*. When she coughs, maggots shoot out of her mouth.

One time, the son of that gypsy family, the Hagerts, was walking home drunk along the seashore when he spotted a burl on a tree. He was sure the burl hadn't been there before. "Hey!" he called out. "Don't you be hiding from me or I'll choke you like a rat." The burl didn't move, so this Hagert boy pulled a knife out of his boot, sat down on the side of the road, and waited. He woke up the next morning with a crumpled piece of paper stuffed in his mouth. As he pulled it out, three baby teeth fell out of the folds. On the paper was a message: *Rokelou yike a chat.*

Afterward, no Suvikylä gypsy ever walked after dusk. They all rushed to the parking lot and piled into an old Mercedes, glowering at people through fogged-up windows as they drove off.

Granny Hatchet despises electric lights. She loathes them. At night, in the dark, you can hear her shrieking and cursing. The noise is frightful—she sounds like a woman who has lost her voice but is still forcing herself to keep on screaming.

She hacks at rotten trees with her hatchet and yanks moss off rocks as she scurries by. She nails squirrels onto tree stumps, leaving their little skeletons for berry pickers to find in the fall. When she sees a robin's nest, she whacks at it until only bloodied feathers remain.

She won't tolerate any sort of screwing around on her land. Should she catch you making out on her property, she won't forget until your shameful deeds are settled with blood the color of an overripe lingonberry.

She drinks brown sewage water straight out of the canal and uses it to brew coffee in an old pot. She has at least a thousand glass jars in her cellar, all filled with what looks like black milk. That's why her tongue is always so black. Nobody knows what the black milk actually is, but it keeps her alive. She never gets sick, not even when she eats poisonous white amanita mushrooms and weaves ropes out of live adders.

Someone saw her dragging a boat in the canal one misty morning with one of those ropes made of adders, and the boat brimmed with a thousand live adders. A human child was seen struggling underneath the pile of snakes, but nobody saw the child's face.

She won't set foot in that boat herself, no way, because she's afraid of water—except the shallow water in the canal and the sewage water she drinks. She also won't wet her feet in the sea, not even if the shore were on fire. The sea is her enemy. She can't even stand its smell. Yet she stays near the shore and won't leave. The Devil only knows why.

Sometimes when dusk falls, she pretends to be a little girl. She squeezes her bones into her body's cavities and slumps to look shorter. She hides her hatchet between rocks and walks straight up to fishermen on the shore, cooing to them in a child-like voice that there's some fine pussy available and nobody else ever needs to know.

Those who have talked about this have described her pussy looking like a sucking mouth that mumbles and smacks its lips. If you have sex with her, you end up going to the hospital, where they won't be able to recognize the weird bacteria they see under the microscope.

When the first Somalis moved into the apartment buildings, you could hear her hissing at the edge of the woods and parking lots after it got dark. When the first girl was delivered to the Granny, she kept her alive and wondered what the hell this is, this thing that's darker than her sewage-water coffee. She tore the girl's scarf off and allowed the wind to press it to her own face, and then she just stood there blindly facing the sea, probably smelling the bazaars from distant lands. She stood like that for so long that the girl slipped away. Granny's taken many others since her, and now she knows that inside, their hearts are all the same color. They all turn black and tender. They all taste the same as her gums gnaw on them.

Somalis are not safe.

Arabs are not safe.

If you don't respect her or leave gifts for her at the peninsula, then you are not safe, no matter what your religion makes you believe.

If you're home alone or your parents are out singing karaoke, she will use her master key made out of animal bones to let herself into the stairwell and ring your doorbell. You'll see a police officer through the peephole, but when you open the door there she'll be, sticking her tongue out at you.

And then it's curtains.

No one's safe, except the gypsies.

Maybe that Hagert kid made a pact with her.

Rokelou yike a chat.

Nobody knows what she meant by that. Maybe it was her idea of a joke.

Or maybe she killed the entire Hagert family. After all, they each disappeared one by one. Some say they moved, but who knows— maybe their hearts are buried in the potato patch.

Usually, though, she kills kids who have wandered off the beaten path. Kids whose heads are filled with ideas they've learned from the Internet or their teachers. Kids who think they can snoop around.

When she crawls on the rocks at the seashore, she pauses for a second, twists back and forth like reeds, and smells the air with her toothless mouth wide open, breath steaming out of her.

And when she's really excited she lets her hatchet fly at boulders, the blade sparking as it scrapes the rock face. One time a rod of light was seen in the forest during a thunderstorm. The adults claimed it was ball lightning, but what do they know?

Do you wonder what color her heart is? That muscle has been twitching and pumping blood for hundreds of years. Her blood is probably thick and sluggish in her veins, like blueberry jam forced into a tube.

Why is her mouth open?

Does she smell with her nose and mouth? Does she taste with her nose and mouth?

And I haven't even talked about her eyes yet.

It looks like she's blind, but she's not.

She can see in the dark.

Or maybe she's been in Suvikylä for so long that she doesn't need to see—she knows where everything is. Except anything brand new, like the parking lots and apartment buildings and town houses and the homes owned by the rich. Maybe that's why she hates them so much. All that evenly laid asphalt, flashing windows, the echoes from the concrete walls.

Maybe she actually is blind.

Whatever. I've got more important questions.

Why does she shout at the sea?

Why does she sing to the sea?

Why is she out and about during thunderstorms?

Why hasn't she left us?

Is she really guarding something?

Nobody knows.

You don't know.

All you need to know is that Granny Hatchet kills children. But she means no harm. She only kills those who do wrong. She protects this place. Without her, it would be like anywhere else. This place would be like the Ristinummi neighborhood or Hervanta in Tampere or some slum in east Helsinki.

I so wish you could hear her wail. She cries like a child whose mother has drowned. Or a mother whose kid has drowned. It sends chills through you.

So never, ever joke about Granny Hatchet.

Either take her seriously or don't talk about her at all.

Go ahead and laugh at church during a sermon or during your confirmation this summer if the priest can't roll his *r*'s or if he's sniffing his fingers. But you shut your mouth about Granny Hatchet.

If you tell anyone about her you'll come to regret it; you'll regret it even more than the time you cried in front of everyone while you were drunk off your ass or when you accidentally sent your mom a picture of you giving head to a neighbor boy. Granny Hatchet will stick her tongue out at you and then chop you in the back with her hatchet. She'll bury your heart in the potato patch.

Just think about Granny Hatchet and how she'll crouch and dig out your heart in the potato patch. How she'll remember the good old days and how you know shit about life and how she's suffered.

Your heart can't die, no matter how much she gnaws on it and smacks her toothless gums. Is your soul imprisoned inside that heart? And if it is, what happens to your heart when Granny Hatchet swallows it? Only the Devil knows, but you can't help thinking about it, can you?

Sure, try everything once while you're still young, but you'd better not try that.

Whatever Granny Hatchet is mourning is too much for you to even comprehend.

Her insides are so dark that even the blind will beg for light.

There's no use in crying once she's eaten you.

All you'll find is the Ever-Devouring Night and the smell of a damp root cellar filled with potatoes.

Once you're there it's too late for regrets.

All the little brats were dead quiet when the Sermon ended.

The High Priest's hatchet landed on the concrete floor with an echoless thud.

He turned a flashlight on.

The kids blinked as if they'd just woken up. The High Priest's raincoat was moss green and torn. The sleeves and the hem were covered in red stains. Everyone knew it was fake blood, but the sight of it was still unsettling.

The High Priest shone the flashlight on the little brats.

Six huddled in the light beam. The Sermon forced them to grow up. Their pupils flashed and shrunk. Their adult shadows stretched out on the wall behind them, like six larger and older animals standing behind clumsy pups.

The High Priest stood up and flailed for a second; his legs had gone numb. His mask almost fell off as he steadied himself.

The kids lined up to kiss the hatchet. Some, for good luck, ran their tongues along the blade. Someone giggled but stopped abruptly. After the kisses, the High Priest leaned over and whispered a name into each ear—this way the brats will find out which one they're supposed to keep in check. Nobody knows who is whose Guardian. They'll only find out if someone makes a mistake and all goes to hell. That's when the Guardian has to step in to punish the wrongdoer.

"And nobody talks about this," the High Priest said. "Ever."

They repeated these words together.

"Nobody talks about this. Ever."

"Now go."

The High Priest took his seat again and turned the flashlight off. A green afterimage of his raincoat burned into everyone's retina. It twitched in the air when they blinked their eyes again.

The kids got up and felt for their way out, bumping in the darkness and complaining about their numb legs until they found the bomb-shelter door. It was heavy and hard to open in the dark. Too many hands were reaching for the handle at the same time. Someone stubbed a toe on the threshold. Another said, "Fuck." One let out a raspy laugh. The lights in the hallway got turned on. Whoever was last began to close the door.

Before it closed, the last one out saw the High Priest inside the bomb shelter in a beam of light.

He was crouched down, looking up. It was clear now that his mask was made of rubber, but even then, right before the door closed shut, it looked like a burl on a dead tree.

SAGAL YUSUF'S SECRET

"Well, that was fucked up," Mira whispered to Sagal as they emerged from the apartment building's bomb shelter and into the yard.

Sagal was the only girl who could hold Mira's hand without it getting all gross and lesbian-y. Others had taken off to the peninsula for a party, even though it was a school night. They had laughed and joked and pretended like they were fine. *What the hell did he mean by us being grown up now?* But Sagal couldn't help but feel like she'd woken up from a nightmare. She could tell by the furtive looks on the faces of the others that they felt the same way, too. The rest of them were better at returning to reality than she was.

They'd all turned to look at Mira, waiting for her reaction. Nobody had dared to say what they'd thought of the Sermon before she said what she thought. But Mira just told others to leave her and Sagal alone. The others always listened to Mira. They envied Sagal because she was the only one who wasn't afraid to be honest with Mira. She was the only one Mira took care of.

"Yeah, what a story," Sagal said and turned to look behind her. "I was worried that someone was going to touch me in the dark. I would have screamed if they did. I would've screamed *so* loud."

She saw the lights go off in the stairwell behind them.

"Really?" Mira asked. "I meant what a fucked-up situation. I almost started laughing."

She'd stopped trying to light her cigarette to check whether Sagal had been serious. Mira's laugh came out almost aggressive when she found out she *was* serious. That's the way Mira laughed when Sagal was about to embarrass herself in front of everyone with some stupid Muslim opinions. Muslim opinions were anything that Mira—along with everyone else—disagreed with. But now there weren't any other people around.

"Seriously, how could that story have scared you?" Mira said. "It's baby stuff. Ooh, her pussy was a mouth and some shit. Sick. Stupid, sick shit."

Sagal shrugged and crossed her arms. She stared at the door to the building. She could see sparks on her right from the lighter as Mira began to light her cigarette again.

Sagal had squeezed Mira's hand in the bomb shelter. Mira had squeezed back. Sagal had closed her eyes, although it had been so dark it made no difference.

"And that goddamned mask," Mira mumbled with her lips wrapped around the cigarette. "So lame. All that hype and then some . . . some story about a mink? What the fuck is a mink, anyway? Or a burl?"

A mink is a terrifying, small predator of wild animals such as birds, and a burl is a disfiguration on a wounded tree, Sagal said, but only to herself.

She could smell the cigarette before a veil of smoke spread over her eyes. The wind blew it away. She didn't want her scarf smelling of tobacco, so she took a step away from Mira. Her mom would smell it on her immediately.

"Besides, I recognized who that High Priest was," Mira said, now slightly calmer.

Sagal turned to her. "No way."

"I did!" Mira laughed. "It was Tuure. The Condom Washer."

"What?"

"The Condom Washer. Tuure Aulanko from the building next door. One time, he stole his dad's used condom from the trash because he was too embarrassed to buy one. Then he washed it and hung it out to dry in his bathroom. Jonna had gone over to fuck him when his parents were at a bar. When she went to pee she saw the condom hanging on the clothesline. She asked Tuure about it and he told her the whole story. She had a real hard time keeping a straight face! She called me as soon as she got to the stairwell."

"Oh."

Mira was quiet. Then she faced Sagal.

"What's wrong with you?"

"Nothing," Sagal said and looked past Mira. Lately she'd had a hard time looking Mira in the eye.

Mira followed her gaze and turned around. "What are you staring at?"

Sagal sighed. "Why won't he come out?" she asked.

"Who?"

"The High Priest. That Tuure guy."

Mira shrugged and took a final drag from her cigarette. "Maybe he got locked in," she said. "Serves him right. Let him rot there under his rubber mask, blowing on his dad's condoms. I still can't believe how shitty that story was. Ansku warned me that the Sermon is so unbelievably terrifying that she was getting goose bumps just thinking about it. What a fucking loser. She's in ninth grade and supposedly still scared a year after hearing the story."

"He's alone in there—in the dark," Sagal said.

It took a few seconds before Mira figured out that she meant the High Priest.

"I guess so," she said, then looked lost in thought. "Or he lives in the same building and just walked up a few flights of stairs to get home."

"He doesn't. You told me he lives in that other building."

Mira snorted. "Well, it sounded like Tuure, but I don't know for sure. I didn't see his face."

Sagal looked through the door at the stairwell for a moment, then nodded.

"Yeah, he must live in that building," she said and tried blowing cigarette ashes off her scarf. "I have to go now."

"You're not coming to the party?"

Of course she wanted to.

"No," Sagal said. "I have to go. I'll see you in the morning."

She was about to take off when Mira grabbed her shoulder.

"You weren't seriously scared, were you?" she asked.

Light drizzle fell like glitter on Mira's dyed black hair. A gust of wind brought the smell of the sea from the shore. Sagal thought that the raindrops and the sea smell were one and the same. She shook her head.

"I wasn't scared."

"I'm sorry I laughed," Mira said. Sagal saw her eyes behind the glowing butt of the cigarette, and she looked genuinely worried. Sagal couldn't hide her smile.

"Just don't have any nightmares. That story is not worth it. That's just the kind of stuff that goes on around here. Scaring kids, things like that, but it's all done with good intentions. It's about us all belonging to the same community. You remember what I told you about Iida?"

Sagal nodded.

"When we scared her at the shore?"

"Yeah."

"We waited for her for what must've been three hours, but it was so worth it."

Sagal didn't say a word.

"So, that's the kind of stuff we do around here," Mira said. "Pranks. And if someone pulls a prank on you, it just means that you're one of us. Right?"

"Right."

"See, you just witnessed a prank in the Fairy-Tale Cellar. Don't be scared. Besides, I'm here to take care of you."

"I wasn't scared," Sagal said.

"For real?"

"For real," she said. "But thanks anyway, Mira. Have fun at the party."

"I'll try, but remember—if you're having nightmares just call me, and I'll be there to ring your doorbell in the middle of the night."

Sagal smiled. "I'll remember that."

"And you'll call me, all right?"

"I will."

"I'm serious—I'll run over and I'll be at your door. Then your dad will say again, 'What you want, you a crazy girl?'"

Sagal laughed.

Mira hugged her. Sagal forgot about all the scary things in this world. Her dad hated Mira: she always had money on her. New clothes, new phones, new hair dye. He saw it as a red flag, knowing that Mira's single mother was unemployed. Where was all that money coming from, he undoubtedly wondered. Rent was constantly climbing, so where did it come from?

Sagal could have fallen asleep wrapped in Mira's damp hair. It smelled of unfamiliar chemicals and cigarette smoke and everything Sagal didn't know enough about. Mira kissed her on the cheek and walked away.

Sagal turned to walk home until Mira was out of sight. Then she pulled a digital recorder out of her breast pocket, releasing a waft of tobacco smoke from the folds of her coat. The device was smaller than a matchbox and connected to a cord that led to a set of buttons. Sagal pulled the cord out of her sleeve. She'd been afraid that Mira or someone else would notice it in the basement, although it had been pitch black.

She glanced at her window. There was still a light on in the kitchen, but her mom and dad were probably in the living room and her little brother was in bed. Her older brother would be back when he'd be back. Boys could come and go as they pleased. Soon her dad would realize how late it was and would ask her mom to call her cell.

Sagal wrapped the cord around the device and shoved it in her pocket. The stairwell in the building with the bomb shelter was still dark. The wind rustled leaves in front of the door. Sagal took a step back but wasn't sure whether she was heading to the parking lot or back to the bomb shelter. The latter thought sent sharp ripples from her lower back through her shoulder blades into her arms. She was both excited and terrified, like how she felt when she slowly waded into cold water. She took a few steps and there she was, at the door to the bomb-shelter building, looking at her own reflection in the glass door. She saw the bare tree branches swaying in the wind behind her, trying to steal her scarf with their crooked fingers. Sagal leaned into the glass and stopped before her nose touched it.

The stairwell led down into darkness. Sagal could see only a white rectangle where the basement door was. She suddenly squeezed her device and thought about dropping it in the storm drain. It would fit through the grid, and the next storm would take the player away. Rats would wonder if it was edible, trying to bite it. Water would seep into it and destroy every single sound it had recorded until only silence and things never done remained.

Sagal jumped when a light flashed in her reflection. She held her breath and turned around, dead sure that a flashlight was aimed at her.

There was no one in the yard. Only a car had pulled into the parking lot, and Sagal saw afterglow from its headlights for another split second before the lights dimmed. Her heart was pounding in her eardrums. She squeezed the thin, plastic music player in her pocket once more. The headlights didn't flicker a second time.

Sagal looked around, then over her shoulder. An empty yard, lined with buildings and lit windows, surrounded her. Behind her was the dark stairwell. She began to walk toward the parking lot. The gravel crunching under her shoes seemed to echo from the square building walls louder than usual. That was odd. Odd feet, odd hands against warm, smooth plastic. An odd girl.

The driver reached inside the car to open the passenger door for Sagal. A faint light turned on. Sagal didn't dare look around—she yanked the door open and sat down quickly.

"What took you so long?" The woman was nervous. "Were you thinking of going back in there?"

Sagal, an odd girl, was now shrouded in the odd new-car smell.

"Take it easy," the woman said and touched Sagal's shoulder. "There's nothing to worry about."

Suddenly the woman was holding the digital recorder. Sagal saw her unravel the wrapped cord hastily.

"You're no cop," Sagal said.

The woman calmed down when she connected earbuds to the device.

"Yeah, I am," she said, barely paying attention to Sagal, listening to the audio.

"No, you're not. Cops wouldn't ask me to do this."

"Mm-hm." The woman's eyes glazed over—she wasn't listening to a word Sagal said, mesmerized by the sounds stolen from the bomb shelter.

"I'll report you to the police," Sagal said.

The woman pulled her earbuds off. "What did you say?"

"I told my older brother. I asked if he's still selling."

The woman was quiet. She may have held her breath.

"He hasn't done anything since the last time," Sagal continued. "Cops aren't after him."

The woman took a quick breath, but then forgot to breathe out.

"You're just screwing me over and I'll get into trouble."

"You won't get into any sort of trouble," the woman said. "You could have, if you'd gone back to the bomb shelter. I was so worried when I saw you walking back."

Sagal frowned. "You're no cop. And you weren't the least bit worried, liar."

The woman went silent. She was thinking. Why had Sagal returned if it was so clear that she wasn't a cop?

"Listen now, Sagal."

"What?"

"What you did was really brave."

"Are you some sort of gossip writer or . . ."

"I'm conducting research," the woman said. "And you have nothing to worry about. I'd like to thank you, and . . ."

She pulled money out of her wallet and handed it to Sagal. "This is for you."

Sagal didn't move. The rustle of the bills reminded her of Mira, who always had money on her. She kept her arms stiff at her sides. She had a clear line of sight to the building's stairwell door through the windshield. Wind pressed the tree branches down, making them wave right in front of the door.

"I'm sorry I lied to you," the woman said, but Sagal wasn't listening.

It was strange to think that she'd been standing in front of the door to the building just a few moments before. The woman dropped the money onto her lap, where Sagal stared at it. She opened the car door and instinctively grabbed at the bills when a gust of wind was about to blow them away. As soon as she shut the door, the woman started the engine.

"Thanks so *fucking* much," Sagal said as the engine revved. She shoved the bills into her pocket and wiped her palms on the hem of her coat.

She was left alone in the wind that mercilessly tossed around everything not rooted in the ground. Sagal knew she wouldn't report the woman to the police—she never reported anything. This wasn't some immigrant thing; it was a Patteriniemi Road thing. If someone's car got torched next to the city-housing apartments, there was no use reporting it. If you walked a hundred yards to the garages of the nicer town homes and broke a windshield over there, the cops might show up. But if you walked another fifty yards and threw a rock through a rich person's single-family home, at least two cop cars would be on the scene, the cops ready to shake you down. Her dad always said that Patteriniemi Road was like his neighborhood in Somalia before the war—except Patteriniemi Road had the strange distinction of being both kinder and colder at the same time.

Sagal returned to the yard and made fists inside her pockets, reminding herself that she no longer had the device. This piece of incriminating evidence was gone, and there could be any number of reasons why she had money on her. Her head was clear until the wind blew something whirly and sticky in her face. It felt like a bug, and Sagal yelped and shook the damp maple leaf off her, wiping her face and spitting bits of leaf out of her mouth. Gross.

When she looked up someone was staring at her from a second-story window in the bomb-shelter building. Staring right at her.

Sagal's body tingled again, lower this time.

They're not looking at me, she told herself. *They didn't see a thing.* Sagal tried to distract herself by thinking about how boring it would be at school the next day, waiting for the school bus, and all the bad breath in the classroom when someone yawned next to her. She always held her hand in front of her mouth when she yawned. Nobody needed to see her tongue or teeth or smell her breath.

She took determined steps toward the stairwell in her own building. When she grabbed the door's cold handle, she turned once more to look back at the building with the bomb shelter. Now there was a light on in the stairwell. Sagal was relieved. It had to be the High Priest walking up the stairs to his place. He was just a regular guy, this Condom Washer, although he carried a hatchet and a rubber mask in a plastic bag. She might spot Tuure on the bus in the morning if his moped or bike was broken. Sagal opened the door and sneaked in quickly.

She hummed a tune and walked toward the light switch.

Her foot touched something.

Sagal shivered and looked down. Something was stuck to the sole of her left shoe. It made a rubbery flapping sound when she shook her foot. She got the thing off and backed away, holding her breath and walking around until she was sure that it remained still.

In the darkness all she could see was a formless, light-colored lump in the middle of the floor. It was right between her and the light switch. Sagal stared at it as if it were an animal playing dead, and she was suddenly aware of the smell of rubber that had attacked her nostrils as soon as she had stepped into the stairwell.

The Condom Washer, Sagal thought, then berated herself for thinking that the shapeless little pile was a condom. Stupid. It had gaping holes and torn edges, and—

She peered into the corner to the right of the light switch. A green shape slumped there like a human without a head or legs. The coat had slid down the wall, leaving behind streaks of dark, dripping stains.

Sagal couldn't help looking back outside. That's when the light in the bomb-shelter building's stairwell turned off. It didn't seem like a coincidence—it was more like a warning, a planned, secret code. She was a bad, bad girl. No one had committed worse deeds than she had: she had betrayed Mira and all the others.

That same Mira who made her think impure thoughts—whose hair she loved to smell. Bad, bad.

Movement in the corner of her eye made Sagal turn toward the yard. She looked between the picnic shelter and a massive rock. These rocks in the yard and in the Suvikylä woods had always made her feel unfathomably alone, as if these buildings that seemed to have been around forever were just a backdrop on some distant planet where she couldn't expect anyone to understand her. She'd seen a picture of the surface of Mars in a textbook, and that's how she felt sometimes. Deeply alone. She should've framed that picture.

Someone stood in the yard.

Sagal realized she'd been staring at the shape for a while without recognizing it as human. It was wearing a green coat and had a funny face.

A burl in a tree.

Let's pull a prank on you.

Sagal turned to look at the heap on the floor, then the other heap in the corner. How could the mask and that coat be here if they were being worn—

She yelped when her cell phone went off. A silly shriek. She threw both her hands over her mouth and looked around. How embarrassing, causing a scene like this over nothing. It made her forget about everything else except the horror of the masked shape outside hearing her scream through the glass.

Her phone rang, echoing in the stairwell. It was loud, but nothing moved. She didn't know why she had expected anyone to hear her, there in the dark.

Sagal dropped her hands to her sides and turned toward the figure in the yard. She thought about the mask and the heap in the corner. She was sure now that this was a setup to shame her in front of everyone. They had found out what a disgusting girl she was. It was all out in the open now.

Just take it easy.

Everybody thinks that everyone else is keeping an eye on them, Mira once said. Even just thinking about Mira made Sagal feel immensely better. She pulled her phone out of her pocket, checked who was calling, and answered.

"Hi, Mom."

"Where are you? Do you know what time—"

"Yeah, yeah. I'm inside the building already."

"Good. Dad's worried about you."

"I'm coming."

Sagal hung up and began to breathe more evenly. Her mom's voice and the thought of Mira had taken all her fears away. She stood still for a moment and stared at the figure out in the yard. *What right did he have to scare kids?* She walked to the door and opened it.

The wind cooled her face and blew the smell of rubber away.

"What did I ever do to you?" Sagal yelled at the figure.

It didn't respond.

"I'm not scared of you guys," she said. "Even Mira laughs at you and your stupid stories."

The figure didn't move, but Sagal wasn't taking any chances. She started walking faster, her mom's voice still ringing in her ears.

"I'll do whatever I want."

She heard the door open to the building next door. Sagal felt empowered: she was surrounded by others—dog walkers, night shifters, drunks. These buildings were full of ordinary people who didn't let silly boys scare young girls. She was with moms, dads, little sisters, and brothers who brought Sagal's family small presents during Christmastime, even when they knew her family didn't celebrate Christmas.

She heard the door behind her open, too. Sagal turned to look. The stairwell was dark, but the lights from the parking lot flashed in the glass. Someone was approaching her fast from the building. Maybe that person had also seen a strange anorak-clad masked figure in the yard.

"He's trying to scare me," Sagal shouted at the approaching figure.

No reply. The figure picked up its pace.

Sagal looked to her right: another figure was approaching from the neighboring building. It was running.

She held her breath and faced the yard.

The raincoat hem flapped in the wind. The mask was askew, about to fall off—too big for whoever it was hiding. Or maybe whatever it was hiding. Sagal thought about the tree, the burl, the scarecrow. She looked for the figure's legs, but all she saw was a black mess. Maybe the jacket and the mask had just been hung onto a rake that leaned on a rock. Maybe it was a trap.

Sagal stopped and turned around.

She was between two apartment buildings, with a third one in front of her. Three boxes battered by the fall winds. Each had its windows lit, TVs flashing, and shadows moving here and there. They had to be normal people who didn't see what was going on or do anything because they were busy with their evening chores, watching news, gossiping on the phone. Her dad had always warned Sagal: never expect people to take notice or take action. When evil rears its head, people turn blind and become paralyzed.

The mute figures were approaching, only twenty yards away now. They raced to get to Sagal, their faces gleaming in the dark, too big for their bodies.

Sagal's hands were shaking as she took her phone out. Its bright screen turned on. She stared at it and tried not to pay attention to the movement in the corner of her eyes.

Who should she call?

Why should she call?

If you have nightmares.

Surrounded by windows, the rumbling of the last bus of the night leaving its stop.

Call me and I'll be there.

The dog walker from the building behind her would stop and light a cigarette and cough at any moment now. But the figures kept on moving toward her, determined and faceless as if otherworldly—as if they didn't exist here, with these buildings. The damp gravel made strange sounds under their feet—there was no predetermined rhythm; instead it roared like a wave, like bloodhounds.

Sagal dialed Mira, her other hand over her mouth, and closed her eyes. She could hear the steps, too close to her.

She waited for the phone to ring, thinking about the morning bus and the other students who always looked past her, their reflections indifferent ghosts in the windows.

She didn't open her eyes until a hand touched her shoulder and squeezed. A whisper in her ear. Sagal didn't understand the words; her head spun. Her neck muscles were wound tight, ready to accept the whack of a blade in her back; the blade that had been plowing hair, fingers, eyes.

Finally, the phone started ringing. Sagal held it tight. Mira would pick up at any moment. She'd run from the peninsula over mossy rocks and fallen trees, almost flying, her breath steaming. Then this nonsense would be over. She'd stomp on the masks and her yell would make everyone on Patteriniemi Road turn the volume on their TVs down and cock their heads like animals, sensing that a large beast was mighty pissed off somewhere.

Then Sagal realized what was out of place. Just plain wrong. She heard two ringing tones. One came from the phone pressed against her numb ear. The other rang behind her. They sang to each other like birds. First Sagal's phone, then a response behind her—one dampened by clothes. By a jacket. Sagal hung up.

Her world went black. A thick, coarse fabric had been thrown over her head. It stuck to her skin, forcing her to drop the phone. The fabric pricked her face. It smelled like a cellar and her own bad breath as she screamed into its fibers.

"Why did you have to talk?" a voice asked right next to her ear.

That was no granny.

It was an angry girl.

"Nobody talks. Ever."

The girl was furious. She wasn't pretending to be furious, like that time when she'd claimed she was innocent to a teacher who'd accused her of smoking cigarettes at school. This time her fury was real.

Sagal stopped screaming.

You could argue with many. Just not with Mira.

When Sagal was dragged away, she heard her phone ringing on the ground behind her. It was her dad's ringtone.

She wanted to take the call. Not because she wanted to ask anyone to interrupt their important business to come rescue her. She only wanted to tell her dad he'd been right all along.

HIS FATHER'S HAND

Samuel Autio was driving toward his childhood home when a stiff human figure suddenly appeared in his headlights.

No way to brake in time. And it was completely dark. Rain was pouring down. His thoughts were a mist. A thump. Something rolling under the tires.

Samuel stopped the car, although he knew it was too late. He felt a strange pressure on his chest, as if an invisible hand tried to prevent him from flying through the windshield. This feeling knocked loose a memory in his mind, and had he not been so exhausted, it would have come to him clearly. Instead, the car engine hummed and rain drummed on the roof and hood in an even rumble. The windshield fogged up immediately. Droplets appeared out of nowhere, as if the window were sweating. Right before the wipers performed their arc, the water had been dirty, darker, like blood. The image lasted for less than a second and was wiped away by the mechanical movement of the rubber wiper blade before Samuel could confirm what he saw.

He looked in the rearview mirror. A wavering line of streetlights and their reflection on the dark asphalt. Nothing else. He turned the engine off and got out of the car. The rain was freezing cold. There was nothing on the road. Nothing under the car.

Samuel stood in the rain and thought long and hard. He remembered a dark figure had rolled over the hood. There was the softest of squeaks when the stranger's palm had slid against the windshield. It had happened in less than a second, but Samuel remembered it vividly.

Pale, squished skin in a blink of an eye. He walked to the side of the road and peered into the ditch.

Nothing.

The road was between the woods and a parking lot, and behind the parking lot, Samuel saw rows of three- and four-story prefabs built in the seventies. Somewhere among them was Patteriniemi Road and his dad's home. He'd learned how to read—from a milk-carton label—in an apartment on the second story of that building. He had done it just like that, on his own.

Samuel circled the car and felt the wet hood with his fingers. No dents. He leaned over and looked for signs of blood but found none. The rain was deafening.

When he straightened up he saw lights approaching. He waited a moment, weighing his options. He walked back to the driver's seat and started the engine. The windshield wipers squeaked. The approaching car's headlights appeared in the rearview mirror.

Where did that thing go?

Samuel squeezed the steering wheel. He thought about calling the police. It had all happened so fast. There had been fog and traffic on the road all the way from Helsinki. He thought about the phone call six hours earlier, the visit to Central Hospital in Vaasa, seeing his dad sleeping, and the nurse who spoke with a Swedish accent telling him his dad was dead.

None of that had made any waves: the hospital, his dad's body, anything. On the contrary, it had felt safe and comforting. He dealt with bodies at Meilahti Hospital all the time. He'd held an old woman's hand at the precise moment when she turned into a corpse. His voice hadn't wavered once when he'd talked about the details with the nurse. Samuel couldn't have forced it to if he'd tried.

But he had to admit that the first call had made his stomach churn, although nothing had really changed: the office calendar was on the wall like always, with the holiday party marked down although it was three months away; someone requested he call an elevator to the ward; the computer hummed softly. He was still in dire need of a bathroom break and was slightly worried that the ache in his left eye was a symptom of early onset Horton's syndrome. And he imagined fucking Annika from the neighboring ward in the parking garage, forgetting about Krista and the kids completely, he'd just do it and then scream at the sea that he would do as he pleased.

Although nothing had really changed, the news of his dad's death had overwhelmed him, forcing itself into his veins and seeping through his skin.

Samuel began to drive. The car behind him came closer, then turned into the parking lot. The light in his rearview mirror blinded him for a moment, then disappeared. The car hadn't stopped or even slowed when it came to where he thought he'd hit someone. Pushing the incident away for a moment, Samuel turned onto Patteriniemi Road. It was the last street before the woods, the small cluster of islands, and, eventually, the sea. He turned the engine off and looked at the apartment buildings' neat rows of balconies.

The same structures, the same shapes. Their resiliency calmed Samuel down. They spoke of his decades between the legal drinking age and the present moment he found himself in. Sitting in the quiet of his car, he realized that those decades honestly meant nothing to him anymore. All the things that had transpired—his first full-time job, getting married, kids, arguments, affairs, movies—were all just a fog that was wiped away every morning. But these buildings remained, like the pyramids in Egypt and the statues on Easter Island.

Signs of modernity did pop up every now and then in the form of satellite dishes and immigrants. If an African man had strolled onto Patteriniemi Road in the 1980s in Samuel's childhood, the local labor union would've composed songs and performed skits about this bizarre creature at their Christmas party. The Hagert gypsies hadn't been considered representatives of foreign culture, although the neighbors gawked at their garden parties from their windows like anthropologists observing tribal dancing. The neighbors peered in, making bets about who'd get knocked out or stabbed first. People these days talked about immigrants constantly, but the new Somali neighbors must be easier folks to live with than the Hagerts.

Once upon a time a man everyone dubbed "The Prof" lived in one of the Patteriniemi Road apartments. He would play opera all day long at full volume and take long strolls, mumbling to himself. No one ever knew what he was talking about. He never answered when kids prodded him with inappropriate questions, and his peculiar concentration could not be broken, not even when boys sped by him on their mopeds, yelling sarcastic remarks. Samuel's dad always said there was nothing inside The Prof's brain except an opera without an audience.

One time, The Prof was returning from his stroll and happened to find himself in the middle of the Hagert family's garden party in the yard. He'd stopped to listen to one of the early evening solo numbers, when talented young singers performed for the approval and admiration of the entire family. Pertti Ahlanen had been leaning out of his window, smoking, and saw how it all went down. The Prof had been clapping along with everyone else. "Marvelous singing," he said, "but the vibrato was a tad forced." The remark escalated into an attempted murder, a police report, and a new, permanent expression in the Patteriniemi Road vernacular among the adults. "Vibrato was a tad forced again last night," they'd say on Sunday mornings when the yard was littered with empty beer bottles, sausage wrappings, and bloodied shreds of gauze—the aftermath of a Hagert party.

These were all echoes from a world that no longer existed, although its sounds and people had felt immortal at the time.

Samuel watched the buildings and for the first time he wasn't sure what to do. He could follow in Aki's footsteps: he'd told Samuel on the phone that he couldn't simply take off from Shanghai on such short notice, even though his dad had just died. This from Aki, who had excelled at guilt-tripping Samuel for keeping their old man at arm's length, even accusing him of hating his dad because of an old grudge. Yet it had been none other than Samuel who'd had to walk into his dad's apartment when things had gotten real. Not Aki, who had called their dad once a week from across the world, now that his successful career guaranteed he was far enough away from his former time zone. The one who hadn't succeeded had the privilege of seeing his dead father. The one who just held old ladies by the hand when they turned into corpses.

Samuel had a set of keys in his palm. He'd found them among his dad's belongings at the hospital. Three keys. One new grooved key, one old Abloy key, and one unknown key—perhaps to his dad's basement storage. Samuel looked at the set and slowly realized how abandoned the keys looked now that his dad was gone. It was as if the little heat with which the metal pieces warmed his palm had come from his dad's touch.

He closed his fingers around the keys and began to walk. Muscle memory in his legs took him to the correct apartment building, to the correct entrance. He suddenly wanted to bound up the stairwell like he had when he was a little kid, counting how far he could make it up the stairs before the door slammed shut behind him. You always had to reach at least the second floor, or else something terrible would happen. Like your dad would die.

Samuel climbed the stairs to his dad's door, opening it with the grooved key. He paused at the threshold, greeted by the scents of his childhood home. There was a subtle chemical smell he hadn't noticed before, possibly left over from a renovation some twenty years earlier. He stepped in and closed the door behind him, then let out all his breath in a deep sigh and turned on the lights. He looked at the shoes and clothes on the coat rack. There were a pair of sneakers, a pair of brown leather shoes—fake leather, rather—one cream-colored coat, and a long black wool-blend coat, an expensive purchase for his dad's meager earnings.

Samuel took his shoes off and shoved them next to his dad's, then walked around the apartment, turning lights on in each room. His and Aki's room had become makeshift storage, filled with folders and cardboard boxes brimming with tools, old magazines, and greasy engine parts. Miraculously, an Iron Maiden poster was still hanging on the wall, crucified with thumbtacks. A futuristic Eddie from the *Somewhere in Time* era peered into the room with his peculiar camera eye, and Bruce Dickinson stood in a wide stance wearing a ridiculous ruffled shirt. Samuel was briefly amused by the image of his dad rummaging in the tool boxes under the poster's watchful eye.

The window in the room was a black rectangle, its surface beading with drops of water. Samuel thought he saw a faint flash in it, like a pale hand moving across it.

He turned the lights off. That was better. The window became transparent again, revealing a leafless tree branch, the silhouette of the apartment building across the yard, and the dark-gray storm clouds overhead.

Samuel walked through the rooms again, turning the lights off.

He went into the kitchen.

There wasn't much in the fridge: a pack of margarine, an opened milk carton, and a piece of pork tenderloin wrapped in plastic. Samuel pulled out a partially filled garbage bag and began to dump the food in it. The package of tenderloin had a screaming-orange tag that read "50% Off, See Best Before Date." That would have been the only reason his dad would buy tenderloin. He'd never understood vegetarianism, but he also never bought expensive meat.

Samuel dangled the cold meat over the garbage bag, looking at the price tag and the colorful prints on the label. Some poor outsourced graphic designer had finally gotten his tenth iteration past the meat bosses, whose aims were to please average customers of average purchasing power and force them to make quick purchase decisions. And his dad had made that decision, but not until the design had been ruined by an orange tag advertising a steep discount.

The milk carton was red. No low-fat products for his dad. Samuel took turns looking at the pack of meat and the milk. He couldn't take them home, but his dad wouldn't have approved of throwing them in the trash.

"Stingy bastard," Samuel whispered.

He didn't know what to do. He just stood there, the fridge door open and a clammy pack of meat in his hand, looking at the carton of milk his dad had opened before he'd died. He'd clearly had difficulty opening it: he'd mangled the carton by tearing it open, making it hard to pour.

He felt soft pressure on his chest, like someone touching him.

Now Samuel remembered why that feeling was familiar. His dad's palm against his chest, sitting in the car when his dad had to slam on the brakes. That's what he'd always done when Samuel sat next to him. His palm would be on Samuel's chest a second before his foot pumped the brake pedal. A protective reflex. Then, at some point when Samuel was a preteen, his dad stopped doing it, perhaps thinking that Samuel should look out for himself now. Or maybe the gap between the two men had already begun to grow back then. His dad stopped protecting him, wrestling and tickling him.

Was his dad trying to protect him now? The touch was soft, but he felt it as clearly as the cold piece of meat in his palm and the floor beneath his feet.

It suddenly dawned on Samuel that something had just happened; something completely ordinary that he should react to.

The doorbell. Its familiar ring echoed in Samuel's sensory memory.

He looked toward the front door. After setting the garbage bag on the kitchen counter, he closed the fridge and went to the foyer.

He could barely see the shape of the door in the dark. The mail slot embedded in it reflected a distant light and flapped gently. The peephole appeared black. Who would stand in the pitch-black stairwell? For whatever reason, the first thought in Samuel's mind was burglars—the kind who would clean out an apartment as soon as they heard that the tenant had died, but before any relatives would flock in. This plan merely required a contact at the hospital, a childhood friend with questionable ethics who stole drugs and old hospital equipment and sold them on the black market.

Samuel took slow, deliberate steps to the door and listened. First all he heard was the rain drumming against the windows. Then there was a cough. Just an ordinary, harmless cough. Yet Samuel did not want to open the door. He didn't have to. His dad was dead.

But it was bizarre to stand in front of a door you refused to open, knowing that someone was standing on the other side of it.

Samuel stood still, holding his breath. In the background of all this stillness, he could hear a low, steady hum. Like the gentle sound of a machine designed to run everything, made to be unnoticeable.

The mail slot clinked. Samuel looked down at it. The minuscule movement of the metallic flap could've been caused by a draft. Then the flap stopped clinking and began to hinge up. Someone was lifting it up to look inside, and the first thing that someone would see were Samuel's legs in the dark foyer.

Samuel was still holding his breath, realizing what an idiotic situation he had gotten himself into. There was no reason to embarrass himself like this. He could have simply stayed in the kitchen. He could have stomped over loudly and then told the stranger to fuck off. What was happening now was the stupidest option. Standing still and holding his breath.

"I'll show you the way."

The voice echoed in the stairwell. Samuel couldn't quite place it. Was it a man or a woman? Samuel thought of a midget, and he almost burst out laughing. It had been such an odd, exhausting day, so anything was possible. Even a midget dressed in bright-colored circus gear. Samuel covered his mouth, his shoulders heaving silently with the rhythm of his laughter. His eyes welled up with tears.

The mail-slot flap remained up. Samuel now imagined a deranged midget crouching in front of his dad's door, not knowing that the owner of this randomly chosen apartment had just died. That the son of the deceased who had gotten himself into this ridiculous situation was standing alone in the unlit apartment. Who had not thought about Krista and the girls for a long time. Samuel suddenly didn't feel like laughing anymore. His muscles stopped jerking. Only the tears remained on his cheeks and a salty taste in his mouth.

The flap fell down, swinging for a while in its frame. Samuel heard footsteps going down the stairs with a hollow boom.

I'll show you the way.

The hurried echo of footsteps down the stairs. Samuel swung the door open. He caught a glimpse of a hand on the railing on the floor below. An unspecified limb in the dark.

"Hey!" Samuel yelled.

But it was too late. He heard the door to the building open onto the yard and then nothing—just the rustling of the wind and a light breeze on his face.

Samuel ran to the floor below and looked through the balcony window into the yard. Nobody there. He opened the balcony door and leaned over the railing. Nobody.

When he walked back into the stairwell, he could tell he was being watched. Each silent door, each dark peephole stared at him. Samuel didn't care. It must've been kids pulling a prank. He was an adult, though, and wouldn't get hurt. He walked back into the apartment and called Krista. The phone rang for a while, which itself wasn't unusual.

I'll show you the way.

Samuel waited patiently, thought of his dad in the hospital, the hand sliding against the windshield, the light body of a midget hopping down the stairs as if he were flying.

"Hey there," Krista said on the other end. "How are you doing?"

"I'm all right. How about you?"

Krista went into detail about a variety of everyday problems, all relating to how she now suddenly had to run the show without Samuel. Then she seemed to remember why he wasn't there.

"What's it like over there?" she asked.

What's it like? It's like nothing you would know, Samuel wanted to say. *It's about people who have never been to Bali or whose parents do not own a villa in Sipoo.*

"How are you doing?" she repeated.

The phone call took longer than necessary because the girls were in bed and Krista had some time to kill. Finally Samuel played the my-dad's-dead-so-I'm-behaving-a-bit-weird card and interrupted Krista midsentence, informing her that he'd run out of energy for talking.

Samuel sat in his dad's living room, looking at the bookshelf, the old, thick CRT television, and the VHS player. It had a tape in it. Looking at the player, Samuel vividly remembered the sound after pressing the "Eject" button. The forced wail, as if his request was too much for the device.

I'll show you the way.

Samuel knew what came after that phrase. He was aware that he knew, but he refused to think about it.

Instead, he stared at the VHS player. The tape peeking out of the player was probably the last one his dad had watched.

His dad occasionally had taped Soviet movies and then, in the spirit of international proletariat solidarity, tried to watch them for their political message, but he'd always fallen asleep before reaching the end. Samuel and his dad had sometimes watched Bond movies starring Roger Moore together. His dad had complained incessantly about

Western propaganda, but he'd never fallen asleep. Sometimes, Samuel would hear his dad sniffle when he tried to stifle a laugh.

Samuel got off the couch and pushed the tape into the machine. It screeched but didn't fight. The digital screen requested "Play." Samuel began to look for the remote control, but the tape started playing by itself.

First the entire screen was light blue.

Then two quick flashes. One of clouds, and he heard a single syllable, "Oh—" The second flash was of wet grass. After some static, the image sharpened.

Samuel stiffened.

It is a teenage girl.

Dark-red hair.

One eye is purple and swollen shut. Her gaze is serious, focused on the upper corner of the screen. Her right hand is holding the camera, which is shaking like in an earthquake from the minutest of movements. Not exactly good film quality. Hand-held cam.

The girl pulls away from the camera and sits down on a bed, crossing her legs. She is wearing an oversized T-shirt that is hiding everything except a shoulder and a knee.

"All right," the girl says. Then she takes one more quick glance at the camera before looking to her left.

A door opens with a clang. A teenage boy steps into focus.

Samuel leaned closer to the TV.

He wondered whether his dad had done the same while watching the tape. Did his dad lean closer to the TV, too, not knowing that the light in his eyes would be switched off and his hands would stop moving and the pain in his chest wouldn't pass this time?

The boy on the tape sits on the edge of the bed. He's wearing jeans and a blue T-shirt. He pulls his legs up onto the bed. The camcorder microphone picks up the wet smacking sounds of a kiss. The sound continues.

Samuel closed his eyes, and in the darkness behind his eyelids, he saw flashes of color and a pale hand. He opened his eyes.

The girl and the boy don't look confident about what they're doing. They're imitating whatever they've seen and heard, looking like animals dressed up as humans, performing human feats. They live in the now and pant heavily, because even just kissing is new to them.

The girl begins to take her clothes off first.

Her bra is black.

"What the fuck . . ." Samuel mumbled and wrapped his fingers tighter around the remote.

The girl pulls the blue shirt over the boy's head. It's a clumsy act, because the boy doesn't understand that he should stop kissing her. For a long time they appear topless, the boy moving his crotch against the girl and sucking on her lips, as if not knowing that he can take this further and that there's actually a goal to reach. Then the boy unzips his jeans and pulls the girl's pants off.

Those jeans are from the department-store sale rack, Samuel thought. He said it almost out loud. The image on tape warped for a moment in the corner, as if to nod and say, *Correct. How did you know?*

General confusion came next when they tear open the condom wrapping.

Stole that condom from his dad.

The boy rips the plastic, and they're both puzzled, observing the odd plastic ring and looking simultaneously aroused and slightly concerned when the boy pulls it on.

From the department-store sale rack.

Samuel watched the fifteen-year-old boy's overly excited, bouncing erection and the small-breasted girl, who has opened her legs to let it in.

In this grainy image Samuel saw how once upon a time and space one boy had been inside a girl called Julia. He suddenly remembered how it had felt; how it'd been hard to believe it was happening; how he had thought about how real the room and the world outside were; and how the sun was in the sky as if nothing special was happening. He had been trying to comprehend that it was really happening to him, Samuel Autio, yet at the same time he had not been thinking anything.

His dad's living room was filled with loud panting, the panting of two little animals, sounds that were not yet heavy with life experience, blasting from the speakers in waves of distortion.

The girl turns to look at the camera. The boy's head is covered by her hair. Her eyes are first drowsy from pleasure, but then they blink wide open.

She shoots a meaningful look at the camera.

Samuel coughed. He recognized he did it as just something to do, like birds that start to peck at the ground when they're in danger. He coughed again.

The girl's lips begin to move. To form words.

Her mouth moves slowly, deliberately.

Samuel stared so hard that everything else on-screen first became a blur, then disappeared. He stared at the screen as if he were trying to interpret a weak transmission on an emergency broadcast. Then he snapped out of it and realized what he was watching, on whose couch, in whose viewing posture.

Samuel yelled and began to frantically look for the VHS remote. He couldn't find it, so he leaped at the device and hammered on the "Eject" button. The machine began its laborious toil and for a split second Samuel was sure it wouldn't want to part with the tape. It had been able to hold on to it for too long, replaying it, and when his dad had watched that same part over and over and—

Samuel yanked the tape out as soon as it emerged. He paced the apartment, realizing he was looking for any tool he could use to smash this piece of his past into such small shrapnel that it would cease to exist. He couldn't force himself to return to his old room, so instead he looked around and saw an ashtray next to the TV. Cigarette butts flew everywhere as Samuel dropped the tape onto the floor and raised his hand to strike.

The two white reels on the tape stared at him like idiotic eyes. Expressionless and ready to record and play back anything. No shame. The player wasn't picky. The thought of Julia having videotaped the two of them. The thought that his dad had watched it. The thought that Samuel would destroy it. It didn't matter. *The sun was in the sky as if nothing special was happening.*

Why did his dad have to see it? What meaning could such humiliation provide in a world already full of shit?

This is really happening to me.

Samuel paused in midstrike, ashtray still in his hand.

His skin remembered how the girl had stiffened underneath him, pushed against him with her hips, her wrinkled brow, her panting like an animal in distress. His skin desired such memories, wanted to protect them. He remembered the girl's smile; how she sniffled in July; and how he'd felt willing to do anything, even lick her nose despite her snot-inducing hay allergies.

The ashtray fell onto the rug with a thump and rolled away. Samuel grabbed the tape and twisted it. The plastic strained against his grasp, but of course it didn't give. He let go, stood up, and wobbled as if he were drunk.

Just take it easy, he said to the living room, to that stupid videotape, to the erection pressing against his zipper. Now is now, no matter what had happened on that tape. His dad was gone, Julia was gone.

Samuel began to cry in a guttural, confused howl. There were no tears, just first syllables of words and moans. Each detail in the room was attacking him. The old electrical outlets, the crown molding, the familiar smells that a quick renovation had not been able to hide. That smell penetrated his clothes and sank into his pores, digging for a memory of itself. Samuel covered his mouth to stop himself from wailing.

Once he was done, he left the apartment without cleaning out the fridge.

When he reached the freeway, he glanced at the tape riding shotgun with him.

It flashed Samuel its idiotic gaze, one that didn't care about grief or the burden of memories. It was all the same, something to record onto a magnetic strip and repeat forever.

MAISA RIIPINEN'S NAILS

"Nobody talks about this. Ever."

Maisa took her headphones off and looked at the muted TV screen. She saw a rain forest shrouded in fog, then a close-up of a green insect that wavered back and forth, camouflaged as a leaf.

Maisa stared at the insect and tried to decide whether she was disappointed or excited. She was overjoyed for having been able to record what happened in the Fairy-Tale Cellar. The guilt of using an innocent Somali girl as a middleman gnawed at her a little. She tried to keep her journalist friend's motto in mind: even the friendliest of wolves have to eat. The world wasn't conquered by feeling guilty.

The insect pretending to be a leaf caught a butterfly, as if to convince Maisa she was right. The frantic flapping of its wings quickly slowed down to resigned jerks.

She went to the window, where she could glimpse the sea through the trees lining Ranta Street. Although her apartment was next to the hospital in the center of the city, this view was nice enough to have been from Suvikylä. She saw pine trees straight as needles and a path through the woods where an overweight jogger tried to keep up with his dog.

Suvikylä was her childhood. It was one of those issues she couldn't shake off as an adult, although it would've been much nicer to remember blowing bubbles and lazy summer days. She didn't care what people said about humans living in the present and how it was never too late to have a happy childhood and all that crap. Maisa knew exactly where her panic attacks came from.

You get those if you are, say, locked up at fifteen in a cellar for, say, twenty-four hours. What a lovely teen memory. Wish everyone could have one.

Maisa was one of the peculiar members of the welfare state, because she knew what it felt like to scratch at a wooden door so hard until her fingernails tore off. What it felt like to realize you've pissed your pants—or even worse—when someone finally let you out. The shame of it didn't even register until later on. An animal without nails isn't interested in shame: it just wants to claw its way out. It holds tight to the first human standing in clear daylight and prays that the light won't be taken away again. It doesn't care what the world's cutest boy thinks or whether it should be losing its virginity already.

Maisa's breathing turned shallow. She realized she had been staring at her own reflection instead of the view. That wasn't good. She needed to look beyond herself.

She went back to the couch and unmuted the TV. The narrator talked about hatching and eggs and ideal circumstances. She watched these incomprehensible, messy events and the determined motions of the newborn insects. She liked insects, because she could see life in its rawest form in them. No traumatized kissing and hugging that the mammals covered in hair performed—it was all pure action.

Maisa had found out about Sagal Yusuf through Kirsi, who taught at the grade school in Suvikylä. She and Kirsi had met once a week over a glass of wine since Maisa had returned to her hometown. They could have been called childhood friends, except once they'd reached high school age, they hardly saw each other outside of school. Apparently both of them had felt they could've seen each other more, because they hit it off immediately upon meeting again. Maisa hadn't kept in touch with any of her high school friends, but for whatever reason— perhaps because they had such a different set of memories—she got along well with Kirsi. They'd gone to different parties, had crushes on different boys, had a different history yet still the same childhood and just enough common ground. The economic depression, Finland's winning the '95 ice hockey world championship, watching news about the World Trade Center attacks. They didn't share much from the time Maisa was fifteen.

She'd gotten tipsy and shamelessly asked Kirsi whether she taught anyone from Patteriniemi Road. And she'd been a little more than tipsy when Kirsi had told her everything about Sagal and her older brother, who had been caught selling drugs at his trade school. This serious, intelligent, and extremely diligent girl had tried to protect her brother to the bitter end. Apparently their father had been beaten on multiple occasions in Somalia, maybe even tortured. Kirsi had seen scars under his sleeve when he'd raised his hand to ask a question at parent-teacher night. He had nothing but pale scars above his wrists.

Now, I don't know if it was scarring from a burn or whether his hand had been . . . skinned or something.

A welfare state didn't have to make a distinction between a burn and a skinning.

A serious, intelligent, and diligent girl. Maisa felt like such a jerk. If she were caught pressuring a preteen and pretending to be a criminal investigator, the worst punishment wouldn't be dealt through the justice system. Her pure, debilitating shame would take care of it. And for what? A good research subject? Maybe. Something applicable to the larger scheme of things. Something beyond a childhood issue for a girl with no nails.

The strip of forest on Ranta Street and the sea behind the pine trees didn't take sides on this. Maisa made her decision, grabbed her phone, and called Pasi. When she heard the phone ring, she pretended to be confident of her decision.

"Hey, it's Maisa," she said when Pasi picked up the phone. "I have a story that'll blow you away."

"Great. The Awakening movement or the Laestadians?"

"Neither."

"But you're in Ostrobothnia, home of these religious movements. Either the Awakening or the Laestadians, pretty please."

"Listen to me. I have a recording from that Fairy-Tale Cellar where the teens go."

Pasi was quiet for a moment. "I'd love to congratulate you," he said, "but instead I am compelled to ask an academic question that lays the groundwork for your project: what the fuck?"

"You'll congratulate me soon enough. I have a session on tape where kids are initiated into adulthood by being told a story that they're not allowed to tell anyone else. They then become adult members of their community. It's super spontaneous, just like I told you. Incredible stuff. The genre is absolutely bizarre."

"But what about the Laestadians—"

"Listen." Maisa put Pasi on speaker and played the recording. He listened.

"Those are just ghost stories," he said when the recording ended. "I mean, 'Granny Hatchet'? That even sounds like kid stuff. A little funny, a little exciting, and stupendously useless."

"It's not," Maisa said, "if it's been going on since the 1980s. Maybe even before then. You know the prognosis for urban legends."

"Two generations max."

"But this thing . . ." She tapped the MP3 player with her finger although Pasi couldn't see her gesture. "This thing hasn't gone away. It hasn't even waned. On the contrary . . ."

"What, it's getting stronger?"

"Yeah."

"Maybe it's an Internet meme," Pasi said.

"It's not. This is genuinely old, organic, and spontaneous."

"I'm still not buying it."

"Just think about it," Maisa said. "They don't need a reason for Granny Hatchet's existence. She just *is*. She's the embodiment of all that's scary and threatening. Everything you need to appease."

"Did you hear that sound?" Pasi asked.

"What sound?"

"The sound of the definition of religion being stretched to its breaking point."

"Surely it's allowed to stretch," Maisa said. "Or are we sticking to organized religion until the end of the world? One more century of secularism and the entire field of religious studies will be wiped out."

"It's in the lap of the gods, as they say."

"So should we not include the gods of Arabic nomads in the definition of religion? 'In practice they're nothing but wandering demonstrative pronouns.' Ever heard of that one? It's a quote you should be familiar with."

"Rudolf Otto," Pasi said. "Stop being so pedantic. I'm sure there's a suburb where the same store window has been broken during alcohol-fueled Midsummer Eve festivities since the 1970s. Is that religious behavior to you?"

"It's not the same thing."

"Why not? They had a rite of passage in Nivala where you'd become a real man if you shot yourself with a BB gun in the foot on your eighteenth birthday. I was in the army with a guy who showed me his scar."

"But this is different," Maisa said. "Just think about it. They manipulate all these teenagers to think that they have to take part in the rite—that they won't be adult members of the community until they do. And this is happening in modern times, in an urban environment, and restricted to a very small area. My informant, Sagal, is a goddamned second-generation Somali from a religious family. Can you imagine the hurdles she's had to overcome to participate?"

Just a tiny jab of guilt hit Maisa then. The memory of a figure wearing a dark-blue veil, walking away from the parking lot with contempt on her heels. The memory of the thumb on her left hand where the nail had cracked, a white, unexplained line running into the cuticle.

"What it means is that there's a place where the same ghost story has been told for over thirty years, and for whatever reason it's become somewhat organized. And Muslims are now invited, too. It's certainly curious, but it's just a ghost story," Pasi said.

"It's not," Maisa said, frustration rising in her voice. "A primitive system is involved. Taboos, initiation rites, sacrificial gifts, punishments. We could use this to research how a religious drive tries to—"

"Careful with the word 'drive,'" Pasi interrupted her. "'Propensity,' please."

"You know what I mean . . . How a religious *propensity* tries to push through in an urban environment when there's even the slightest possibility of isolating individuals from the mainstream culture. This must be researched, and it must be done now. These things are like butterflies; soon they'll be gone because there is no paradigm to keep them grounded. This girl I talked to wasn't very convinced herself because teenagers see and hear things that are much worse all the time. I don't know where it came from, but it could disappear any day now."

Pasi was quiet for longer this time. "They talked about sacrificial gifts. At the peninsula."

"Right."

"What's there?"

"It's the boundary."

"The boundary?"

"Patteriniemi Road is an area of social interest. On one side you have public housing provided by the city, and on the other side you have mansions, with some townhomes between them. Such an arrangement stems from the Nordic school of thought on equality, where a variety of social classes are placed in the same area. Of course invisible barriers form between the classes, but the most important boundary, and the one nobody should cross, is at the shore: the boundary between them and the cabin owners who've been there forever. You'd think that telling the teens not to go there would just egg them on, but no. Going there wasn't just prohibited, it was . . . a taboo."

"Oh, dear me," Pasi wailed. "I cower before your formidable academic terminology!"

Maisa closed her eyes. Her father had talked about the cabin owners with a loathing rivaled only by his attitude toward neighbors who were renting from the city. White trash. Those who ruled Patteriniemi Road lived in the apartment buildings, or that's how the teenagers saw it. They always told the best stories, had the best music, and they were stocked to the gills with cigarettes, beer, and fruit wine. They had the toughest and cutest boys. They were the ones to pass on the local folklore. Kids who were all about mopeds, and the band Accept, and who they'd fucked and where they'd gone drinking. They talked about Granny Hatchet with such reverence that in retrospect it seemed ludicrous that Maisa and the rest of the kids had ever bought those stories.

She looked down at her nails. Her hand wasn't shaking. Good.

"A taboo?" Pasi said. "Can't you use a term that's a little less loaded?"

"I can collect enough materials to convince you," she said.

He sighed. "Is there no way you could check in on the Laestadians? It's easy to dig up something there that would arouse interest across the board. Just find a lamb that's about to leave its flock, and investigate—"

"Just fucking trust me this one time. It'll pay off for you."

She could hear only Pasi's breathing for a while as he either digested the curse word or the insinuation that personal gain was the only thing that drove him.

"OK," he said. "But just remember that an inherited ghost story is not religion; it's urban folklore. It's been researched to death."

"I'll keep that in mind."

"It's the same with Yakuza—despite their initiations and other rites, they are not a religious cult. Keep this distinction in mind. You're surrounded by your childhood, and I get it; you're experiencing some lost youth out there, so it makes sense to be excited about the possibility of an urban religion that's about to kick off, but to be honest, I'm not convinced."

"I get that," Maisa said.

"And in the form you've presented this story to me—it won't convince the research-grant committee, either."

"Soon it will."

"We'll see about that. Later."

Maisa hung up and felt her confidence drain out of her, writhe in pain, then die in misery. Pasi knew how to clip her wings. Old grudges reared their heads. Pasi was a professor, waiting for a young researcher to land on a story only to then swoop in like he always did as soon as the media got involved and claim credit. There was evidence of him fucking at least two of his protégés. Or three, but Maisa was too disgusted to count herself among them. Pasi had an uncanny ability to convince people to be grateful to him, and it was hard to explain how he succeeded. He was supposedly a relaxed, self-deprecating, calculating little shit who fucked with his socks on and whose wife smiled so hard at the department holiday party that her cheeks forced tears out of her eyes.

Maisa listened to the recording once more. She walked over to her desk with her headphones on and looked at the quote she had on the wall: "Should it happen that all traditions in the world were cut off with a single blow, the whole mythology and history of religion would start over again with the succeeding generation." It was framed and hung at eye level when she sat down at the computer. These days it was unwise to use Jung as a reliable source, but to Maisa this quote meant everything. It was her personal creed.

Pasi's doubts had managed to poison her confidence. She listened with closed eyes, trying to transport herself to the bomb-shelter ritual, to the Fairy-Tale Cellar.

It wasn't easy. Panic was settling in.

There were times when Maisa had been so excited about her research subject that she couldn't sleep. She'd pace her apartment and chew on her cuticles until the morning newspaper dropped through the mail slot in her door in the early morning hours.

And then there was always Pasi.

Nothing but crap. Ghost stories. Wishful thinking. No future. You should've gone to business school like your father told you to. Why travel to India and go nuts about the Parsi fire temples and the piss-poor people who performed beautiful acts of worship in the eternal light of the morning, as if they'd just invented the sun?

And then there was the newspaper clipping next to the quote from Jung: *The police are requesting any information on Samuel Autio, who disappeared . . .*

Maisa had been surprised to see how much the adult Samuel looked like he did as a teen. Of course his face was wider and his eyes were colder, but that's how men aged. They got wider and more cynical.

He was last seen September 29, 2012, in Vaasa. He left Helsinki in his blue-gray . . .

But what did anything matter? Just keep on trudging to retirement, if those days ever come.

On the day he disappeared he wore . . .

Maisa fixed herself a gin and tonic, then took it with her to the bathroom and started applying makeup.

She decided she was beautiful when she finished lining her lips. Beautiful enough even for a miracle such as Samuel Autio, who had gone missing two years earlier walking toward her in a dark alley like the resurrected Christ. It was a stupid thought, but it awakened a hint of teenage excitement in Maisa. Anything could happen. Anything was possible.

She pursed her flawlessly lined lips and thought of Pasi. She couldn't help grimacing and sticking her tongue out at her reflection.

As Samuel exited the freeway he sped past traffic cameras, going a hundred kilometers an hour. He realized this wasn't a good idea on a rain-slicked road. He could've lost his license if he'd been caught.

He slowed down to eighty and immediately saw headlights in his rearview mirror. They moved from one edge of the mirror to another, looking for a chance to pass. Samuel didn't care. He drove a steady fifty for a couple of hours.

At some point the lights in the rearview disappeared. They had probably disappeared awhile back, but Samuel just hadn't noticed that he was the only one on the road. He and the videotape.

Why had Julia filmed it?

What a stupid question.

Samuel squeezed the steering wheel so hard his knuckles turned white. Everything had been so much simpler when his dad was still alive. He hadn't needed to stay in touch or return to Suvikylä to know what was going on there.

Tears began to blur his vision, so he quickly turned off the road into a gas station. He filled the tank although he didn't really need to. It just felt good to do normal things. He parked the car and went inside to buy a coffee. He punched in the first number of his debit-card PIN with his index finger and then stopped. He stared at his finger, defying it to move. No visible shaking.

"Forgot your PIN?" the young woman behind the counter asked.

"Almost." Samuel laughed and entered the rest of the numbers. The woman told him she'd had to request a new card twice because she'd forgotten the PIN. He quipped, "Just you wait until you get older." They both laughed.

On his way to an empty table, Samuel observed completely ordinary people reading newspapers, staring intently at their phones, yawning. He first sat at a table the farthest away from everyone else, but the incessant noise and flashing lights from the slot machine next to it made him restless. He moved one table over. He'd already had half of his coffee.

Samuel felt safe among people. He thought about the tape and his dad, but with a detachment that kept him calm. Gas stations like these were built on practicality. They were pit stops far away from home. Anyone could get out of their car, walk in, and be whoever they wanted to be.

"Did you forget your PIN?"

This question could've been aimed at anyone, but Samuel made the mistake of turning toward the voice.

The woman at a nearby table became visibly excited about the eye contact they'd just made. She was an odd-looking character. Samuel didn't reply, just kept on drinking the weak coffee. He took his smartphone out of his pocket and started reading his emails.

"You tried to forget your PIN."

Samuel continued to stare at his phone, although he'd already seen everything on the screen. Somewhere to his left the woman let out a deep sigh. Maybe she was losing interest in her victim. He heard a down jacket rustle. Samuel put the phone back in his breast pocket.

"People try to forget their PINs."

Samuel aimed his gaze firmly at the register. A disabled man was trying to place an order at the fast-food counter, and the cashier leaned over with a sympathetic look on her face. Samuel would've given positive customer feedback about the girl if there was an easy way to do it. There had to be.

"Did ya hear me?"

Samuel kept on watching the man order his food and thought about how the fast-food counter, the colorful posters, and the entire gas station were designed for people like him—ordinary folks who didn't think too much.

"Did ya hear?"

Samuel tapped the table with his fingertips.

"Did ya hear?"

He could just finish his coffee and leave. Or leave the coffee and walk out. Nobody would even notice.

"People try to forget their PINs."

The woman had switched tables. She was now sitting right next to Samuel.

"Excuse me?" he said.

He had to look at the woman.

Black hair, at least forty years old. Some shades of gray here and there. Her light-green eyes could've still mesmerized men if she hadn't been so cross-eyed. Her stare was penetrating, expressionless. She was obviously a drug fiend or mentally ill.

"I just . . ." the woman started.

Her gaze traveled straight through Samuel. Maybe she was blind. It was easy to mistake the mute and the blind for wise people, but they were just mute and blind.

"You've lost someone."

Samuel stirred his coffee and stared at the blown-up, sickeningly colorful version of the fast-food menu.

"Am I right?"

A burger and fries for €8.10 and a drink of your choice.

"Everyone's lost someone," he said, hoping that his remark would kill the conversation. He turned to look away at a group of teenagers sitting down at a table. One of them was oblivious to how uncool piercings were these days. But then again, how would Samuel know what was cool?

"I'm an actress," the woman said.

Of course you are, he thought. *You're an actress when you get liquored up or forget your meds.* Samuel was no longer feeling safe.

"I was in a movie with Chuck Norris."

Listen to this bullshit.

"My dad organized it. That is, if I hadn't died."

"I see," Samuel said and gripped his coffee cup tighter. The woman's confusion made him laugh, but then he remembered the discounted tenderloin in his dad's fridge. Everything was so unreasonable. This life wasn't easy on anyone. Why should he laugh at this sad, insane woman? She was driftwood, and the waves had tossed her onto the same shore where he already lay. There was no need to pretend he was better than anyone else.

"What's your name?" he asked, looking at the woman. She was a pretty woman, a real person. Nothing was forcing him to do this. He could get up anytime. His car was outside, the keys in his pocket.

The woman was delighted by the attention. Her shoulders shot up. A charming smile from days long gone spread across her face.

"Video Tape," the woman said quietly.

Samuel stared into her light-green eyes. One of the eyes looked past him.

"Excuse me?" he blurted.

"Video Tape."

The woman was absolutely ecstatic that Samuel had asked her. She looked like an employee who'd gotten a promotion and then realized she wasn't supposed to tell anyone yet.

Samuel looked intently into her eyes, demanding to make some sort of sense of this conversation. But no. Doll eyes stared back at him.

He chuckled. "Nobody's called Video Tape," he said calmly.

A trickle of sweat tickled his back.

"My name is Video Tape."

They kept facing each other. Her immobility was distressing. It was sick. Samuel was suddenly certain that something extremely important had happened while he wasn't paying attention. As if he'd nodded off and it had snowed in the meantime. Someone had been observing him. His dad's death and the invisible victim of his hit-and-run. This was sick as hell. Who would do this to him? Yet the sliding doors at the gas station kept on moving back and forth, letting people in and out. Customers kept on chatting behind him. Everything appeared normal.

"What do you mean by that?" Samuel asked, clutching his coffee cup.

The woman smiled and watched him with her doll eyes. "This," she said.

There was no gesture, no indication of what she was talking about. Her light-green plastic eyes stared at Samuel, gray hair here and there among the black crow's nest.

"And by 'this' you mean . . . ?" Samuel asked, although his mouth had gone dry.

I'll show you the w—

He should've kept on driving.

"Well . . ." The woman pulled something out of her pocket. It got stuck in the fabric of her coat before it came loose. She shoved the object in her mouth before Samuel got a glimpse of it. Her jaws began their work.

"Yes?" Samuel said. He was suddenly afraid he might cry again. Maybe because of his dad, or Julia, or because he was just so damned exhausted.

The woman opened her mouth.

It brimmed with blood.

Samuel looked away.

One of the teens was sitting on the table, an earbud in one ear. He was gabbing away while the others listened to him. His friend was tapping a rhythm on the table. Samuel turned back to the woman.

He saw a tiny fish in her mouth; he saw its eye. He saw the fish hook. Then the mouth clamped shut.

The woman tilted her head. *What the hell are you ogling at?* the gesture inquired.

"You have a lure in your mouth," Samuel said.

He said it just like that, calmly and coolly. He even took a sip of coffee to punctuate the end of his sentence.

"Ee nah," she responded and squeezed her mouth into a tight line.

Her pale lips spasmed into a smile, then were forced back into a line. A small red dot appeared in the left corner of her mouth. It began to expand as the blood spread slowly, first in small fractals into the wrinkles around the lips. Samuel wouldn't have noticed the wrinkles in the gas station light without the revealing red.

"Excuse me?"

"Ee nah luah," she muttered, barely opening her mouth. Blood spurted out in thin lines from both corners of her mouth, sliding down as dark spittle onto her neck and dripping in a rapid rhythm off her chin. Samuel looked around. The man at the nearby table was reading a newspaper and yawned.

"Nawwhan wio heop you," she said and wiped her mouth, smearing blood all over her upper lip and cheek.

Samuel thought of his dad's protective hand. He wished he could feel it again. Instead he felt the smooth, warm surface of the coffee cup slipping away from him although he held it in his palm as firmly as a marble column or a doorknob.

"I don't understand what you're trying to say," he said.

How incredibly calm he sounded, although his heart was beating out of his chest.

The woman leaned toward Samuel, looking him in the eye. One of her pupils was a minuscule dot. The other was enlarged, covering almost the entire iris.

"Naw. Whan. Wio. Heop. You."

She nodded toward the man with the newspaper.

"Eh doh see oh heoh."

The woman burst out laughing. Blood sputtered onto her chin, droplets falling onto the table. Her swollen tongue lolled, pierced with hooks. It was split in half. Lolled in red foam like a mouthless, eyeless prey.

Samuel considered the possibility of having a heart attack. Not because he was panicked, but because he thought it was time to think about it rationally. He was in his forties. It wasn't impossible. People his age collapsed when they were jogging or lifting weights at the gym all the time. He thought about himself in the violent throes of death at a gas station after midnight.

"Excuse me," he whispered to the man with the newspaper.

He just kept on reading, ignoring Samuel and turning the pages.

Eh doh heoh.

Samuel felt his lungs slowly collapsing. Some large animal was squeezing his chest, and it caved in like a mouse's rib cage.

"Excuse me," he said. A little louder this time.

The man jumped but didn't turn to look. He pretended to read for a while longer, then glanced at Samuel briefly. Their eyes met.

"Yes?" the man said.

Samuel was relieved, although he could hear the woman's cackling in his left ear, the lure jangling. The man didn't pay any attention to her.

"Yes?" he repeated and put his newspaper down. His expression was cautiously friendly.

Samuel stared at him until he was sure. The man didn't even glance at the woman.

"What's the time, please?" he asked.

The man first turned to look over his shoulder, then took his cell phone out.

"It's ten past midnight," he said.

"Thanks," Samuel blurted, a bit too fast.

"No problem," the man mumbled with a smile and continued reading the newspaper.

Samuel knew he had to get out of there. He finished his coffee and got up.

Nawwhan weo—

Samuel stuck around to buy the daily paper, which was something he never did. He didn't let Krista buy them, either, no matter how interesting the headlines were. It was all crap. He folded the paper under his arm like any normal human being and fished his car keys out of his pocket. He saw the woman's reflection in the sliding doors before they opened. She was sticking her tongue out at him in protest. Her pitch-black tongue.

Samuel walked to his car, sat down, and focused on his breathing. He called Krista.

"I have to stay here for a while," he told her voice mail, imagining all the hardships this caused Krista—taking the kids to school and losing her temper from all the added stress—but right now it didn't matter. "I'll be back as soon as I can. I'm sorry."

Samuel started the car and headed back to Suvikylä and his dad's apartment.

I'll show you the way . . .

". . . that I went," Samuel finished his thought. His voice sounded drowsy in the hum of the car.

It was from a poem by Eeva-Liisa Manner from the collection *Inscribed Stone.* The book cover was pale yellow, drawn over with sharp, vertical black lines, like a seismograph reading imitating the surface of a stone. The book's spine audibly cracked each time it was opened, making Samuel worry that one day the pages would come off, and the library would send them a bill.

If you should one day come back to look for me.

Samuel pushed harder on the gas pedal although the rain had fogged up all the windows. He tossed the daily paper over the video-tape on the front seat to cover its stupid, staring eyes.

Maisa woke up way too early. She had set her alarm for ten, but she was already up before six thirty. Her mouth tasted like hangover.

She managed until afternoon before opening a fresh bottle of wine and calling Kirsi. They chatted for a while about anything but Sagal and Maisa's research. Kirsi agreed to go out with Maisa in the middle of the week, although she was slightly worried about her reputation at the school.

More repetition of the same followed. Kirsi sat with Maisa at Crystal Bar until eleven, but Maisa continuing drinking by herself at the apartment until three in the morning, writing in her notebook and on the computer, drawing graphs, leafing through Nasr, Eck, and even good old Corbin in search of choice quotes that would confirm her hunch that she had something more meaningful than a ghost story within her grasp. She looked at the newspaper clipping about Samuel, touching its dry surface. She was sure she felt two souls reaching out to each other in a drunken haze. She decided to call Kirsi again before going to bed to seek absolution for how she had wronged the Somali girl, but Kirsi had turned her phone off.

Maisa kept at it for two more days. She started drinking already at three in the afternoon and then she was off to a bar, where she could easily convince herself that everyone led the same kind of life. Everyone had been granted a gift at birth, and Maisa's was the ability to drink all day, every day. When she stopped it wasn't because she couldn't go on any longer; she stopped because she got bored.

On her last hungover morning Maisa got out of bed and was determined to not think or be ashamed about anything that had recently happened. The sun shone into her apartment; she could pay the rent for at least six months with the grant she'd get. Once the grant was squeezed dry, the only option would be to leap off the Raippaluoto Bridge like all the desperate, abandoned mail-order brides. She'd never ask her mother and father for money. Other people had it way worse than she did, and they couldn't ask their parents for money because they had no parents.

Maisa slipped into her tracksuit before her hangover even registered. She ran north along the Prison Shore over to Hoviska Park and then to the small island of Vaskiluoto. She stopped to catch her breath on the jogging path for fifteen minutes, allowing herself to admire what a determined woman she was. Yet she wondered whether she should've done everything differently when she was twenty; she could be on the deck of a sailing boat right now, stretched out on top of fiberglass worth a million dollars while some tanned man in a white cotton shirt who had graduated from the Hanken School of Economics steered the boat and told her how the wind would certainly turn in their favor before they'd dock at Bora-Bora.

Maisa ran all the way back home, wishing either for a heart attack or Bora-Bora. Or she could simply transform into a blue-collar woman who has been painfully aware since childhood that the last person she should take advice from was her drunken father. She'd work as an office cleaner, and on her smoking break with her cleaning buddy, she'd talk about how that no-good husband of hers was unemployed again and the band Yö would be playing at Hullu Pullo, a bar just down the road. No self-doubts, no ethical choices about food; just pure survival and poorly sung karaoke straight from the heart.

She kicked the morning newspaper and the envelope on top of it out of her way in the doorway, took a shower, and turned the coffeemaker on. She sat on her towel, naked, watching the last leaves of the summer hanging on to the trees and the sea behind them. Memories of the conversations she'd had the past few nights flooded back; the unknown men and women who'd assumed she belonged to their party just because she'd shamelessly sat down at their table.

Her thoughts led her back to the envelope on top of the newspaper. How come the mail had been delivered already? It wasn't even ten yet. The mail didn't usually come before noon.

Maisa walked into the foyer and picked up the envelope.

No address. It hadn't been glued shut, either. She opened it and pulled out a piece of paper. Something dropped onto the floor. Maisa expected an invitation to the HOAS fall picnic or something equally inspiring, but as she looked down she saw it was a photo. A warped, old-timey photo. She crouched down to pick it up.

She stared at the photo, not quite understanding what she was seeing. Her hangover and the uselessly long run had exhausted her, and her brain wasn't putting two and two together. Slowly she began to comprehend.

It was a plate. A knife set on the right. A fork on the left.

An eyeball on the plate.

Next to the eyeball was a collection of teeth.

It had to be an invitation to a premiere at a theater in Turku. Maisa had been getting such invitations for years although she'd left the university theater group. She unfolded the accompanying piece of paper. The text had been written with a good old typewriter.

Dear Miss,

A learned "old spinster" like yourself would likely find it most unpleasant to be tied to a chair and observe this sight with your one remaining eye and swollen gums, all the while knowing that there will be no sons or daughters left behind to grieve you or maintain your grave. In the serving suggestion you see in the image, the eye and the teeth were removed from an old sow who'd oft given birth, so of course they are much too large and otherwise inappropriate for your case.

With kind regards,
The Ever-Devouring Night

P.S. You leave the lights on too often. You sit on your windowsill, drinking wine in your underwear. Picking your nose and shoving your finger in your mouth. You piss in the Holy Trinity Church park in the wee hours of the morning. I assume you are trying to rid yourself of these vices, especially that one. You know which one.

Maisa shrieked in laughter. Once she was in control of herself again, she read the letter five more times, then laughed some more. She walked into the kitchen, sat down, and read the letter once more. It had to be a sick joke, but it had been committed with too much care for a joke.

The threat revolted her. An eye and those teeth with an arching line of discoloration between the root and the rest of the tooth—right where the gum line had been. Did her teeth look like that, too? The thought made her nauseous.

The accusations in the postscript brought up hazy memories from the past few days, manifesting themselves as a sharp ache behind her eyes. Shame and fear stirred their heads. She'd never leave the apartment again. How could she? What had all the passersby thought and what had she looked like? Memories of faces, snippets of conversation. Maisa Riipinen was a disgusting human being: shameful through and through, overly pontifical when she was drunk, ready to take on anything, too useless a whore to be a mother, a childish, unskilled naysayer wholly dependent on grant money. She didn't care about others and never knew when to stop. Her life was a series of failures, whose misery enforced her deluded notion that she was somehow special and one day other people would see it, too. How pathetic. So pathetic that she should've just died. That would have been the easiest solution: dying. To one day suddenly be overcome by an odd sensation at the breakfast table and have just enough time to ask the empty kitchen, "What now?" before she'd smash her face into the cereal bowl.

Maisa collected herself. She read the letter out loud.

"Dear Miss. A learned 'old spinster' like yourself . . ."

She imagined a teenager, a loser smelling of moped grease, writing these words.

"In the serving suggestion . . ."

Highly unlikely.

"I assume you are trying to rid yourself of . . ."

No way. Teenagers living in these suburbs wouldn't approach her with such a respectful tone, let alone spare a single second to think about old spinsters and sows who had birthed "oft."

Maisa looked at the photo again. It was still revolting, but this time she felt like she had the upper hand. Most likely it was an image from some old film that has since been used to scare people for decades. That thought felt even better.

"A ghost story, huh?" Maisa chuckled.

The hot winds of Bora-Bora caressed her face. In her mind she saw the vastness of an open ocean, the undiscovered shadows on the approaching island, the natives greeting her from their canoes, if Bora-Bora had any inhabitants. No man of Hanken behind the steering wheel—she'd steer the boat herself.

Maisa went back to the foyer to get her cell phone from her purse.

"There's been a so-called development," she said when Pasi picked up. "Listen to this."

She read the letter out loud without a trace of fear. She sounded confident. She felt no shame about peeing in the church park.

The yard in front of the Patteriniemi apartment buildings was strange, yet familiar.

As Samuel stood at his dad's kitchen window in the morning, he tried to grasp at details that had changed. The brick barbecue pit was now covered by a corrugated steel shelter. The sandbox had been replaced by a jungle gym and a device that looked like a carousel, but Samuel didn't quite understand what it was used for.

The most obvious change took the longest to understand. There was nobody in the yard. No daycare staff with hordes of children in tow. No neighbors huddled together in serious conversation, no men leaving for work and stopping for a few words on politics (the world's most boring topic, but fascinating to listen to because of the tense exchanges). No retirees sitting on benches, occasionally scolding, then instructing and entertaining, groups of children, sometimes even handing out a chocolate bar without anyone thinking they must be pedophiles.

It looked like everyone kept indoors and to themselves these days. Samuel stood at the window for hours and saw only three signs of life: two people walking quickly across the yard, an elderly man, and a woman exiting a building, pushing a stroller. The only larger group of people consisted of immigrants, all men, gathering under the barbecue shelter for a moment. The fiery ends of cigarettes waved in the air for a quarter hour before the group split up again.

The yard and the buildings around it gave off an air of a temporary rest stop for people passing through. Their real lives were somewhere else, where single-family homes were built and people looked like actors in ads for insurance companies and SUVs. The years had stolen something important. They'd stolen the feeling that this was good enough. Despite all the vices and closed-mindedness and the urge to stifle anything that stood out of the ordinary, these buildings had acted as walls against the darkness emanating from the sea and the villas, its source some inhumane, unknown place. That dark wind chilled bones all over the world. But never before had it reached all the way here. Until now.

Suddenly Samuel felt guilty, as if he'd played a part in how empty the yard had become. After all, he had always been fixing to leave, wanting to be anywhere else but here.

The thought of leaving brought the gas station and the woman to mind. He turned away and tried to force other thoughts into his head. He randomly pulled a book off his dad's shelf and turned its pages. An old-book smell flooded him, reminding him of pipe tobacco and wall-to-wall carpets. He'd picked out a book that had been there since his childhood, with its dark leather covers.

"Where the proletariat fights consciously, the liberal bourgeoisie ceases to be revolutionary!"

Samuel looked at the spine.

J. Stalin, Works, Volume 2.

He had been gone for too long to remember how his dad had been a Stalinist all the way into the '80s. He only remembered the terms uttered with excitement: scientific socialism, the proletariat, class traitors. His dad's rants about how Finland was being unnecessarily held back by the bourgeoisie when revolution was inevitable.

Samuel leafed through the book, finding sections with thick underlining.

"Down with capitalism!"

"Long live socialism!"

"Down with the Czarist monarchy!"

He stopped at each exclamation point as if he'd located a piece of unknown inspiration right in front of them—the kind of inspiration that had forced his dad to get out of bed even in his final mornings. He had fought every day, viewed himself as a hero. Maybe he had been happier than the young unemployed and individuals beaten down by their poorly paid jobs because he had an ideology and his exclamation points. He never bowed down to anyone, and he hadn't been afraid of the future. Even nuclear war hadn't scared him.

"The bourgeoisie will collapse regardless," he'd guffawed when Samuel had asked how inevitable a nuclear war was. "You don't need a war for the downfall to come. Finland has enough Communists—the Soviets will protect us should we end up in a war."

His dad had always crossed the yard with his head held up high. No one had dared to debate politics with him. Did anyone walk with their heads held up high these days?

Suddenly Samuel realized how empty the apartment was. The space was filled with an unidentifiable whirring sound and the ticking of a clock, perhaps in the kitchen.

He had to return to the TV, to press "Play" on the VHS player. To watch a moment from twenty-six years earlier, a moment that had suddenly become available for outsiders to observe, yet he couldn't go back and change the memory of it, or forget it, or smooth over any of the details.

Of course Samuel had to jerk off, even when it caused intolerable shame. But how else was he going to focus on what was important?

And that was to focus on the slow movements of the lips on-screen. On the hand that simultaneously stroked fifteen-year-old Samuel's neck. On the gaze that appeared different with each viewing: first sarcastic, then condescending, indifferent, finally abysmally mournful. The yearning gaze of a lost memory. A cry for help.

Samuel rewound the tape and played it from the beginning.

A few seconds of black, crackling sounds, then static that warped in the upper edges of the screen. Then a clear image. In the background a buzzing sound and a hint of an echoing room, although all he heard was white noise.

Then a hollow click and the screen goes dark. The white noise grows louder while the screen remains black.

Then Julia is standing there. Looking serious, in a slightly amusing way, like a precocious actor. Not sad or contemplative, but calculatingly dramatic. Her pale green gaze does not waver (he couldn't tell the color of her eyes on the tape, but Samuel's memory filled in the gaps). Her hair moves in the wind. Julia had always looked odd, like a glittering piece of meteorite half-buried on a sandy beach. Her hair wasn't one of the primped, permed, or relaxed messes that everyone else but punk-rock kids wore. She didn't even wash her hair with shampoo— she'd said so herself.

"Suvikylä is a beautiful and peaceful place on the western coast of Finland, right by the sea," Julia says on camera. "Little would you think that—"

Samuel moved his lips along with her. The delay was barely noticeable as his memories stirred and turned into words. How effectively he'd soaked it all in: each gesture, intonation, and word. And yet that delay existed. He needed an old VHS tape and a living image on a CRT screen to bring his memories back and transmit them disjointedly onto his lips to form rudimentary words.

Images changed on the screen. Samuel recognized each take. Toward the end he had been behind the camera more often, and not because he was better at filming—Julia had been better in front of the camera. She was naturally fake, self-assured, made to be a celebrity. She could've been anything.

Samuel's eyelids twitched as familiar scenery and sounds were revealed to him. He felt like he was about to fall asleep, about to drift through the screen, grasping at the notion that time was remarkably relative.

Then, the villa.

Samuel stopped breathing. He continued gulping shallow breaths as he stared at the frozen image.

It shows a large, three-story wooden villa, with a tower on the left side like a fairy-tale castle. Julia stood in front of it.

Her actress's charisma disappeared. There stands Julia in windless scenery. The evening sun and its color of thick, bubbling honey are supposed to make her look gorgeous. They should keep her warm. But Julia is pale like a ghost, as if she were freezing.

"Ew, what stinks?" she asks the camera.

"No idea," Samuel said.

Not on tape. He said it there, on his dad's couch. The fifteen-year-old Samuel says nothing.

"This is . . ." Julia stops and gags, pressing her arm against her nose and mouth.

The camera stays on her, except for a small nudge that cuts the top of her head out of the frame. There's a faint buzzing of bugs in the background. They're the little dots rushing across the screen.

"This is so gross," Julia says.

Suddenly Samuel remembered the smell that the tape had not been able to transmit. He remembered throwing up on the large rocks at the shore. A wave had cleaned the vomit off right away.

The camera is raised slightly, and for a moment Julia is there entirely, head and all. Then the image is nudged again.

"What's that sound?"

Samuel's voice, a young boy's voice, is so near that it cuts through the white noise, keeping it almost muted for a while. Julia lets her arm fall off her face and leans over. Her eyes jerk from side to side, as if controlled by a mechanical arm.

Then, among the white noise and the buzzing of the bugs comes a high-pitched shriek. Like someone screaming inside a bottle.

"It's coming from over there," Julia says and lifts her left hand.

The camera turns toward the sound. A large white villa comes into focus.

"Come on," Julia says outside the frame. You can hear she's covered her nose and mouth again.

She goes first. The image follows her with a reckless bounce. Despite the quality, what Samuel saw on-screen now was much clearer than what he'd seen back then. The tears that had followed his vomiting had blurred his vision.

Julia walks up the stairs into the house. The shriek grows louder.

"It's coming from the cellar," she says and points at the stairs that lead down below. "Come on."

The dark rectangle of the door grows larger.

There's a woman's voice.

"What are you doing here?"

The camera is yanked down.

"Let's get the fuck out of here—"

All Samuel saw was grass flying by quickly.

That's where the recording stopped.

Samuel jumped off his dad's couch and rushed to the bathroom. He leaned on the edge of his dad's piss-stained toilet bowl and heaved a couple of times, but nothing came out.

"We have to go . . ."

It was the TV in the living room. The water in the toilet bowl was barely moving.

". . . back there . . ."

Samuel's ears popped. Then his left ear began to ring. His old fear of getting tinnitus came back. It was all those late evenings from five to nine at band practice when he was a teenager, and the volume had always been turned all the way up. All those shows, completely wasted while standing right next to the loudspeakers. Peer Günt, Mana Mana, Death Angel, Suicidal Tendencies, Bad Religion, and all the bands he couldn't even remember. Later he'd wear wireless headphones at home while the children were asleep. He'd open a can of beer and blast Nirvana or Pearl Jam or Tool as loud as he could to relive that feeling of freedom, when he could just walk out the door and think, *Today I can do anything my meager income allows, and after that I'll borrow more.* The sky was enormous above him. He didn't need to travel. The sky and his hometown were infinite.

But already that feeling of freedom he experienced as a twenty-year-old had become a yearning for the impossible. He had become infected by sorrow. Julia had been gone for a while, the early glimpses of happiness had been lost, tainted in something so evil and incomprehensible that he couldn't bring himself to talk about it.

Samuel did not throw up. Instead, he cried. His tears fell into the toilet where the water had sunk below the stain ring when no one had been around to use it.

When he got back to the living room, the screen shows Julia on the bed again and his own skinny fifteen-year-old body. Julia's eyes focus on the camera.

Too much happened in one lifetime; nobody could trudge along, pulling a full sled of experiences. Something had to give. Yet this here had been a part of every single thing Samuel had ever done. It had been in everything he'd ever said to Krista when they first met. In the drunken waltz they danced in the hotel hallway after their wedding. In the birth of Aada and Iines and their baptisms. In Krista morphing into a stranger who merely shared his bed. All of this had been echoing in the background, hundreds of miles away, but at the same time it had been near to him, as if it had shared his basement when he closed his eyes at night and listened to the hum in his ears.

Samuel realized he was whispering words. The same words Julia's mouth mutely formed on-screen. Again and again.

He walked into the foyer and threw his coat on. The door slammed with a loud bang as he left, sending an echo through the stairwell. It was all just one big basement to him.

The rain had finally stopped. Samuel walked with determination, trying to keep his head up high like his dad.

The woods behind the townhome garages had been ravaged by the storm. The soaked tree trunks looked like the limbs of large, strong animals. Their yellow leaves flitted in the wind like a beast's lure waiting to catch its prey.

The path began where it always had, under the beech and its twisted branches. The path would take him through a marsh, through sinking mud where the sea and the land hadn't quite decided which of them should rule over the other.

Reeds swayed along the path. Someone must've used it all these decades. The distant glow from the streetlights was enough to light part of the way along the path, but it quickly turned pitch-black. Samuel took his first step into the darkness. When his feet began to sink in the mud, he tried to remember Julia's sad eyes and her mute words.

"I hate you," she'd mouthed on tape.

She'd repeated it like a bitter mantra. Or a curse.

As Samuel waded on, he thought he could see Julia's figure like a shadow in front of him. Her eyes full of rage, yet at the same time fearful. Her hair was glued to her forehead and pale cheeks like shiny calligraphy.

Julia showed him the way. Julia, who hated him.

THE MORONIC
MOON

When Samuel was fifteen he realized he was never alone: he shared a room with his little brother Aki, and when he walked out to the yard, it was filled with daycare staff with groups of children, or men smoking cigarettes on the benches, or that bully Jape with his crew revving their mopeds. If Samuel was in his room and began to hum to music on his headphones, soon either his dad or Aki would emerge out of nowhere to grin idiotically at him. He never had longer than five minutes in the bathroom before someone knocked on the door.

When Samuel looked in the mirror, he entertained the thought that a camera was hidden behind it. It made no sense, but he'd never had any reason to think otherwise.

Someone always saw him. Someone was always watching, listening, judging, keeping tabs on him. Samuel didn't own a single moment. He accepted his fate like a prisoner who was well aware that the flap in the door could open at any time. A faceless pair of eyes would stare at him and judge his deeds.

Then came Julia and everything changed. She showed him that the cell door was ajar. That two people could be one, yet alone, in their own realities.

Julia had appeared unexpectedly and fearlessly in the summer of 1987. Samuel saw immediately that she was of a different, more wondrous breed. Usually odd people looked somewhat familiar, like you'd seen a relative somewhere. Samuel thought about how there were only about ten types of people, and everyone's facial features, body structure, and tone of voice were determined by these types. But not Julia's. Julia was something else. Julia was a promise.

She appeared in the middle of a block party. The adults were grilling sausages, with at least three cases of beer keeping them company. Cranky Raimo from Building Two, who always told kids not to kick soccer balls against the wall, was everyone's best buddy that night, even the kids'. He offered a swig from his flask to Samuel's dad. They were surrounded by a ridiculous swarm of mosquitoes, but everyone was having a great time. Adults started asking the teenagers about music, and even his dad put his Walkman on to listen to Kreator's *Pleasure to Kill* before handing it off to Raimo, who quipped that his Anglia made a similar sound when the exhaust was busted. "Should I record my car, then sing in English over the sound and send it to the radio station? Let's buy leather pants and take Anglia on an American tour! Let's leave our wives behind and steal both women and money from the capitalists." Anita from downstairs, who usually remained quiet, said that she thought the Beatles were pretty good. "Boys, you should listen to the Beatles. They've got some fine *meldodies*." Foreign words weren't her forte.

Samuel and Harri nibbled at their charred sausages. One good thing about block parties was that Jape and his crew didn't dare to come slap them around when adults were present. They'd go talk to the adults in packs of five, even to the ones they talked shit about behind their backs. They didn't even glance at Samuel and Harri. Instead, predictably, they talked about mopeds and cars. Harri was bullied even worse than Samuel in those days. They said Slayer and Motörhead sucked, and they should listen to Finnish bands like Popeda and Eppu Normaali—the bands Jape played loudly on his boom box while standing on his balcony topless, arms spread out, singing along to the lyrics about galloping to the liquor store. The world was made for people like Jape. Samuel just had to accept it.

"Who's that?" Harri said and nodded toward the parking lot.

Samuel looked over, expecting to see a second cousin of the son of a second cousin from the Hagert gypsy family.

An odd girl stood between the two apartment buildings. Her head was tilted, and a strange device covered one of her eyes. First Samuel thought it was a spyglass, because nobody had video cameras. Julia represented something never before seen on Patteriniemi Road, but only Samuel understood this. Harri had already returned to eating his burned sausage.

"I'll go ask her," Samuel said.

"Why?" Harri asked.

Good question. The only time girls on Patteriniemi Road even looked at them was to yell, "Your commie dads were marching again in the first of May parade," or "Come here, you commies, so we can suck you off," which was an outright lie. The girls' dads were at least Social Democrats, but only people taking part in the annual May marches were included in the taunts, and those were Harri's and Samuel's dads. The band Venom made these girls pretend that they had to puke. They'd never play Metallica on the radio, unlike Eppu Normaali and Yö.

"Just because," Samuel said casually. He had a chance at acting casual when he was drunk, as long as he didn't draw any attention from the moped boys. He stood up and walked over to the girl. She didn't put her camera down until he was right next to her.

"Hi."

"Hey," Julia said.

"What are you filming?"

"Everything."

"Is that supposed to be a video camera?"

"Yeah."

"But it's so small."

"It's a camcorder. It has a VHS-C tape in it."

Julia turned the camera over and opened it. A funny-looking tape was nestled inside. It looked like a normal VHS tape, but much smaller.

"Where can you get those?"

"Maybe nowhere," she said, "around here."

That last sentence sounded annoyingly cocky, so Samuel stopped talking.

"Is this supposed to be a barbecue?" Julia asked.

"A what?"

"Like a grilling party."

Samuel thought for a second. Then he nodded. "A grilling party, yeah."

"Cool."

"Right," he said. "Where do you live?"

Julia nodded to the left, meaning that she lived in either a townhome or a single-family home. Either way, her parents owned their place. Samuel's dad had always said that tiny parasites sucking on the common workingman's veins inhabited the townhomes, while the single-family homes were nests for the big-boss bloodsuckers. The only occupied single-family homes in Suvikylä were right next to Patteriniemi Road, and those houses were huge. Only people who voted for the Coalition Party lived there, and that one traitor Social Democrat who had been getting money from the CIA.

"Want a sausage?" Samuel asked.

Julia smiled, shook her head.

They managed to introduce themselves. Just as he couldn't come up with anything else to say, Anita appeared.

"And who are you?" she asked, teetering.

"I'm Julia, *ma'am*."

"What the hell is a 'ma'am'?" Anita laughed.

"It's spelled like 'madam,'" Julia explained calmly. "But you pronounce it 'ma'am.'"

"Like in the TV show *Dallas*?" Anita giggled.

"Mm-hm."

"What's that on your shirt?"

"You can probably read it for yourself."

It said "D.A.R.E. To Keep Kids Off Drugs" in English. Samuel didn't get it.

"Raimo is looking for you," he told Anita, who was spelling the text on the shirt out loud, one letter at a time. He was embarrassed for her. Luckily Anita was so drunk she didn't even notice the camera. Otherwise she would've asked Julia to record her drunken bullshitting. Anita jumped and turned toward the crowd, which had started singing a song by Kirka.

"It's. Your time."

Anita began to sing along and started on unsteady feet back toward the grill.

"I'm sorry." Samuel knew she had saved Julia from an inane conversation about the Beatles, but he felt it was polite to apologize.

"It's all right."

"Why do you say *ma'am*?" he asked.

Julia shrugged. "We used to live in the States."

"For real?"

"Mm-hm. In LA."

"And you moved here?"

Julia nodded.

"Are you pretending to be something?"

"Like what?"

"Like an American or something."

"No. My grandmother still lives there, but I was born in Finland and went to school here for the first three grades. I'm not pretending to be anything."

"You'll get your ass kicked here if you speak English," Samuel said quietly. "Everyone will think you're trying to be better than everyone else."

Another shrug. Samuel wasn't sure whether the girl really would be beaten up, but he'd heard how Maisa from the townhomes had been shoved against a wall really hard for some reason that wasn't meant for kids to hear. Most of the perpetrators had been girls the same age as Samuel, but they all dated boys who owned cars.

"When did you get here?"

"Yesterday, duh."

"So you don't even know anyone yet."

Julia nodded, and the nod revealed how scared she was. Samuel wouldn't have paid any attention to it if he hadn't secretly drank out of his dad's bottle with Aki right before the party. Now he wasn't afraid anymore and could clearly see the fear in her. How could someone from America be so afraid of Patteriniemi Road?

"Don't worry," Samuel said. "I'll introduce you to everyone."

He felt as if he could command Jape and his pals. His ears hummed.

"You mean, to those guys?" Julia nodded toward the party.

"No, I mean to all the good people. Like Harri, and . . . the rest of them."

"What are the rest of them called?"

Samuel hadn't expected such a direct question. All the reasonable names in the world disappeared from his brain and the only ones he could think of were Arthur and Väinö.

"Well, let's just start with Harri."

Harri was the only boy on Patteriniemi Road who hadn't had Samuel in a headlock. He listened to Mercyful Fate because his older brother made him. Samuel could always go to his place to listen to the kinds of records the neighborhood idiots knew nothing about. He wouldn't have dared to even store some of the records on his shelves. Mercyful Fate's *Don't Break the Oath* was the worst. Looking at its cover, Samuel started thinking how it might actually pay off to go to church and pray, as long as no friend would ever see him do it. They'd had the guts to listen to Venom's *At War with Satan* backwards, but only for ten seconds.

"All right." Julia smiled. "Introduce me to Harri."

Samuel knew she'd called his bluff, but it wasn't the end of the world. He could tell by the way she smiled.

"Where exactly do you live?"

"Oh, you want to walk me home?"

"Sure."

They walked past the town houses toward the homes occupied by the small parasites' hosts.

"Your mom and dad are rich," Samuel said when they stopped at a single-family home. It had at least three floors, if you counted the garages downstairs. And there were two garages, as if it were obvious that the people living there had two cars. It was the last house before the woods began, the woods that stretched all the way to the sea. Samuel had always thought that the previous family moved out because the house was too close to the wilderness. In the dark it looked like bears and wolves and who knows what lived there.

"My dad is," Julia said. "Super rich. He knows Chuck Norris."

Listen to this bullshit.

"Where's your mom, then?" Samuel asked, because he didn't want to catch Julia lying.

"Dead."

Samuel didn't ask anything else. He just said, "My mom's dead, too." He then worked up the courage to ask her, "Want to hang out tomorrow?"

"Sure."

He walked back to the party as if he weren't walking at all. He glided through the air that had been softly scented with rain and reeds and the sea, and he looked up and saw the tops of the trees with the sky behind them, and the sky stretched all the way out into space.

Later in the evening, as he sat around with the other kids and drank Raimo's liquor and beer that the adults had forgotten next to the grill, he thought about the tilt of Julia's head, her greenish-blue eyes, and how America had landed on Patteriniemi Road.

Maisa's reaction to the threat she had received was completely opposite from its apparent intention. She did not draw her curtains in the evenings. She didn't glance over her shoulder as she jogged through Hoviska Park and on Palosaari Island. Or at least she didn't admit to it.

When she thought about it, the photo and the threatening note quickly became an integral part of her bedtime ritual. Their memory haunted her behind her eyelids when she turned off her reading light. Sometimes she turned the light back on and read the letter, which she'd placed on her night table. She looked at the grotesque photo, enchanted, clutching it triumphantly like a kid with a glass jar in which she had captured a baby snake.

She drove to Suvikylä every day and strolled to the point in the peninsula. Her childhood memories led her to the Boundary effortlessly, to the place with the twisted beech. Leafless, its branches looked like tentacles. There used to be a small single-family home nearby, but all she could see from the path was a foundation covered in grass. A wet path that began at the beech led to the shore, which was overrun by reeds. But the path was still visible. Once she'd get to the shore, she'd see the Bondorff villa.

Maisa realized she'd been holding her breath, so she stepped over the Boundary as if to mock it, letting her adult weight crush the wet branches and bits of reed. She looked down the path until her breathing had evened out, then turned back.

On her way to the car, she noticed a police van next to the Patteriniemi Road apartment buildings. The sight jabbed at a corner of her soul, but she didn't want to get in touch with Sagal again. The girl's phone records would already show nearly ten calls from Maisa. She didn't want to think about all the questions and what she'd give as answers—that would just mess up her thinking patterns.

Everything would've been fine if she only knew for sure that Sagal was all right. She felt energetic, cocksure, and optimistic. She slept well, and when she couldn't it didn't matter; for whatever reason, three hours of sleep had sufficed lately.

If Sagal had only answered her phone or at least sent her a *fuck you* in a text message, everything would've been as perfect as it possibly could've been in Maisa's world.

She got into her car and buckled up. She'd already started the car when a group of girls gathered at the corner of one of the buildings. They lit their cigarettes and formed a broken circle in unison. It was easy to tell who was the leader, who was the ass-kisser, and who barely had permission to be there. Without a soundtrack it was easy to see how naturally these roles were filled.

Maisa watched the girls for a while. Her hand was still on the key. She nudged it and the engine turned off.

"Excuse me," she said, approaching the girls.

None of them heard her, so she repeated it slightly louder, not sure whether she should've aimed for an adult's authority or peer-like youth. She ended up sounding somewhere in between and insecure.

The entire circle turned toward her. Judging by their faces Maisa had accused them of something she wasn't allowed to bring up.

"Do you girls happen to know why that police van is here?"

One of the girls whispered to another.

"The fuck should we know?" the apparent leader of the group said. "Ask them."

"What's your name?" Maisa asked, trying to stare the girl down. She wanted to show her that she could see through the exaggerated makeup and the nonchalant pose all the way to the girl's fragile self-esteem.

"What's it to you?" the girl asked.

The group froze. Their faces flickered with fearful defiance.

"You better answer," Maisa said and walked unnecessarily close.

"Are you some social-worker bitch or what?"

"Your name," Maisa demanded. "Or you bet I'll go talk to those cops."

Abracadabra. The girl's mask cracked. The *c*-word always worked, no matter how vague the threat was.

"Mira."

"Last name?"

A long drag from the cigarette. The answer came on the wings of smoke. "Mickey fucking Mouse. It's an honorary title."

The group chuckled quietly, but the mask on the girl who had introduced herself as Mira continued to crack.

"Listen, Mira Mickey fucking Mouse," Maisa said. "Do you know why the police are here?"

"Someone ran away from home."

"Ran away."

"Yeah."

"How do you know that?"

"Because she's fucking talked about it for a year. Can I finish this cigarette or not?"

Maisa weighed her options, and while doing so she realized her own facade could come crumbling down any moment. All it took was an unsure glance for a split second.

"Who's the kid?"

"This one Somali girl," a girl hiding on the outer edge of the circle piped up. "Her dad doesn't even let her use the Internet. He beats her. Now he's yelling up there, being all 'Me love me girl.'"

Some more laughing, but less enthusiastic than when the leader had cracked a joke.

"What's your name, then?" Maisa asked.

"Mine? Yunomi," she said and blew smoke. "My dad's Japanese. My last name is Fukuyu."

The group let out a lazy guffaw. Only the leader remained stone-faced.

Maisa looked at the girl who'd just spoken, not knowing whether she should be relieved or worried more than before. Kirsi had given no indication that Sagal had problems with her father when they'd talked about her. Actually, quite the opposite: the father had sounded like a responsible parent.

Maisa jumped when a cigarette butt flew past her. Not that close, but close enough. Mira stared at her quizzically, feigning innocence.

"Can we go home now, miss?" she said. "We have such a dreadful amount of homework."

Maisa was quiet. Whatever authority she had had was gone.

"Thank you all," she muttered and walked back to her car.

She expected to hear shouting or sarcastic comments behind her, but instead she heard absolutely nothing.

Once she sat in her car, she saw the girls leaning in to each other, whispering. The leader, Mira, stood with her head held high and talked to each girl in turn with a relaxed face, but the circle around her had gotten tighter. Only one of the girls was looking at Maisa, but just briefly before she snapped her head back to Mira, as if by command.

Maisa turned on the engine and tried to find something positive from her exchange with the girls. Teenage girls ran away from home all the time—maybe even more often now than back in her day. Most of them came home when their barely adult friend kicked them out, or the older boyfriend who'd promised the girl the moon didn't get what he wanted. There were plenty of explanations.

Unfortunately none of those scenarios explained Sagal's disappearance.

The phone kept on ringing in the morning, but it didn't interrupt Aki's sleepy breathing on the lower of the bunk beds. He just ground his teeth and snored. Samuel could've fallen asleep again to the sound of the phone, but Aki's teeth-grinding was too much. Once, Samuel had decided to sacrifice a piece of Juicy Fruit and smuggle it between his brother's teeth, but it had only been soaked in drool and bent against the teeth. Screech, screech!

"Hello?" Finally, their dad's annoyed voice in the foyer. It would remain annoyed unless the caller was from the labor union or a member of the Communist Party.

"Who's this? Yes . . . he is," he said. "Just a moment."

Samuel tried to shut his eyes quickly, but his dad had already opened the door.

"It's for Samuel," he said and wobbled back into the living room.

That sentence sounded weird. Even Aki stopped grinding his teeth for a moment before launching back into it again. Their dad would've eavesdropped and teased Samuel about the call if he hadn't been hungover from the party.

Samuel jumped out of bed and went to the phone. The receiver rested on a small table in the foyer. He picked it up, catching a glimpse of his knotted hair in the mirror. He needed a haircut again.

"This is Samuel," he said.

"It's Julia. How are you?"

How are you? What the hell kind of a question was that?

"Just a bit tired, otherwise I'm all right."

"Good. I was just wondering if you'd want to go for a walk."

"Where?"

"Anywhere, I don't know."

"Sure. Right now?"

"Why not?"

They agreed to meet in front of Julia's house. Samuel ran back into his room to put his pants on. Suddenly Aki's head popped up.

"Where are you going?"

"None of your business."

"I'm coming, too."

"Just stay here and grind your yellow buckteeth."

"So what? You've got pubic hair!"

"Why do you have to be such a goddamned brat?" Samuel mumbled. "Go get yourself checked."

He wore the same shirt he'd worn the day before, although he was slightly worried it smelled and Julia would be wearing a fresh set of clothes. His dad hadn't had the energy to do laundry in the communal laundry room after work, so Samuel had to look for clothes that smelled the least. Right now he had no time, though; Aki could get dressed any moment now and follow him. His brother was clearly frustrated: their dad had taken him home from the party already at nine in the evening.

"You're pretending to read fancy poetry by some French 'Ballselaire,' and you're just sitting around growing your pubes."

Aki's voice sounded on the verge of tears. He was coming really close to tagging along. Samuel wouldn't have time to brush his teeth if he wanted to duck out in time. He had to be careful which way he was breathing. And he had to worry about smelling like sweat. And to look around to make sure Aki wouldn't jump out of some bush and attack him and Julia. What a joy to have a little brother.

"I'm going," Samuel said. "You keep scratching your ass and sniffing your fingers."

He didn't stay for Aki's rebuttals but instead rushed out of the room and slammed the door behind him. His dad stopped snoring then, but he would have forgotten about it by the time Samuel came back. Only in the stairwell did he notice he'd locked himself out without keys, but that couldn't be helped right now.

Old lady Huhtala was collecting empty bottles that had been left next to the grill. She placed the rain-washed bottles into a plastic bag. She'd been staring at the party below all evening from her window, like a reflection of a full moon.

Julia was already waiting on the street in front of her home. Samuel could tell from afar that she'd brought her video camera. She was filming Samuel approaching, which made him pay too much attention to the way he walked. He looked natural. So natural that he stumbled once and almost face-planted on the asphalt. Julia didn't laugh; she just kept filming. She was wearing a fresh shirt, Samuel could tell that from afar as well. It was blue, with a graphic of a surfboard and letters spelling "Los Angeles" and something else. It was tucked into her jeans, revealing the shape of her breasts. The shirt she'd worn the previous day had been so loose that these thoughts hadn't even crossed Samuel's mind. All of this made him feel anxious, especially since he was hungover. He wasn't really feeling it, but because adults always complained about a hangover after drinking a bit, he probably had one, too.

"Hi," Samuel said and looked Julia directly in the eye.

"Hi." She lowered the camera.

"What are you filming now?" he asked.

He'd think about her tits later when he'd go to the communal sauna in his building to jerk off. He wouldn't necessarily think of Julia's tits, because that would be wrong; he'd think of tits in general. He could lock the dressing room in the sauna from the inside, making sure that not even Aki would come knocking. Then again, Aki was too afraid to even go down into the basement by himself.

"Where do you want to walk?" Samuel asked.

"I don't know," Julia said and forced a laugh. "I thought you'd know what's worth seeing around here."

He thought about it. He looked down at Julia's shirt without a dirty thought in mind, and without realizing he was even looking. The shirt said "Santa Monica Blvd." and "Los Angeles, CA." He looked at the surfboard and thought about places worth seeing.

"I don't think anyone else is out at this time," he said.

"Well, let's do a sightseeing tour, then. I want to film my new haunts."

"You want to film Patteriniemi Road?"

"Yeah."

She was from Los Angeles and wanted to film this place.

"There are some cool rocks at the shore over there." Julia pointed. "I took a stroll this morning."

"Oh, those rocks. You shouldn't go too far. They are . . ."

Samuel rummaged inside his memory like in a toolbox for a tool he'd never expected to use. That time he'd gone on a field trip with his history class to the shore had been forever ago. Harri had gone to the movies with his older brother to watch *Krull* and told him about all the good parts. Samuel remembered all of that, including the magical ninja stars, but he had a hard time remembering what his teacher had said. Something about the Crimean War and that there'd been cannons and that's why the place was called Patteriniemi, Battery Bay.

"They used to have cannons there," he said. "But that was about a thousand years ago. People climb those rocks sometimes and drink booze and fu—"

"Hey, junior," a male voice boomed above them.

For one terrifying moment Samuel was sure God himself was interfering in his miserable attempt to come off as a ladies' man.

A man leaned over the balcony at Julia's house, looking like he was on his way to a masquerade ball. Mirrored aviators, colorful shorts, a white sleeveless shirt with shiny jewelry peeking over the neckline. Samuel assumed he was talking to Julia. Maybe he was her brother. No adult dressed like that.

"This is Samuel," Julia yelled back, annoyed.

"OK," he replied. Or actually, it was more like "okay," with a long *a*, and sounded like a question, even if it wasn't.

"He introduced me to some neighbors yesterday," Julia said and rolled her eyes.

The man let that information sink in for a moment behind his aviators.

"Cool, cool," he said. "Nice to meet you, Samuel."

He raised his hand in a lazy salute, just like in the movies. Samuel smiled because he was sure the man had meant it to be funny, but he looked serious.

"Let's go," Julia said and walked past Samuel.

The man lifted his elbows off the balcony and tapped on a red-and-white box for a cigarette. The tapping didn't stop even when a woman dressed in a shiny nightgown appeared behind him and put a hand on his shoulder. She didn't acknowledge Samuel; she just yawned and kissed the man's shoulder. Samuel had no doubt in his mind that the woman was wearing nothing under the nightgown; and he was just as sure that nothing like that could ever happen to him.

"See you around, Samuel," the man said and twirled the cigarette into the corner of his mouth with a gesture he'd had to have repeated a thousand times.

"Yeah."

They walked in silence. It seemed like Julia didn't want to talk while her dad was within earshot, because she became chatty once they reached the townhomes.

"The camera's battery is pretty low," she said. "I forgot to charge it. So you have to choose one subject to film."

"A subject?"

"A subject. To film."

Samuel wanted to tell her he wasn't a complete moron, but that's not how you talked to a woman you were trying to hit on. Or had he already succeeded? Dating was scarier than anything having to do with the occult.

"Or I could just keep on filming you," Julia suggested.

She raised the camera to her eye and turned it on Samuel.

"State your name, cowboy," she said in English.

The camera's lifeless and cruel stare reminded Samuel of a sniper's sights. Julia's face had changed, melted into the expressionless observation of the camera.

He froze. He gasped for breath and blushed. He didn't even realize he'd stated his name before its stupid echo reached the back of his mind.

"Samuel," Julia repeated. "Now tell me, Samuel, what do you desire the most in this world?"

To walk with you.

The answer that popped into his head surprised him completely. His face turned a shade redder. The camera's eye was observing a fiery red face that had lost the ability to speak. The camera recorded it for anyone to wonder what the hell was up with that guy. Did he have a rash? Couldn't he talk? Was it cerebral palsy?

"I know something better to film," the horror made him blurt out.

"Too late," Julia mumbled, concentrating.

The camera was fixed on Samuel. Centuries went by.

"Just kidding," she said. "It's not even on."

She let the camera drop to her hips. A harmless block of Japanese plastic. Only now did Samuel realize he'd never heard the machine hum. Thank God or whoever it was who decided what went down on this Earth.

"Oh," he said. "I was just getting warmed up."

All of humanity and some rain-forest amphibians stopped in their tracks and laughed.

"All right, what do you suggest?" Julia asked. "I have battery left for maybe another fifteen minutes."

"Helge's cabin," he said.

"OK. And what's so special about it?"

"He's . . ."

A former grade school teacher who got fired for being a perv. He had to move into his mom's tiny cabin, where he now lived alone. He'd been beaten up a bunch of times. "He always was after the boys," his dad had said when he'd heard about Helge's getting fired. His dad had gone to the same Lutheran confirmation summer camp with Helge as fourteen-year-olds, and occasionally hung out with him. Apparently the last straw had been when Helge lured the headmaster's young male relative to his house. When Samuel had been younger he'd joined groups of kids in breaking Helge's windows with rocks, their favorite pastime. No one had done it recently. Maybe kids had gotten tired of it. Or maybe the dog Helge cared for so lovingly had finally turned people sympathetic toward him. Or maybe the reason was that one time Helge had begun to cry and scream, "What do you want me to do?" and nobody had known what to say. Except Jape, who'd said, "Go hang yourself," but this quip wasn't followed by approving laughs— just silence. Even Jape had apologized and asked Helge if he could buy the kids some booze. That had been the beginning of a permanent, secret arrangement that benefited everyone involved. That was the real reason why Helge was left alone.

"It's a pretty nice place, actually," Samuel said. "You can see the sea from there."

"Sounds wonderful. I love the sea. Our balconies have always had an ocean view. Except here—trees are in the way."

"You can see the sea from our balcony, too," he said. "You just need to lean over the railing a little."

"You should show me sometime. How about we go now?"

Samuel looked around. Besides one dog walker, they were alone.

"Let's go," he said.

He chose the more difficult route. The invisible route behind the garages. The small path was hidden by trees and reeds.

When they got closer to Helge's cabin, he turned around, reconsidering this plan.

"I need to tell you something about Helge."

"Tell me."

"He's a queer."

"Oh."

His statement didn't appear to register—Julia didn't react. Samuel thought he'd best repeat it.

"I mean a fag. He fondles other men."

"So what? Our neighbor in LA was gay. He organized huge parties where guys with mustaches sucked on each other naked."

Samuel waited for a cue that would let him know Julia was joking.

"Once, these two gay guys were fucking in the swimming pool. It looked so crazy. Then they held memorials. Lots of memorials."

"For what?"

"AIDS."

"All right," Samuel said. He tried to imagine mustached men in a swimming pool and AIDS funerals. The only swimming pool in

Patteriniemi was in that traitor Social Democrat's backyard, built with CIA money. Trade-union men with mustaches did make an appearance, but Samuel was sure nobody fucked anyone in that house.

"I just thought you should know," he said.

Something crashed in the reeds behind them. At first Samuel didn't think the sound was scary, but then she saw Julia's horrified face and the hand over her mouth.

"Don't worry, it's—"

The creature jumped at Julia, almost toppling her over. The hand holding the camera shot up above her head by reflex, just like when Jape still held on to a bottle of beer when he fell over on his moped.

"It's Arvid," Samuel said.

Arvid wagged his tail and licked Julia's hand. They heard Helge shouting, "Arvid! Get over here!" in the distance. Arvid was an idiotic-looking spitz-poodle mix.

"He's *won*derful," Julia said, stretching out the first syllable.

She forgot about the camera and let Arvid lick her chin, face, and mouth.

"Get over here!" Helge shouted. Huffing and puffing, his figure waddled toward them.

"Don't worry, we're fine," Samuel shouted back at him and turned to look at Julia. He couldn't help but envy the dog and his straightforward, stupid charm.

"How are you doing?" Helge asked as he finally reached them.

"I'm all right. We were actually thinking of coming to see you, if you don't mind. Julia here wants to film with her video camera."

"Fine by me," Helge said without hesitation.

He always responded the same way. His predictability and eagerness to comply made Samuel feel sorry for him.

They walked together the rest of the way with Arvid running rings around Julia and Samuel.

"Did you two want something to drink?" Helge asked when they arrived at the small one-story wooden house with a sauna built next to it. A grill fashioned out of loose bricks stood in the middle of the yard with a rusty smoker placed on top of it. There was a well next to the cabin. Samuel's dad had told him that salty seawater had ruined the well a long time ago, but Samuel had seen Helge hoist up drinking water from it. The house was in ruins: paint had chipped off in patches and the roof buckled, but Helge had somehow survived here even through the roughest of winters. Sometimes Samuel thought about Helge and Arvid while he waited for the school bus in freezing morning temperatures. Quivering, he would wonder how on earth they could make it another winter. He'd even walked to the cabin to check up on them and was always relieved to see light shining through the frosted windows.

"I could use a beer," Samuel said nonchalantly.

Helge looked confused. The beer game wasn't supposed to go like this. If the teens gave him money, he'd buy alcohol for them. Freebies weren't a part of the deal. Samuel looked away but didn't stand down. Julia scratched Arvid.

"Right . . ."

Helge went into the cabin and appeared with three bottles of beer. Samuel felt a pang of guilt but did his best to ignore it. He grabbed two bottles from him and handed one to Julia.

"This is great," she shrieked. "In the middle of the day!"

Samuel did his best to look as if this were completely normal to him. He even opened Julia's bottle with a piece of chopped birch he'd pulled out of Helge's firewood pile. He didn't succeed on first try, but the overall impression he made was decent.

They sat down on the chairs facing the grill. They couldn't lean back because the backs were covered in purple bird shit. The sun was shining. Arvid nuzzled Julia. Things could've been worse.

"Can I film now?" Julia asked.

"Of course," Samuel answered on Helge's behalf.

Julia messed around with her camera before lifting it to her eye.

"Helge," she said. "Why is Arvid called Arvid?"

That's a good question, Samuel thought, one that had never crossed his mind.

Helge squirmed in his chair. "Well, it was my great-grandfather's name."

"Great-grandfather's?"

"That's right. Arvid Fager was my great-grandfather. A lawyer from Raippaluoto who—"

"Great-grand?" Julia said. "He had to be alive in the Middle Ages."

"In the 1800s."

"That's still a long time ago."

"Yes. Arvid was keen on learning about fish, and eventually he even quit his job so that he could move right next to the shore. He collected fourhorn sculpins while everyone else hated them. They'd get stuck by their horns in the fishermen's nets and never let go. A lot of their skulls are in the shed out there."

"What are fourhorn sculpins?" Julia asked.

"They're great." Samuel tried to sound convincing. "You have to see them. They're like that monster in Jabba's palace's basement in *Return of the Jedi*, just smaller."

Helge always took kids who came up to the cabin to drink to see the skull collection. And in a way it was pretty cool to see at least a hundred horned fish skulls lined up neatly on the wall.

They went to the shed right away. Julia's camera whirred.

"It's too dark in here," she complained but kept on filming.

They returned to their chairs. Julia seemed a little drunk.

"That was amazing. And I hear you're gay," she said and drank out of the beer bottle.

Helge looked confused again.

"A fag," Julia tried, and looked at Samuel as if he were some goddamned interpreter.

"Yes, I am," Helge said.

"Do you throw a lot of gay parties?"

A shocked silence ensued.

"So, been getting any fish lately?" Samuel asked Helge.

For a while they talked about fishing. Helge used to sit at the end of the peninsula, staring at the tiny buoy's minuscule movements. That was one thing the kids joked about. He supposedly ate all the fish he caught raw, but actually it was Arvid who ate them, and they had to be cooked.

"What's that big house over there?" Julia asked suddenly.

"Which one?" Helge said.

"That one with the roof peeking through the trees."

Helge and Samuel turned to look where Julia was pointing. Between the swaying birch trees in the distance, you could see the top of a roof and a little turret. You wouldn't have been able to see them if they hadn't stayed still while the birches in front of them swayed.

"That's the Bondorff villa," Helge said and slurped on his beer.

"It must be amazing," Julia said.

Samuel looked at the uncomfortable expression on Helge's face, then said, "You can't go there. Isn't that right, Helge?"

The beer was making Samuel talk. It was hitting him so hard that his ears were humming. Helge shook his head and wiped his mouth with the back of his hand.

"Why not?" Julia asked.

Samuel knew that the question was inappropriate. For whatever reason Helge, the man who said "Yeah, yeah" to everything else, had always told them not to go to Bondorff Island.

Julia was now leaning forward. She had a curious look on her face, at the same time absent and completely present, as if someone had turned her face off so that she could concentrate on every single word.

Great, Samuel thought. "They even killed someone, right?" he half-muttered into his bottle. "Old man Harjula used to rant about it on his balcony on the weekends."

Helge chuckled and looked toward the sea. The villa roof was visible behind him. Samuel knew Helge wanted to say that old man Harjula had drank his brains out years ago. That's what they all said, but Helge never judged others. He honestly couldn't afford to. Samuel looked at the man's tired face, his eternally forced smile, his damp eyes. Samuel was embarrassed.

"I think those are just little boys' stories."

They sat in silence. The reeds shuffled louder to fill in for their absent words. A branch broke somewhere with a loud crack. Usually Arvid ran around with his nose on the ground, but he was still calmly sitting right beside Julia.

"Sure, they could be made-up stories," Samuel said, scratching the label off the bottle. "Harjula just was one of those—"

"Let's go there."

Julia's face had returned from the land of the expressionless observation.

"Go where? To the villa?" Samuel asked.

"Yeah. Let's film some footage there."

He wasn't sure what to say. He looked at Helge, who had a pained expression on his face as he shook his head. The wind played with the hairs on top of his head.

"There's nothing to film there," he said quietly.

"So you've been there?" Julia asked.

It looked like Helge nodded and shook his head in one motion. "I haven't . . . Inside the house, that is."

"I want to film it," she said.

Her tone meant business. No room for negotiations. She didn't threaten or beg—she just stated a fact that was bound to happen. Her face shone with adult-like certainty.

"We're going there."

Samuel heard the wind hissing in the trees. He thought about how it would sound once they'd reach the villa. He'd never thought about it before.

"Come on," Julia said and pushed herself off the chair so quickly that her beer spilled onto the ground. She picked up the bottle, drank the foamy liquid, and wiped her mouth. Arvid got excited from the sudden commotion and ran a quick circle around her.

"Or at least *I'm* going," she declared and began to march toward the shore.

"Wait up!" Samuel yelled and went after her.

"Samuel . . ." Helge said softly behind him, but it was too late. His legs were leading him already. Julia had found a narrow path in the reeds. She went first, with the camera in her right hand, pushing the reeds out of her way with the other. The path turned quickly into the muddy bottom of the sea, cracking and sinking under their shoes. Samuel's sneakers were soaking wet, but he didn't dare to complain. The reeds hid what was coming up in front of them until they reached a taller rock, at knee height. Julia hopped onto it.

"Yay," she said and focused the camera on something.

Samuel jumped up next to her.

"It's the villa," she said. "I want to get closer."

He saw right away that they couldn't just walk there directly: the bay was between them and the white villa. And water up to their waists, at least. He was relieved.

"Can you go around through there?" Julia lowered her camera and pointed.

Samuel shrugged. "I don't know."

"You don't know?"

"We never come here."

"You and that Harri?"

Sarcasm.

"Nobody does," Samuel said, now irritated. "We shouldn't go there. It's private property."

"But doesn't that make it more exciting?" Julia asked. "My dad said that Finland has this commie thing called everyman's right. That you can walk anywhere."

"Well, you can't walk over there."

"But can't we—"

Julia was interrupted by a loud hiss. Samuel felt a gust of wind right next to his ear. He lost his balance and almost fell off the rock.

Something jangly and shiny moved in the reeds.

"What's your business?"

They turned toward the voice. A man stood in a boat. He wore a rain hat, although the sun was shining. He reeled the fishing line back in. The lure stretched and ripped the reeds next to them.

"Our business!" Julia shouted back rebelliously and began to film the man.

"Go, get back to your homes."

Julia laughed and glanced at Samuel with playful eyes.

"But it's so boring there," she said.

"Julia, come on . . ." Samuel said, but Julia wasn't listening.

"You don't own the fish here!" she yelled at the man in an alarmingly know-it-all tone.

Samuel swallowed. He should've apologized for Julia's behavior, but butting in seemed dangerous.

The lure came off the last of the reeds and plunged into the water. It glittered under the surface. The man reeled it back calmly, occasionally yanking when the lure got stuck. The rain hat covered his eyes, but Samuel could see the lower part of his face: it was pale and immobile. When the lure jumped out of the water, a fish was struggling at the end of it. A small baby pike.

"This is your final warning."

The man didn't remove the hook gently with pliers. He didn't clobber the fish unconscious like Samuel's dad had taught him. Instead, the man wrapped the fishing line around his gloved hand and yanked. They both heard the hollow crunch on the shore. And then another. The lure flew out of the fish's mouth with shreds of gills trailing after it. The head was almost severed. The fish's tail moved uselessly, overcome by its reflexes to flee.

"Back to your homes," the man said and threw the fish back in the sea. It floated on the surface between them and the man, the sun reflecting off its scales. Samuel was sure that the fin on the surface was still moving, but it could've been just the waves rocking the fish. He saw the way Julia watched it. She was still smiling, but her expression was frozen with shock and rage.

The reeds behind them rustled before Julia had a chance to open her mouth.

"Get out of there, right now," Helge huffed. Arvid ran past him and lifted his front paw on the rock. Julia couldn't help but scratch him, although her eyes were fixed firmly on the figure standing in the boat.

The man didn't react to Helge at all. The fishing line swished in the air again and landed in the nearby reeds, this time slightly farther away.

"That guy has a real attitude problem," Julia said, way too loud. Her voice would've been tenser if she hadn't been scratching Arvid. "He's a sick animal torturer," she whispered to him.

"Come now," Helge said and apologized to the man with his shaking voice.

"Let's go," Samuel said and jumped off the rock. He started walking on the path without looking behind him.

"Mother*fucker*!" Julia muttered in English, screaming the last syllables. Samuel was glad to hear two pairs of feet behind him in addition to Arvid's jaunty steps.

Then Julia yelped.

He turned around.

Julia's shirt was pulled so tight in the back that her belly button was visible.

"What the fuck?" she screamed and tried to turn around.

"Don't move," Helge said. "Don't move a muscle."

Samuel saw the lure stuck in Julia's shirt collar. The hooks were ripping the fabric apart.

Helge shoved his way past Samuel and loosened the lure. It made a clinking sound against the rocks as it bounced back toward the man.

"Did that fucking sadist just throw—"

The man standing in the boat reeled the lure back silently.

"Shut up," Helge said and pushed Julia onward.

They walked the way they'd come back to the cabin.

"What kind of a nutcase was that?" she asked.

"He's a dangerous man," Helge said, almost whispering. "You better not make him angry."

"He could have hit her in the neck," Samuel said.

"If he'd wanted to really hurt her, he could have," Helge said.

They eyed Helge suspiciously.

"No one is that accurate," Samuel said.

"They can be. That's all they do."

"Who are 'they'?" Julia asked.

"That's just how it is," Helge said and gestured for them to move.

Once they reached the yard, Julia turned back toward the shore. Samuel waited for another tantrum, but she began to laugh instead.

"Fucking great," she said. "I could get killed here."

She didn't seem to mind the torn collar, or the idea of a hook sinking into her flesh. Samuel and Helge watched Julia, terrified. Maybe she didn't realize how dangerous a lure's hook under her skin would be. She'd have to go to the doctor, unless she had the guts to push the hook in farther to force the barbs out and cut them with pliers.

"He's an accurate man," Helge finally said. "He's been throwing lures in the reeds for so long, he knows exactly where he's throwing. He catches seagulls out of the air. And you, Samuel, should know how easy it is for seagulls to avoid lures."

His voice trembled, and his hands began to massage his thighs nervously. His pant legs were covered in mud up to his knees.

"Why would he torture birds like that?" Julia asked. She didn't sound angry, just genuinely surprised.

"That's just what he does. I guess he practices."

They *practice,* Samuel thought, but didn't want to say it out loud.

They talked for a while, but only Julia sounded as cheerful as she had before they'd gone to the shore.

"Hey, Julia, don't cross that boundary," Helge told her as they were heading back home. "I know you're new here and don't know all the rules, but they really don't like it if you walk on their lands. It's just the way things have been around here."

His tone was nonchalant, but Samuel could tell he was faking it— Helge had practiced what to say for a long time.

"You can film in those yards over there and elsewhere, but you shouldn't go to the villa. And that Reino there . . . He doesn't mean any harm. He's just doing what he has to do."

"Fine," Julia said and kissed Arvid on top of his furry head. "But who's Reino?"

"He's the Bondorff villa caretaker. He's not a bad man. He's just a little strict."

"Not bad?" Julia laughed. "He's a sadist and an idiot."

Helge didn't argue, nor did he agree. He said he should start fixing the shed roof, so they decided to leave.

When they'd walked about twenty yards from the cabin, Julia whispered, "So, when are we going there to film?"

"To the villa?"

Julia nodded.

Samuel let out a short, joyless chuckle. She must've been insane.

"Today?" Julia suggested.

"No . . ."

"Tomorrow?"

"You did hear what Helge said, right?" he said. "This place has its rules."

"All right, I believe you." Julia laughed. "See you tomorrow, though?"

"OK," he said.

"OK."

She took Samuel by the hand.

For that one moment everything seemed possible. They could go anywhere. It was an intoxicating feeling, mixed with the smell of rocks covered in moss and the rustling of treetops and the light breaking through the woods. Somewhere, strange lands and huge waves and people speaking foreign languages who lived in major cities existed, and nobody asked where you were going and whether you were trying to be better than anyone else.

"I should go," Julia said. "Dad's annoying bitch is making burritos and I can't stand her screaming if I'm not there to eat with them."

What are burritos?

"When should we meet tomorrow?" Samuel asked as her fingers escaped his.

"At ten. Right here."

"All right."

When they split up Samuel skipped twice on the asphalt, then quickly glanced around. The windows in the houses around him reflected the burning sun of a summer day, and he could hear happy screams of children. Everything was in its place, except his eyes were so wide open they were chock-full of light.

Samuel had to ring the doorbell because he'd forgotten the keys in his rush to get out. Aki came to the door. He looked suspiciously cheerful. Samuel kicked his sneakers off and stared back at him.

"All right, what the fuck is it now?" he hissed.

"Nothing," Aki purred and went into his room.

Samuel didn't think his little brother could've followed him and seen Julia. Aki sucked as a stalker. He would've walked out from his hiding place with his mouth gaping wide if he'd seen someone like Julia with Samuel.

As he walked toward the kitchen, he caught a glimpse of Aki coming out of his room, then turning quickly back in.

"'Life slips away at every moment.'"

His dad's voice in the living room. Samuel stopped. He recognized this tone immediately. The Funny Dad, but it took a moment longer for him to recognize the words.

"'Life is not here, it is elsewhere.'"

Poet Eeva-Liisa Manner. From the library. Due date well in the past. Aki burst out laughing somewhere behind him. Samuel marched into the living room.

"'I do not miss it, why would I miss a fragile substance—'"

"Give me that," he said.

His dad was on the couch in his underwear, hair like a crow's nest and the book in his left hand. His right hand gestured dramatically.

"'—that barely throbs!'"

He couldn't keep a straight face when he uttered the last word. He laughed easily when he was hungover. Easier still if he'd started drinking again.

"Just give it to me," Samuel said, his cheeks all red.

"'—smokes like a . . .' What the hell is this word . . ."

"Come on, give it to me already."

Samuel felt his brother's slimy presence behind his back, his muffled giggles and the faint aroma of the undies he'd peed in.

"'—smokes like tormented lightning in a bottle!'" His dad fell over laughing. "The goddamned things the bourgeoisie come up with."

Samuel lunged at his dad, who lifted the book high above his head. Its pages crumpled, but it didn't matter. If the pages were torn it wouldn't be Samuel's fault. His dad struggled free and got off the couch. Samuel chased him around the coffee table while his dad opened the book at another section and continued.

"'To witness this with one's body!'"

"Fuck, you're stupid," Samuel said and stopped chasing him. "A grown man."

In the worst case, Samuel started laughing, too. Every time he tried to keep a straight face until the very end.

His dad recited a couple more stanzas, but he was clearly past his most exhilarating high, although Aki shrieked in fake laughter to entice him to recite more. Samuel yanked the book out of his hand. He walked into the bedroom, brushing past Aki at the door.

"This is exactly why I want to get the fuck out of here."

He turned to his dad. Or not directly to him, but close enough, and said, "Just like Mom did."

"Don't swear," Aki said.

Their dad said nothing.

Samuel banged the door shut behind him as loud as he could. He knew his dad would soon walk in to talk about something else as an olive branch. That was his way of making sure they were cool. This time, though, his joy seemed to still carry a spark. Samuel took it as a sign that playing the mom card might not work any longer.

"Like a tormented fart caught in ice-fishing coveralls," his voice echoed from the living room, slightly quieter now to make sure he didn't annoy the kids so much, which just made it all the more annoying. And then: "Why would I miss the fragile Marketta from next door . . ."

Marketta was over eighty. Samuel shoved the book back into his drawer on top of an Arto Melleri book. Then he pulled the drawer open again and threw Melleri on top of the poetry book. It should be less of a source of entertainment for his dad.

"To witness this with my asshole!" his dad now declared right behind the door.

"Just fuck off already," Samuel whispered.

His dad could be the most annoying man in the world. He had to have been born with that skill. If his dad would've had any say, Samuel's name would be Yuri or Vladimir. Luckily his mom had been slightly religious and had demanded a biblical name. Sometimes Samuel thought his mom had been an angel who'd merely fallen onto this Earth to prevent the naming catastrophe his dad had planned.

Samuel dropped the Walkman headphones over his ears and slumped on the bed. A Kreator tape was still inside the deck from the night before, so it had to do. He cranked up the volume so loud that the tape's hissing melted under the noise, and Samuel was able to forget everything else. That's why he liked poetry and Kreator. They both charged at him, overloading his senses, making him mercifully invisible.

He drifted through the wall of noise into the sun, where reeds swayed back and forth and the wind blew Julia's hair. Together they were allowed to go anywhere.

He didn't stir until he felt someone poking his ribs. Samuel opened his eyes. His dad stood next to his bed. He lifted the headphones off his left ear.

"What kind of toppings do you want on your pizza?" his dad asked.

His smile was sad like the time he'd told Samuel that Mom might not come back from the hospital.

"Tuna and ham," he said.

"All right. Aki can go get it."

His dad ruffled his hair and then walked out of the room. He closed the door slowly behind him not to make a sound, the way he'd always done when he still read bedtime stories to Samuel and thought the child had fallen asleep.

Samuel put the headphones back on. Usually he would've relished his little brother's arguments against running errands like picking up pizzas for them, but this time he had better things to think about.

The reeds and Julia returned as soon as he closed his eyes.

Maisa's phone rang just as she'd gone out for her evening run at seven. It was Kirsi.

She slowed down to a walk and looked at the glowing screen, weighing her options. Kirsi could've heard from Sagal. Her body could've been found in the Suvikylä woods or on the shore. This news spread quickly in the teachers' lounge. Or maybe Sagal had come back home and told everyone how a strange lady had lied to her and blackmailed her to get a recording of a stupid teenage ritual. Maisa caught her breath for a moment and then answered.

"I have a message for you," Kirsi said after a rushed hello.

Maisa stopped.

"From Sagal?" she asked.

Kirsi was quiet.

"No . . ." she said, sounding slightly confused. "It's from another former student of mine. A girl called Mira Haataja. She wants to meet you. Right now."

"Why?"

"She didn't tell me. She said she met you earlier today in Suvikylä."

Maisa tried to remember the faces in the circle of teenage girls. She remembered Mickey fucking Mouse.

"Oh, yeah," she said. "We exchanged a couple of words."

"She told me to ask you if you could meet at seven thirty today."

"I guess so . . ." Maisa checked the time on the phone. "It's going to be a bit tight. I need to take a shower and then drive to Suvikylä."

"No, she wants to meet you at Brage Park. Remember where that is?"

She tried to remember. "Of course," she said. "I'm about fifteen minutes away."

"Good. And listen."

"Yeah?"

"She sounded pretty anxious."

Maisa frowned. "How come?"

"I don't know. Just . . . anxious. As if she were afraid of something."

"I see."

"Do you know what this is about?"

Maisa thought about the teachers' lounge and the fog of gossip floating over the coffee mugs.

"I haven't got a clue."

"She made me promise not to tell anyone about this. I used to sit in on her detention when she was at our school, and we talked quite often. I think she trusts me."

"All right."

Kirsi was quiet again, probably hoping that Maisa would use the silence as an opportunity to spill the beans.

"Hey, I really appreciate it. Thanks for letting me know," Maisa said.

She promised to tell Kirsi all about it later, although she knew it was a lie. When she hung up she thought about how Mira had not actually trusted Kirsi, although they were supposed to be buddy-buddy. Then she thought about the cigarette butt flying past her face and how Brage Park was barely lit. It wasn't hard to imagine a group of teenagers mugging her there. Girls could be evil if they wanted to be. Maisa had seen how a girl in her class had been beaten unconscious at the market square. Teenage girls, all of them—the victim and the perpetrators.

Tied to a chair. Swollen gums.

Maisa checked the time of the call and started a leisurely jog toward Brage. According to Kirsi the girl had sounded anxious. There had been no signs of that on the girls' faces earlier, but their defiance may have been just for show. Behind their act they were overly romantic, crying into their pillows.

Maisa slowed down before reaching Brage and was glad to see other joggers and dog walkers on the shore road. She left the road and walked on the grass, away from the lights. Their glow reached fairly far, but soon she realized how large the park was. It might be hard to find the girl in the darkness.

"Hey," a voice said behind her.

Maisa turned around. "Hey," she said.

The girl stood in an odd pose. Earlier that day she'd looked like she knew what she was doing, and all her gestures were honed and precise. Now the rules were different. She had no audience to perform to.

"Are you Mira?"

The girl nodded. In the dusk her face looked even paler than before. The ember glow of her cigarette shook nervously in the air.

"You wanted to see me?" Maisa said and glanced around.

"I didn't," Mira said. "But I had to."

"Why?"

"You asked about that girl who ran away."

"Sagal."

"Yeah. She didn't run away."

Maisa waited for more information, but the girl had turned to look at the shore road. A biker looked their way and slowed down. There was no way anyone could recognize them in the dark, but the girl remained tense and quiet until the biker was gone.

"We had to give her up," she said.

"Give her up?"

A nod. "She broke the rules by talking to you. I saw you there."

Maisa was puzzled. "Saw me where?"

"In the car. In the parking lot. And a week before that you stopped Sagal at the bus stop. Did you really think nobody would notice?"

Maisa let the words sink in. She thought about the lit windows of the Patteriniemi apartment buildings and the shadows surrounding the parking lot. The thought of having been watched was uncomfortable.

"Sagal gave you something in the car and that was the last straw."

The girl sounded bitter. Maisa was overcome with guilt but couldn't let it show.

"Mira, listen to me." She put her hand in her jacket pocket and took a cautious step toward the girl. She hoped her cell phone's recorder had turned on.

"What are these rules you're talking about?" she asked.

Mira crushed the half-smoked cigarette with the toe of her shoe and lit another one right away.

"Aren't you interested in finding out where Sagal is?" she asked.

Maisa swallowed. "Of course."

"Well, figure it out. All I know about is the place where we left her."

"Where?"

"In one of the storage spaces in the building basement. Hooded and with Ami's used sock shoved into her mouth. That, by the way, was Ami's idea. I had nothing to do with it. But Sagal is no longer in the basement, so there's no use for you to go there. I went there first thing the next morning. I didn't sleep a fucking second. I would've let her go, but what can you do?"

The hood and a sock shoved into a mouth played a trick on Maisa's thoughts for a second.

"Then why are you even a part of this?" she asked.

"Because of the rules. According to the rules, Sagal was my responsibility."

"There can't be rules where another person would—"

"Yes, there can!" Mira shouted.

Maisa flinched. She realized how cold she felt. Her sweaty running jacket was glued to her back.

"We didn't come up with those rules, you fucking cow. We just do what we're told. And we've never had to take any action until you came around to stir shit up."

Maisa didn't know what to say. Guilt gnawed at her, although the voice inside her head said she had no reason to feel that way. The voice told her other things, too. The material she was recording would be unique, as long as the phone did what it was supposed to do.

"Who comes up with these rules?" she asked.

Mira shook her head. Crushed her cigarette on the ground. Lit another one.

"How would I know who they are?"

"Which 'they'? How can they tell you to do anything if you—"

"We receive letters."

"Letters? In the mail?"

"No, the letters are dropped off at this one place that you don't need to know about."

"So someone leaves you letters that tell you what you should do?"

"Yeah. They contain the Sermon, and—"

"The Sermon?"

"Don't fucking play dumb. You probably made Sagal record it for you, so cut the bullshit. I'm responsible for fetching the letters and I'm paid in cash and cigarettes and some other stuff, but that's not why I'm doing it."

"Why, then?"

She shrugged. "You're just . . . supposed to."

Excellent, Maisa thought. Pasi would drop his sarcasm at this point in listening to the recording.

"It's an old thing."

"Do adults know about it?"

"I guess so. At least some of them do. They say that the Granny catches you if you walk to the woods at the shore at night, but we can't start asking them questions. You just don't do that. Some leave gifts under the octopus tree. Like I told you, it's an old thing."

The octopus tree. Maisa thought about the twisted beech but didn't recall anyone calling it the octopus tree when she was a teenager. She had seen shopping bags full of stuff underneath it, and you weren't supposed to touch the bags no matter what.

"Mira," she said, searching for a voice that would evoke confidence. "I need to ask you one important thing."

Mira didn't say a word.

"I received a note. A threat."

"Oh."

"It came with a photo. It was pretty gross."

Mira dug into her empty cigarette pack, then dropped it onto the ground.

"Do you know who sent it?" Maisa asked.

"No."

"Are you sure?"

"Are you fucking deaf?"

"Are you absolutely sure?"

"All right, it was me!" she shouted.

This time she didn't sound angry, just relieved. Mira stepped on the cigarette pack and twisted her heel as if she were crushing a snake.

"But I don't write them," she said. "And I don't take any pictures. I just deliver the letters where I'm supposed to. I don't really believe in any of that shit in the letters. I'm not interested in some fucking . . . hatchets and grannies and what's under the island."

"There's something under the island?"

"Yeah. There're supposedly caves and some old shit that nobody should be talking about."

"What do you mean?" Maisa chuckled. Her light tone was meant to encourage Mira, but she got even more worked up.

"It doesn't matter," she muttered. "If you don't want to help me, then whatever."

She turned to leave. Maisa panicked and grabbed Mira's sleeve.

"Can you sit down for a second with me?" she asked.

Mira yanked her sleeve away, but stopped walking.

Maisa waited. "There's a bench over there." She pointed.

The girl remained quiet until they sat down. Then Maisa heard a sound she didn't recognize at first.

Mira was sobbing.

"I don't want anything bad to happen to Sagal," she said. "She's suffered enough."

This should be reported to the police, Maisa thought. *Tell Mira to call the police. Or call them yourself.*

Something prevented her from doing it. Either it was the fear that her own dishonesty with Sagal would come to light, or that this wondrous and now almost unraveled secret would be taken away from her right under her nose and committed to dry interrogation reports, typed up by some older constable with his index fingers one letter at a time without realizing how important it was.

"Mira," she said and touched the girl's shoulder, carefully, like approaching an unpredictable animal. "I can help you."

She was prepared for the girl to pull away or to throw her hand off. But she just wiped her eyes and looked away.

"Does anyone on Patteriniemi Road know what these rules and letters are all about? Any adults?"

Mira shook her head.

"Someone older? Someone who's been talking about a hatchet and how you should avoid it?"

The girl looked toward the hospital. She was still breathing hard. Maisa could feel her breathing against her palm, the helpless confusion of a young human being.

"Maybe Anni."

Maisa leaned closer. "Who?"

"Anni Saarikivi. There are rumors that she once burst into the bomb shelter right in the middle of a Fairy-Tale Cellar session. She said those stories shouldn't be repeated anymore. She even attacked someone, causing a huge ruckus. The adults got involved, too. It caused a lot of fighting, although it had been innocent back then."

"What was innocent?" Maisa asked and repeated Anni Saarikivi's name in her mind in case the recording hadn't caught it.

"The Fairy-Tale Cellar and all that. That's when we still used the old Sermon. It was just something everyone did. You know how adults do things just because that's the way things have always been done. Especially the people who are still around, fishing."

"Tell me more about the old Sermon."

"It was just this story that older kids read to the younger kids in the bomb shelter. We're just having fun. We laughed if someone was really afraid."

"Who wrote it?"

"How the fuck should I know?"

"And then there was the new Sermon."

"Yeah," Mira said.

"When did this happen?"

Mira thought about it for a moment. "Maybe two years ago."

"And you have no idea who sent it?"

"No."

"Some older guy from your building, or—"

"I don't know."

They were both quiet for a while before Mira spoke again.

"Anni might know something. My dad says she's lived in Suvikylä since she was a kid—that was when the apartment buildings were built. She moved to Patteriniemi Road when her house was torn down. She's at least eighty. She lives in one of the apartment buildings. The first building on the left, second floor."

"Why did she get so upset about the Fairy-Tale Cellar?"

"I don't know. I was in sixth grade so I wasn't taking part yet. The adults fought about it publicly, out in the yard. Anni said she'd call the cops, but everyone just laughed at her."

The cops. An unfortunate topic. Maisa was about to say something when Mira turned to her and looked her straight in the eyes.

"You'll find Sagal, won't you?"

"Of course," Maisa said before she even thought about it.

Mira nodded, then pulled away from under Maisa's hand and started walking toward the hospital, probably to catch a bus. Maisa thought about offering her a ride, but she was sure Mira would've said no. *You really thought nobody would notice?*

Besides, Maisa had better things to do. She waited until the girl was back on the lit road where no one could see into the dark park. Her cell phone was still recording. She stopped it and played the file back.

First white noise, then mumbling in the background. If she hadn't known that they were human voices, there would've been no way of telling. Maisa cursed out loud, dug out her earbuds from her pocket, and tried again.

White noise. Mumbling. A couple of curse words and then something she could perhaps interpret if she tried hard.

Some old shit that you don't—

Maisa stopped the recording and deleted it. So much for that material.

She slumped onto the bench and looked out to the sea, contemplating the promise she'd hastily made.

Of course she'd find Sagal.

Samuel saw Julia every day that week. They'd walk over to see Helge, they'd sit at the tip of the peninsula long into the evening, filming seagulls and reeds floating on the water, despite the hordes of mosquitoes surrounding them.

Julia had a dream. She wanted to make the world's best tourism clip about Suvikylä. She told Samuel about America, how large the sodas they sold over there were, and how many TV channels everyone had. All movies were shown in theaters a year before anyone saw them in Finland.

Once, Jape and the other idiots spotted Samuel and Julia together. They had a lot to comment on. Samuel briefly worried about Julia developing a crush on Jape when he showed off wheelies on his moped and gave her cigarettes. Later he grew even more worried when Julia suggested that Jape should move to the States.

"Really?" he said as coolly as he could. "Why's that?"

"He would fit in perfectly in the Georgia backwoods where people yell *Praise Jesus!* while having sex with animals. *Squeal like a pig.* Do you know that one in English?"

Samuel guffawed loudly. "Yeah, I do."

"*Deliverance*. What an awesome movie. I don't know what it's called in Finnish."

He told her. They laughed together about how great Jape would've been in that movie, if he only knew how to play the banjo. Samuel and Julia, they wouldn't have fit the scene. They were a different breed altogether. He began to read poetry to her. She had asked what kind of books he read, and he had told her about Stephen King and James Bond. Julia thought they were boring, so he quickly blurted how he also read poets like Manner, Meller, Harmaja, and even Leino, although his poems had lame words in them, like "oh!" or "taketh" or "shroudee."

Julia had never read poetry—her dad considered it commie literature. When Samuel brought books to her one evening and began to read them at the tip of the peninsula, a curious expression spread over her face. They sat on the rocks. The sun had almost disappeared behind the trees. Julia's face was illuminated in heavenly light, and her hair waved in the wind as she listened to Samuel. Her video camera lay on the ground, untouched.

Soon the sun glowed only faintly over the horizon's thick, black line. A pale moon had risen, the kind nobody usually noticed. Just a ghost of a moon, as if ants had gnawed on it.

"You need to write me a poem," Julia said.

"I can't," Samuel said, looking at the ghost of a moon.

"Yes, you can. I can tell by the way you're reading them."

"What do you mean?"

"Your voice changes."

What a strange thought. Samuel had never considered that.

"Maybe I will write one," he said.

This was followed by a silence that nearly convinced him to start writing straight away. If he'd only brought a pen and paper, his words would've flowed. The words felt like breathing; they organized effortlessly into beautiful lines in his mind. He didn't quite understand them, but they made him feel good the same way music did.

I know how to do this, Samuel thought. What an astonishing thought. Maybe he could be like Eeva-Liisa Manner or Arto Melleri. Maybe he, too, could piece words together to reveal completely new sceneries, the kind that were descriptions of a simultaneously unknown yet familiar world.

"What's over there, on Bondorff Island?"

The question barely penetrated his internal wordplay.

"You hear me?"

"Yeah, I did," Samuel said. "That's where Granny Hatchet lives."

"Granny?"

"Yeah."

Julia laughed. "Why does she have a hatchet?"

"Because she kills children," he said. "It's just this story we tell each other."

"She's a bogeyman?"

"What's that?"

"Like a . . . troll."

"Sort of, yeah."

He wished he had a pen and paper.

"Why does she kill children?"

"I don't know," Samuel said. "Nobody asks that kind of stuff. She just does."

How wrong was it for no one to ever have thought about it? Words in his head began to flow around the singular puzzle of Granny Hatchet.

"How is it even physically possible for some old lady to catch kids?" Julia asked.

"She smells them," Samuel said. "Like that half-blind witch in 'Hansel and Gretel.' You know that story?"

"Of course."

"She can smell children from miles away. She sniffs the air like a fox that's been sniffing gas out of Jape's moped tank."

Julia laughed so hard that tears began to run down her cheeks.

"She runs like a mink at terrifying speeds, and when her hatchet swipes at rocks you can see sparks fly."

Julia turned on her side. It sounded like she was choking.

"Don't laugh," Samuel said, trying to keep a straight face. "You're allowed to laugh if you catch Helge sniffing his own fingers, but you better not laugh about Granny Hatchet."

"Stop!"

"Otherwise she'll appear one day when you're least expecting her," he continued. "And she'll wait for you to turn your back on her. Then she'll whack you with her hatchet between your shoulder blades so hard that the air is knocked out of your lungs and your legs go numb. And she'll roll you over. She'll stick her black tongue out at you . . ."

Julia suddenly wasn't laughing anymore.

"That's gross," she said, wiping her tears. "I'm getting scared. Tell me something else."

She sat up and looked around in the summer dusk.

"I'm sorry," Samuel said immediately. "What kind of a story would you like to hear?"

"You can tell me about that island, but please—not one more word about any grannies."

He looked up at the sky and pondered. Then he said, "That island is a piece that was broken off the moon."

"What?"

"The moon forgot to take it along when it separated from Earth."

Julia's clothes rustled as she turned to face Samuel.

"Ooh. Tell me more."

"Our geography textbook has a picture showing the moon breaking off from Earth about a hundred thousand million trillion years ago."

"So?"

"The moon's left eye was created when Bondorff Island refused to follow it, instead staying here."

"Really?"

"Really."

Julia chuckled. "Did you just make that up?"

"I didn't make it up—Harri did. He remembered that picture in the book and one day just started telling this as a fact. Sure, we'd had some moonshine that day, but only now I understand what a great story it was."

Words finding their places, wrong words replaced by the right ones, causing chain reactions that were beautiful even at their ugliest.

"And when the moon's eye was left behind, so was Granny Hatchet. And some creature that ought to belong on the moon."

Samuel could feel his words coming now, bubbling up inside of him . . . *How does it feel to dive into the green waters of early summer through algae that wraps around the ankles like a forgotten—*

"Moonshine? Does it mean home-made alcohol here, too?" Julia asked.

"Yeah. Made of yeast and sugar. Makes you really drunk."

The mud on the bottom of the sea is soft and light brown, the damp ashes of the ancient separation—

"All right. Where did the moon's right eye come from?"

"It's another island," Samuel muttered. "Near Iceland. It's inhabited by people made out of rocks who can hold burning lava in their hands, and when they do, their faces glow in its light, making them look like . . ."

Words became muddled as soon as they were spoken. They became mechanical toys that lost their magic. He should've been writing them down instead.

"What about its mouth?"

"That's America," Samuel said without hesitation.

"California?"

"Maybe. Yeah. California is big enough."

Julia was getting excited.

"That's the reason why California could fall into the ocean if there's an earthquake," she said. "The moon tried to pull it along for the ride, but some of it fell back to Earth. That's why the moon's smile looks so moronic."

"Yeah," Samuel said and put this enormous catastrophe of an earthquake into words in his head, although he wouldn't have been able to find California on a map. It just seemed to fit the story. Some things were true, even if they really weren't. But somewhere deep within their cells and between cells, they were true. This thought caused another chain reaction of words. Tens of new words. Hundreds. The algae braided itself into tentacles, the soft mud on the bottom of the sea puffed up like a mushroom cloud, piercing the surface like the aftermath of a nuclear explosion, rising high into the sky where the moon shook and buzzed as ants gnawed on its insides. The hum of the sea became louder, devastating his eardrums. The words took Samuel away and his sense of where he was, what day it was, where he lived.

Julia saved him by taking his hand.

The mud settled.

The algae unraveled.

The gnawed moon steadied.

The waves found a rhythm.

There was only Julia. In the pale full moon.

And the realization that words could whisk you away from this world.

*

Neither of them wore a watch so they had no idea what time it was when they finally headed back home along the path in the woods. Their exhaustion manifested only in increasingly ridiculous stories.

"My dad will have a fit," Julia said. "He thinks I should always be home on time."

Samuel thought this was strange. Usually when he got home, he had to shake his dad awake, who'd fallen asleep in front of the TV. Nobody ever asked him what time it was.

The path was narrow, so Julia went ahead. She skipped over rocks and roots sticking out of the ground, exaggerating the obstacles, as if she were a ballet dancer. It was a completely still night. They heard only the seagulls screeching out on the sea. It was so quiet Samuel thought that the world had turned itself off, and they could do whatever they wanted.

"What if we don't go home?" he suggested.

He liked the world when it stood still like this. He could've spent the rest of his life this way.

He didn't hear an answer, and was about to repeat his question when he bumped into Julia.

"Shh."

"What?" Samuel said.

Julia was looking off the path to the right, into the woods.

"That wasn't there last time," she whispered.

Samuel tried to pinpoint where she was looking and saw nothing special. All he saw was a bunch of tree trunks and piles of rocks in the darkening summer night. Far behind them the sea glittered. Julia came closer to him and pointed. Now he followed her arm all the way to her fingertip. Her hair tickled his cheek.

"There, on the tree trunk."

"Yeah?" Samuel said, although he wasn't sure he was even looking at the right tree.

"That weird . . . lump."

"That burl?"

"Whatever. It wasn't there last we walked by."

Samuel focused his eyes. "Are you pulling my leg?" he asked.

"Come on. No."

"How can you even remember what all these trees look like?"

"I was filming here earlier, remember? I was shooting right between these two birches out to the sea."

Samuel noticed the back of his neck had gone cold ever since Julia had stopped in her tracks, and the cold was spreading down to his back, arms, and belly.

"There's someone there."

"No, there isn't," he said. "You remembered wrong."

Julia shook her head slowly, still looking ahead.

"Someone's standing behind that tree." She was dead serious.

Samuel tried to make out any details in the figure, just to prove to Julia that she was wrong, but the more he squinted, the more the burl seemed to transform. It kind of did look like a human shoulder poking out behind a tree. Or, maybe, a face peering from behind the tree. Dusk had blurred the details. Julia lifted her video camera toward the tree trunk.

"Shoot," she said. "Out of battery."

Samuel was about to ask the immobile group of trees if anyone was out there. *That's one way to find out,* he thought, and he'd show Julia that he wasn't scared.

The burl moved.

Julia screamed. Her scream startled Samuel and he yelped. They took off running as if it were a part of an agreement they'd signed. Julia sprinted so fast that Samuel had a hard time keeping up. His back was tingling, as if preparing to be touched, waiting for a cold blade to sink in all the way to the spine. The screams of the seagulls in his ears began to change, and all he heard was the attack call of a hunter running like a mink.

They didn't turn to look back until they felt asphalt under their feet. They leaned against the garage wall, panting, ready to run again at the first sight of movement in the corner of their eyes.

Suddenly the idea of the world having stopped turning and leaving them alone didn't sound that great. Samuel would've loved to hear just one car coming around the corner.

"What the fuck was that?" Julia asked, like he was supposed to know. This was where he grew up, after all.

The memory of the figure in the woods began to instantly fade. The screams from the sea were nothing but seagulls again.

"Maybe it was nothing," Samuel said. "Maybe we're just tired and we're imagining stuff."

Julia panted and breathed out a muttered protest.

"I heard its steps," she said. "It was running right behind us."

He didn't have another rebuttal. Maybe she had heard his steps. How could you be sure of anything when you ran for your life and your heart beat in your ears like a drum?

Talking about it began to change the way Samuel remembered what had happened. Maybe there had been a third, faster pace mixed in with the rhythm of their feet. It had sounded softer and lighter, like someone running barefoot.

Samuel noticed again how his back felt clammy and cold, as if a corpse were breathing on his sweaty skin right behind him.

After that eventful night, the days grew longer again, just like in Samuel's childhood. The fear they now shared had brought Samuel and Julia even closer together. It was their unspoken secret that made the daylight seem so much brighter.

They could hear the waves. The wood grain in the utility poles told them that the poles hadn't always been there—someone had made them. Jape's mean laugh and threats were meaningless as they walked across the yard. They knew that Jape was a deeply sad human being and lived in a pathetic alternate reality, and they almost pitied him.

They didn't pity the girl living in the townhomes, Maisa, nearly as much. She'd had a crush on Samuel since January. Earlier her flirting had just been awkward: she'd push her way through the crowd on the bus to sit next to Samuel. She even called him on the phone. His dad had once picked up the phone and told Samuel right away that he'd better not start planning to marry any of "them townhome brats." For once they agreed on something.

Jape had noticed how badly Maisa was crushing on Samuel, and that had made it even worse. The bastard wrote a little ditty about it.

"Maisa, Maisa, will you let Samuel fuck ya . . ."

He composed a whole song. When Samuel couldn't fall asleep he entertained horrifying thoughts of Jape becoming the singer of a popular rock band and recording and releasing that song. All sorts of nonsense had become hit songs for yokels like Jape to sing along to when they were drunk. Samuel's shame would never end, and he'd have to move abroad or drown himself in the sea. That would crown Jape the ultimate winner.

When these thoughts pummeled him, Samuel tossed and turned until three in the morning and did his best to convince himself that it wasn't that easy to become a rock star. But someone always became a star, and Jape had already been a singer in one band until playing drums was banned in the garages. On other occasions Samuel thought about the ways he could silence Jape. He could wait near the path in the woods until Jape was drunk and wobbling his way back home alone. He'd hit him with a rock from behind. He'd beat him until he was unmistakably dead. He'd walk to the shore and throw the rock as far into the sea as he could. Teachers would give kids an opportunity to share their thoughts about Jape in school, and cops would launch an investigation, but nobody would suspect Samuel if his plan were flawless. He'd wear plastic bags over his feet and agree on an alibi with Harri: he had been at Harri's place listening to records all night. Eventually, it would all turn into a story. Jape's disappearance would be another Granny Hatchet job. The sea monster ate him. There would never be a rock star called Jape, and there would never be any mean songs about Samuel.

When Julia arrived, these horrifying thoughts disappeared. Jape became delightfully meaningless.

But now there was Maisa. Even just seeing her made Samuel despise and loathe her so much it scared him. He used to pity her, but now he could've spat on Maisa's face to get the message across.

Maisa once appeared out of nowhere at the shore with her golden retriever when Samuel and Julia were there. That was the worst.

"Who are you?" she asked Julia. Maisa's voice betrayed how close she was to a breakdown, but only Samuel recognized the signs.

Julia introduced herself and chatted politely, yet she was reserved. Any mention of the United States made Maisa yell at her dog, who was tugging on the leash, trying to get back to the path. Her admiring voice at Julia's stories was sickeningly fake.

"How nice. How exciting."

When they ran out of things to talk about, Samuel started to worry that Maisa might cause a scene. He made sure to keep his back turned to her and not look at her.

"What are you filming?" Maisa asked.

"The Bondorff villa," Julia said. "Apparently you're not supposed to go there."

Maisa yanked the dog back to her.

"Why not?" she asked defiantly.

Julia shrugged. "I don't know. Ask Samuel."

He felt Maisa's eyes on the back of his neck.

"Come on, tell her," Julia said.

"Maisa already knows," Samuel said. "She's just bullshitting to say something."

Julia looked puzzled. She laughed a little at Maisa and escaped the situation by hiding behind the camera. The uncomfortable silence continued for an eternity. Even the swooshing of the waves seemed to demand someone to speak up.

"Do you know how it feels," Maisa said, holding back tears, barely audible, "when your heart is ripped out of your chest?"

So embarrassing. Samuel was so ashamed for her that it hurt. Her voice was so helpless and humiliated that he couldn't bear to listen to it.

Go away, he kept thinking to himself. *Die, or whatever, but just disappear.*

It took awhile, but Maisa eventually left. Samuel could hear her shoes crushing the tree branches and her sobbing disappearing into the woods. He didn't see where she went, but he noticed Julia had turned her camera around.

It followed Maisa. A thin, cruel smile slowly spread across her face.

That's when Samuel felt sick, but only for a moment. He decided to drop by at Maisa's on his way home and apologize to her. Nobody should tolerate cruelty like this.

But when Julia suddenly kissed him, he forgot about apologies, along with everything else.

"Did you bring a condom?" she whispered, lips touching his ears.

Of course he did, but Samuel had been hiding the condom for so long he almost lied about it. He'd found it in the bottom of one of his dad's drawers. The "Use By" date had passed almost a year before.

He worried about a lot of things. Would he be as good as the men in pornos? Would someone see him? What if the condom broke? He'd get AIDS or worse, a child.

Then he forgot everything again.

When Samuel walked back home later, Maisa no longer existed to him.

When Samuel called Julia on Sunday, he was greeted by an angry man's voice on the other end.

"Are you that *loverman?*" the voice asked with a sneer, in a mix of English and Finnish.

Samuel froze, terrified, not knowing what to say. He shrieked like Aki, "Yes."

"I'd like to have a little chat with you." The man's anger changed to forced politeness. "Your name is Samuel, right?"

He could hear Julia in the background, *"Come on, give it to me."*

"Come over."

"Uh . . . right now?"

"Yup."

The man hung up.

Samuel got dressed and looked at himself in the mirror, breathed deep into his lungs, and blew all the air out. He aimed for a steady stream of air, but instead he breathed in gulps. Surely Julia hadn't told her dad. Why would she?

"Where are you going?" Aki yelled at him from behind his Fantastic Four comic.

"It is *so* none of your business," Samuel said as coolly as he could muster. Good thing their dad hadn't come back from work yet. He wouldn't have to come up with lies in this mental state he was in. If his dad found out, he would start preaching about how his sons weren't going to grovel in front of capitalists in their homes, and how he should get himself a proper blue-collar girl, and so on.

"We're going to see Grandma today as soon as Dad gets back!" Aki shouted from his room.

"I know," Samuel said and tied his shoelaces. "Tell Dad I can't make it."

"But Grandma will be sad."

"She won't even realize I'm not there. Tell Dad I promised to fix Harri's bike—I owe him for a record he got me. I can see Grandma alone some other time."

"You won't."

Samuel didn't want to argue. He took off.

As he approached the end of Patteriniemi Road, he realized this would be the first time he'd see a rich man's house from the inside. Behind his fear he felt a jolt of guilt. His grandma was lying in bed in a nursing home, she made no sense when she spoke, and she could move only in a wheelchair. Samuel wouldn't be there, holding her hand awkwardly, unless he was forced to. Instead, he walked toward a house with two garages and more rooms than his grandma could count.

"Welcome," Julia's dad said as he opened the door.

He wore a white dress shirt with a stained apron draped over it. He had ridiculously bright-colored shorts on. His hair had been slicked back with gel, like Don Johnson's in *Miami Vice*.

"The man is in the house," he yelled in English over his shoulder, turned back, and extended his hand.

"Mike," he said. "Movie mogul and master of barbecue. Nice to meet you." His handshake was swift and loose. "Come on in."

Samuel followed him and began to take his shoes off.

"No, no," he said. "We wear shoes inside. None of these Finnish traditions in this house, please. Walk through with me—we're having lunch in the yard. Julia will be right there."

Samuel walked through the house in his shoes, treading lightly as if that would prevent him from tracking dirt onto the rugs. The walls were covered in framed posters. *The Octagon. The Legacy. The Evil Dead.*

"You have really nice posters," Samuel said, about to shriek in falsetto.

"Of course," Mike said. "I import them. Come over here."

His hand crushed Samuel's shoulder, pulling him into the living room. His breath smelled of alcohol.

"Just look at that," he said, pointing at a black-and-white photo in a frame. "You recognize that guy next to me?"

Two men in black suits and bow ties. Mike and a shorter man.

"Chuck Norris," Samuel said, not believing his eyes.

"Exactly. And I'm going to bring him to Finland. I'll bring him here, to Vaasa. Can you believe it?"

"No," Samuel said. He really couldn't.

So Julia had told him the truth. He had assumed that of course Julia would tell an innocent lie. He'd even forgiven her for that lie a hundred times in his mind. Who wouldn't want to make a lasting impression on the first person they meet in their new neighborhood?

Mike laughed. "Of course you can't. Folks here are not used to the ways of the big world, but believe you me, he'll come. I talked with him on the phone just yesterday. But enough of that, let's eat."

Samuel followed him in a trance, trying to forget the photo. For a reason he couldn't quite place, he was ashamed of everything he'd ever told Julia and of every single poem he'd read to her. Compared to Chuck Norris they were meaningless.

A large electric grill and a table had been set up outside. A woman in a pink bikini and sunglasses was sprawled on a lounge chair on the grass.

"You speak English?" Mike asked in English.

"Yes," Samuel said, "but not much."

He laughed again. "It's all right. There's no point in talking to her, anyway. I usually just say *yes* or *no.* Usually *no.*"

More laughing. The woman lifted her hand lazily and said something behind her sunglasses that Samuel didn't understand. Then he realized the words were aimed at Mike.

"Fuck you, too," he muttered and walked up to the grill.

Samuel didn't know where to look. He just hoped Julia would come soon.

"Samuel, did you know that a real live Communist lives right next door?"

"Um, no."

"I hear he's a commie, but he owns a pool and other flashy stuff. In LA no practicing commie would flaunt their KGB money that openly. If we were in LA, or especially somewhere in Texas, I could fucking shoot him, and the cops and the feds would only thank me for making their jobs easier. But here these commies can do whatever the hell they want."

Samuel finally knew who the man was talking about. He could've said that the neighbor was not a Communist but a Social Democrat, but he thought it was best to keep his mouth shut.

"Do you know any other commies around here?" Mike asked, then took a swig out of a Bacardi bottle and turned over a smoking piece of meat on the grill.

Samuel shrugged. His dad did come to mind. He certainly was no Social Democrat.

"Where's your bathroom?" he asked.

"All these commie stories making you shit your pants, kid?" Mike laughed. "The nearest one is over there by the front door. And no jerking off in there, all right? Just do your business, and then we'll talk about you and Julia *man to man.*"

Samuel laughed when Mike laughed, although the promise of a chat sounded a little too ominous. His voice had turned cold when he'd mentioned Julia. Samuel was relieved to be back in the house, away from the hissing grill and the burning sun. He marched down the hallway lined with posters and was about to walk out of the house when Julia appeared and grabbed him by the sleeve.

"Let's get the hell out of here," she said.

"All right."

She slipped sandals on her bare feet and pushed the door open. By the time the door banged shut, they were at the edge of the woods, running toward the tip of the peninsula.

"Does your dad really know Chuck Norris?" Samuel asked, out of breath.

Julia ran in front of him, holding her video camera.

"Yeah. Or at least he used to."

"How is that even possible?"

She slowed down to a walk.

"He was a hotshot back in LA. Then he started getting drunk more often than not and snorting coke first thing in the morning."

Samuel knew about coke, but had never thought someone outside of *Miami Vice* would be doing it.

Julia stopped and turned to him. Her left eye was swollen.

In a couple of days it would bloom in all possible colors. Samuel knew: Jape had once kicked his ass. Now these same marks on Julia's face looked much worse. They looked criminal.

"Who did this to you?" he asked.

"Dad, who else? Who the fuck else?"

The posters and Chuck Norris all disappeared, replaced by helpless rage and a burning desire for vendetta. Samuel could've pushed Mike's face onto the hot grill, and he wouldn't have felt any remorse. Except Julia's dad was bigger than him. He could feel helplessness all the way in the marrow of his weak arms.

"Why did he—"

"Just forget about it. And don't come around anymore if he calls you."

"What right does—"

"He goes insane whenever I'm seeing someone," Julia explained, annoyed, like to a petulant child. "Ever since Mom died he's been like that. End of story."

Samuel was left alone with his rage. Julia left him alone with it on purpose. He was insulted: why did she want to keep this to herself? Didn't he mean enough to her to share this pain? But he couldn't say anything. How could he, when she stood there with her eye all swollen and her mom dead? Samuel wanted to console her, to say he knew how she felt, but Julia's expression was like drawn curtains at a theater. The show's over. Go home.

Samuel dragged his feet toward the shore, angrily kicking little rocks until he sat down. The waves sparkled in the sunlight. There were no clouds in the sky.

He stared at the horizon until he detected a faint buzzing behind his back. He looked over his shoulder. Julia was crouching there, her video camera blocking the swollen eye.

"What are we filming today?"

Samuel knew he could never be angry at her. Realizing this made him happy, yet unspeakably horrified. He really couldn't be angry at her, not even if he wanted to be. A man like that would be trapped and would never take things lightly again.

"I don't know," she responded and then paused. "How about we go to your place?"

Samuel laughed at the absurdity. Then he remembered. His dad and Aki were visiting his grandma. They'd be gone for at least two hours: they'd take her to the pond in her wheelchair, and his dad would recite old stories and correct her stories, patiently, with his hand placed gently over her wrinkled hand.

"Maybe," Samuel said.

"What does your dad think?"

"He's not at home."

Julia smiled.

He was trapped.

Samuel walked in first to make sure that his dad and Aki were gone. Julia waited one floor down in the stairwell until she heard him call to her. The coast was clear.

"Where's your room?" she asked as soon as she walked in.

Samuel showed her and ashamedly revealed that he still shared a room with his little brother, but Julia didn't seem to listen. She turned her camera on and began to walk through the apartment. Samuel walked behind her, excusing the mess and the stains on the wallpaper and why there was a black circle on the kitchen's plastic rug. His dad had been about to move a hot pot of soup off the stove when he heard the news on TV that Yuri Andropov was dead. Samuel had been sitting at the kitchen table drinking juice when his dad's back had stiffened and he'd said, "Not again," lowered the pot onto the floor, and ran into the living room. Samuel had smelled the burning plastic and moved the pot onto the kitchen counter. His dad hadn't even noticed. He'd spent the rest of the evening running between the TV and the phone. Samuel didn't tell this version to Julia. Instead, he blamed Aki for the mess.

Once Julia had seen everything, they went back to Samuel's room. She walked to the middle of the room and let the camera pan. Then she put it down.

"Go away for a bit," she said.

"Why?"

"I'll get ready."

"For what?"

"You know, you dork."

"All right."

Samuel closed the door and strode into his dad's bedroom. He went through all the drawers until he found a pack of condoms. There were three left. His dad would notice one missing, but there was nothing Samuel could do about it. There was a girl in his room who was ready to fuck, as unbelievable as it sounded. A girl who may have met Chuck Norris and who was prettier than Madonna on the cover of *Like a Virgin*.

Samuel went back to the hallway and waited at his bedroom door. He squeezed the condom in his palm and kept telling himself that his dad and Aki wouldn't be back for another hour, that their landlord wouldn't walk in with the master key to check the radiators, that Harri wouldn't ring the doorbell and call for Samuel through the mail slot in the door, horrified to relay the news that King Diamond has left Mercyful Fate or whatever he'd read in *Metal Hammer* with his older brother and a dictionary.

"I'm ready," Julia's voice came through the door.

Samuel walked in. Julia sat on his bed, wearing his T-shirt that looked comically large on her. His dad had bought it and Samuel hadn't worn it once. He didn't understand why Julia had needed to dig through his stuff for the shirt. Maybe she had planned on being naked, then had gotten shy, but did it really matter? Everything about her was perfect. Her oddities, her bashfulness, her swollen eye. She was an angel sent to Earth where Samuel thought no laws could ever be rewritten.

As he closed the door behind him and walked to Julia, he felt free for the first time in his life. He was self-assured and inside a world of his own where no one could hurt or humiliate him. Only the two of them existed in this room. Nobody was watching, listening, searching for flaws. Nobody saw how he pressed his face into her hair and breathed in its scent as if he'd just woken up in a deep, infinite forest.

As the outline of the Bondorff villa began to emerge from the stormy darkness, Samuel felt like he was fifteen again.

His limbs were heavier, more vulnerable. The angular shape of the rooftop and the lonely turret against the dark-gray clouds forced him to slow down and eventually stop. The reeds hissed all around him. The woods hummed loudly at him from a distance. It was easy to be transported to a time when networks or cell phones didn't exist to check for location or call for help.

The mere thought of it made Samuel fumble for his phone. He pulled it out and used the screen as a flashlight to light the way ahead. He was sure he'd heard the low churning of waves right next to his feet. The cell phone shone on the rocks that led the way to the island.

Samuel hopped onto the first rock, wobbled, then hopped onto the next one. On the third rock his foot slipped and dipped into the sea. His shoe was immediately soaked in freezing-cold water. Nothing left to lose, he continued on less carefully. The water was shallow, up to mid-calf, but each time he pulled his foot up, the stench of muddy clay surrounded him.

The rocks in the water soon became a shore. Samuel stopped walking, put the cell phone back into his pocket, and tried not to think about his legs that had gone numb from the cold water. He noticed how the wind sounded different on the island. There were only two birch trees on the shore, so the wind could blow straight through. Samuel's coat hem flapped and a gust of air forced its way under his shirt. He pulled his collar up and began to trudge toward the villa. He looked around but didn't see anything moving, except a bush and some saplings waving in the wind behind the building. Samuel noticed something in one of the villa's windows.

He slowed his pace.

Light shone through one of the windows downstairs. It flickered, like a candle in a drafty room. But it was no candle. The light was paler, lifeless. It had to come from an artificial source, maybe from a dusty, broken lamp, as if no one had taken the time to screw the bulb in properly.

Samuel stopped. He expected to feel his dad's hand on his chest, but the hand never came. He was alone now. He'd crossed the line into a territory that no memory of a protective hand could reach. He was growing concerned about his numb legs. He had to either get inside the villa or turn back.

He took a few more determined steps to reach the house, then a few slower, cautious steps up the stairs onto the porch. It didn't dawn on him until he stood at the front door.

Someone was inside the villa. Someone lived here. He had no business being here.

The light shone dimly through the glass. Samuel knocked on the window. First he knocked loudly, but it just made the glass shake and rattle in its weather stripping, eaten away by the salty winds from the sea. Then he knocked more quietly. Three cautious knocks.

Nothing changed in the dimly lit darkness beyond the dirty window, but he did hear sounds. Samuel cocked his head and listened.

Thumps. A high-pitched hollering that was immediately lost in the howling wind. He pressed his ear closer to the glass, shivering when the cold surface touched his face. He covered his other ear, facing the sea, with his palm.

The high-pitched sound was gone. It was replaced by low mumbling. Like stifled speech.

Samuel took a step back and pressed down on the door handle. The door squeaked, fought back, then opened a little. An unfamiliar smell flooded his nose. It was thick and stuffy.

I remember, Samuel mouthed to himself. *I remember this.*

The memory didn't quite turn into images in his mind, but it had an immediate effect regardless. His muscles tensed and shriveled slowly into a small lump. He pushed the door open wider. It led him inside a narrow vestibule. Another door was ahead of him. He pulled his cell phone out again. Its cold light shone on the wooden floorboards and patterned wallpaper that had buckled and cracked at the seams. Samuel moved the light slowly to the right until the wall disappeared, and he saw a narrow hallway leading down. He walked further into the house.

He felt like he was supposed to announce his arrival, to say something, anything, but the thick air inside the house had gagged him. To the left of the wall was another hallway that clearly led deeper into the house. That's where the light was coming from. He wasn't able to locate the mumbling. It resonated through the beams, as if the house were having a conversation with the wind howling outside. Samuel took a few tentative steps toward the light. He turned the phone screen off when there was enough light, but he didn't put the phone away just yet. His fingers clutched the plastic piece like a talisman from another dimension.

The mumbling stopped. Now a steady pecking sound pierced the wind. He took one more step and saw the device.

A movie projector.

The large reels were spinning in overdrive. The projector broadcast a bridge of light through the dust onto the wall across the room. Samuel walked even closer.

A torn piece of fabric hung from the wall. It may have been a sheet. He stood in the glow of a black-and-white image, glancing around the room. He'd forgotten about his numb legs.

The projected image showed a large bed and a woman on it, sitting but leaning back on her elbows. A young man dressed in old-fashioned clothes was sitting next to her. He couldn't see their faces because the two figures had been shot from afar. Both of them looked straight into the camera.

A quick cut to another scene.

A woman, most likely the same one as previously, stood alone on the seashore, slightly hunched. Her entire body jerked as if she were shouting at the camera. Her long nightgown had slipped off her shoulder, and its hem flapped in the wind, mimicking her wild black hair. The nightgown was filthy, covered in black splatters. Samuel still couldn't see her face because the camera was again too far away, as if the person behind it was too scared of the woman's tantrum. Samuel gaped at this mute display of emotion that lasted for what felt like an eternity. Its strangeness was captivating, voiding all rational thoughts—all those thoughts about running away. Thoughts about any reasons he'd had for coming here.

Then the woman began to approach the camera. The camera shook once. Then again.

Her face filled the entire screen.

Samuel stumbled away until he hit a wall.

The wrinkles and imperfections in the sheet distorted her face, but despite them, he saw enough to feel a chilling lump in his throat. The woman's left pupil had shrunk. Her jaw was covered in black splotches. The toothless mouth formed words in exaggerated, jerky movements. Its muted scream raged from beyond the forgotten decades and summoned the wind to shake the villa's foundations, as if to tear off the entire roof.

The image cut to another, but the muted scream remained.

First the shapes in the dark looked like folds in the sheet. Then the folds began to move.

The wind kept on howling.

An image like large earthworms writhing against each other unfolded. The camera light reflected off their slimy skins. Samuel caught glimpses of a white circle with a black dot in the middle among the slippery earthworms. It was revolting. Like a rotten black egg yolk in a frying pan. It disappeared, then reappeared. Even the thought of it watching him, hiding a primitive form of intelligence behind it, nauseated him. His throat rattled as he bent over, not quite sure whether he was about to throw up or simply kneel down. He grabbed ahold of the projector, twisted each button and lever, then tore the reels off. Out of the corner of his eye he saw the lit image on the wall first shake, then go dark.

Samuel panted in the dark room, doing his best not to spit because it had been drilled into him at an early age: spitting on the floor was rude and not allowed under any circumstances. He lit the cell-phone screen again. The floor near the projector was covered in shreds of film. Shoddily cut pieces, some taped together. Samuel lifted the phone higher to shine the light into every corner, his feet stomping around rebelliously to scare any attackers. He saw nobody. Only the memory of the woman's face on the torn sheet remained. The memory of slimy shapes sliding against each other. He had heard that the way earthworms and snakes moved evoked primitive feelings of disgust in humans. Samuel had seen only an adder, and only twice, but he knew this claim to be true. The image of whatever he'd seen on the screen made him feel worse.

He gagged again. Wiped tears away from his eyes. Got himself under control. Muttered a curse.

That made him feel better—the ability to say something, anything. Samuel huffed and leaned forward, his palms on his thighs. Now that the projector was quiet, he could hear the mumbling again. The sound was coming from behind a door. He stepped closer. A dim light was shining under it. It looked different than the other lights. Softer, more even. No flickering from an old projector.

Samuel touched the door with his fingertips. The hinges creaked softly as the weight of the old wood shifted to reveal another room. He stood in the doorway.

There was a TV in the room. An old CRT. A VCR player underneath it.

The screen showed a woman, in the same location as in the film he'd watched on the sheet. She was wearing the same kind of dirty nightgown, in the same pose, but this time her body didn't jerk.

She spoke calmly. In color. Samuel could hear the voice. The camera mic picked up the wind, but he could still hear words here and there.

"To swim on God's surface for a gentle . . ."

He recognized that voice.

". . . chosen moment . . ."

He had already recognized the figure, the pose, the way her arms hung over her hips.

". . . on the surface of the cold eyes of gods . . ."

He'd recognized the figure as soon as he'd stepped into the doorway.

". . . who do not stay awake . . ."

Samuel recognized everything. The figure, the voice, the poem. A memory that earlier had been a cramp in his muscles now flooded over him like white water. This had all been set up, just for him. A trap.

He yanked himself out of the hypnotic glow of the screen and rushed back into the dark room. His wet shoe slipped on the floorboards, sending him flying. His cell phone bounced, then slid on the floor.

Samuel lay on the hardwood floor. He looked up.

All he saw in the darkness were the straight edges of the dark windows and the madly waving bushes behind them.

A human-shaped figure was standing in the middle of the room.

Samuel lay helplessly on the floor, staring at the figure. The chill in his legs had migrated into the rest of his body, making his limbs tremble uncontrollably. He'd never felt this way before.

He uttered the woman's name, although he didn't want to. It was the whisper of a man nearing hypothermia. A man who trembled on the surface of a god's cold eyes.

The figure said nothing.

She just stared at him with her one glowing eye. A glowing red dot. A spark that had leapt out of a fire that had been put out.

"The flints brought you back here," the spark said. "Whence you once came."

Decades had scratched her voice hoarse.

But Samuel remembered.

HOW THUNDER GOT ITS NAME

Julia went inside to charge her video camera, the woods nearby darkening as if a velvet shroud had been pulled over the sun. Samuel waited at a safe distance from the house. Just as he saw her at the end of the street, the first heavy drops of rain began to fall.

"Where should we take shelter?" he asked.

"Nowhere," she said. "Let's get wet."

Thunder began to rumble in the distance. Samuel felt it in the pit of his belly.

"Wow," Julia said.

They looked over to the sea. A wall of clouds had risen on the horizon, now visible between the treetops. The wall was black in the middle. They couldn't stay outside, but they couldn't go home, either. And the Suvikylä library was too far away.

"Let's go to Helge's," Samuel suggested.

"You think he won't mind? Last time he seemed a bit down."

"Let's cheer him up, then."

The rain began to fall heavier as they ran into the woods. They heard another rumble, and the woods were illuminated in a bright flash for a second. Samuel grabbed Julia by the hand and pulled her down the shortcut. It meandered through tall ferns and fallen tree trunks, but they had no other option. He pulled her behind him, although his instincts told him to nestle in safety under the first fallen tree trunk he spotted. He realized he'd never experienced a proper thunderstorm before. The rumbling had always been in the distance, followed by a delightful flash of lights that he and Aki both observed from their balcony, excited to count the lightning bolts they saw.

Rain was coming down so hard now that its roar drowned the sounds of their shoes. By the time they reached Helge's cabin, they were soaking wet and out of breath, their ears pounding from exhaustion.

To Samuel's surprise Helge stood outside the cabin in the pouring rain, wobbling like a sleepwalker.

"What are you doing out here?" he yelled over the roar.

Helge yanked his head toward Samuel when he repeated the question.

"Hello, Samuel," he said. "Lousy weather, isn't it?"

"Can we get out of the rain?" Julia shouted.

"Of course."

Helge slurred his words. His face was limp. Samuel saw he was barely holding on to a bottle of vodka.

Samuel led the way up to the porch and wiped water off his face. Julia's breath was steaming. Helge opened the door and gestured to them to walk in.

As soon as the door closed behind them, the rain changed its tone. The drops rustling dully against the corrugated roof played a monotonous tune. The thunder rattled the windows and the glassware inside the house.

"You're fucking drunk," Samuel told Helge angrily, although he didn't mean to.

"Your observation is correct."

Arvid crawled from under the table to greet Julia first. His gait was calmer than usual, but he still managed to jump against her and lick her face. She almost fell over.

"The dog's inside and you're out there in the rain," Samuel said.

Helge nodded.

"But why?"

He shook his head slowly. "What's my life worth, huh?" he asked. "I should just die. A worthless . . . damned . . . How are you two? Is everything all right?"

"Don't say that," Julia said, scratching the dog. The dog panted and rolled his eyes in panic. "Arvid needs you."

Helge muttered something.

"The old man's piss drunk and just wants sympath—"

Thunder interrupted Samuel. The floor shook and the light in the room went off. This time the glassware rattled longer. When the lights came back on, Arvid had disappeared. His eyes gleamed under Helge's wooden bench.

"What's this?" Julia stared at her fingers.

She got up slowly and extended her palm to Samuel. It was covered in blood. First Julia looked at Helge, who swayed in front of the window and stared at the floorboards as if they needed his immediate attention. Then she turned toward Arvid, who was whimpering under the bench.

"What happened here?" she asked.

Now Samuel saw Arvid's paw prints. Red pools all over the light-blue floorboards.

"That damned . . . Reino Raaska, he . . . never yields . . ."

Thunder drowned Helge's soliloquy. As the lights flashed, Samuel watched Julia crawl toward the bench.

"It's because you went to the shore and talked back to him," Helge said. "He never yields, he's never given in . . ."

"Who did this?" Julia demanded.

Samuel wanted to tell her not to touch an injured dog. His dad had warned him about that. The animal does its best to hide its wounds and will bite if you meddle with it. He saw Julia reach under the bench to stroke Arvid's fur in calming motions.

"Reino Raaska. I told you not to go to the shore."

Helge hadn't lifted his eyes off the floor. His hands were balled into fists.

"You mean the fisherman?" Julia asked.

Her voice sounded distant. It was unsettling.

"His mother served them until she died, and I've always listened to them, too, but they've never yielded and they've never thanked me . . ."

Julia got on her knees and put her hands on her thighs, leaving bloody stains on her jeans. She turned to Helge.

"Are you talking about that fucking sadist?"

Helge shook his head miserably. "I understand, he has his reasons, but . . . why hurt Arvid? He's never hurt any—"

This time there was no rumble. The sound escalated quickly, but on another frequency than the thunder. It crackled and hummed at the same time. The noise filled the room and grew louder, until Samuel's ears were ringing. A strange, cold light stretched their shadows against the wall.

Samuel stumbled back until he hit a wall.

Before he noticed the ball lightning that had appeared over Helge's desk, looking exactly like his teacher had described in class, he was already in full fight-or-flight mode. His skin tingled and tensed like in cold water. Papers flew in the air, twisting and turning across his vision. Samuel shouted, but he had no idea he was shouting. He lowered himself onto the floor and began to crawl along the wall to the other side of the room.

Then a loud bang, and the ball lightning was gone. Papers floated down, touching the floorboards softly. He was pressed against Julia, who sat on the floor and hugged Arvid, who was struggling in her arms. Helge had slumped right behind Samuel, so close that he could smell the alcohol on his breath. He wished he had been converted at the Lutheran confirmation summer camp, because this seemed like a good time to pray.

"What was that?" Julia asked.

Samuel blinked, trying to dispel the afterimage.

"We call it ball lightning," he said in a sunken voice, as if he'd just woken up. "But my teacher says they're not real."

The afterimage of a brightly lit sphere stuck. It just kept on changing color and moving in his field of vision.

"I didn't ask you if it was real," Julia said. "I wanted to know what it was called."

They gasped for breath and sat still until the rain and thunder began to wane. The drops on the corrugated roof became louder twice more, but the time between the flash and the rumble grew longer. Samuel counted the seconds in between, although he didn't quite remember what the point of it was. How many kilometers one second was equal to.

He came out of his reverie to hear Julia sobbing.

The sound was so surprising that it broke the ball lightning's spell.

Julia lowered Arvid gently onto the floor. He was panting fast. His fur was matted with blood. When she put her hand in front of Arvid, his pink tongue licked her fingers twice, then remained stuck between his teeth.

Samuel hadn't seen Julia cry before. He hadn't even imagined it was possible. The swollen eye had been nowhere this bad. She was an angel who had arrived to save him from all this shit. She was supposed to be endlessly free and strong and confident. And here she was, tears streaming down her face. Samuel looked at Arvid. His belly was rising and sinking too fast. He didn't need a vet to know it wasn't normal.

"He's suffering," Julia said, wiping snot from her nose.

Helge stood up. He didn't want to look at them. His voice was now clearer than before.

"There was no reason for this sort of . . . unreasonable after everything . . . what had Arvid ever done to them . . ."

Julia stroked the dog's fur gently.

"You have to help us . . . Arvid and I have never been to the vet . . . He's not comfortable on that cold floor . . . he usually sleeps over there . . ."

Helge pointed at another room.

Arvid wheezed. His legs jerked every now and then, as if he were trying to run.

"How are we supposed to help?" Julia asked.

"We've never been to a vet . . ."

Samuel understood that Helge expected them to take on a vet's responsibilities. The thought was so bizarre he wasn't sure if he'd understood correctly.

"We don't . . ."

Samuel didn't look at Julia, but he knew that she understood, too.

Helge just stood there, watching them. "I can't do it," he said.

"What happened to Arvid?" Samuel asked to avoid the subject.

Helge opened his mouth, but then shook his head.

"Anyway," Samuel said. "We're not going to—"

The movement in the corner of his eye cut him off. Julia had swiftly leaned over Arvid, and before he knew it her hands were wrapped around the dog's throat. She pressed down with straight arms, putting all her weight into it.

Arvid started convulsing. He bared his teeth, slowly and helplessly. It had to be instinctual. Samuel couldn't call it a struggle, although it seemed to last forever. If Arvid had been healthy he would've struggled free, bitten Julia's hand, then calmed down and slinked back to lick her fingers. But now he was losing the battle, his world turned upside down. The same hands that had petted him and scratched him and handed him pieces of sausage were choking him to death. That would be the last thing he'd ever experience on this Earth. The pain and the notion that even the most reliable of humans turned evil in the end. He saw the people who scratched and fed him, and one of them was strangling him.

Arvid's eyes relaxed, as if he were getting tired. His legs were still jumping. His right paw was tapping on Julia's arm as if to tell her, *There, there.*

Julia didn't let go, although the dog had stopped moving. Her body was stiff and immobile, except for her arms, which shook from exertion.

Then she fell back onto her elbows and gasped for breath, as if she'd just surfaced from a sinking ship. She clambered up and wiped her face with the back of her hand.

"Why did he do it?"

Her eyes had the same distant look like that time when Helge had told them about the Bondorff villa. The back of her hand had left a smear of blood on her face.

When Helge said nothing she began to scream.

The sight terrified Samuel. The thunder's crackling rage seemed to have returned and squeezed itself inside Julia's fragile frame.

Maisa's finger hovered over the doorbell. She listened. The stained plastic letters on the door read "Saarikivi." She could hear music through the door. She pressed the doorbell, then hesitated, and waited for a couple of beats before removing her finger. That was how an insecure woman rang a doorbell. *Not a great way to start,* she thought.

The music was turned down immediately, but Maisa didn't hear footsteps until they were right behind the door.

"What's your business?" a tired falsetto asked from inside.

"Are you Mrs. Saarikivi?" Maisa asked, leaning toward the door. She was annoyed how her words echoed loudly in the stairwell. However loud she was, the neighbors didn't seem to take notice—the TV soaps and screaming children hadn't been interrupted.

"Yes, I am," the voice said.

"I'm a researcher, and I wondered if I could ask you a few questions?"

Silence. Then: "Are you single?"

Maisa frowned, not sure if she'd heard right. "Yes. Yes, I am."

"Well, all right, then," the voice said before she heard the chain lock rattle and the door open.

"Good afternoon," Maisa said, still trying to figure out the logic behind her question.

The woman, in full makeup and flashy earrings, responded to her politely.

"Is this about the church-board elections?" she asked, eyeing Maisa suspiciously.

Maisa looked at the long Oriental rug in the hallway behind Mrs. Saarikivi. The red walls were lined with large, gold-framed paintings of nature scenes. She could hear a faint tango in the background.

"No," she replied. "A friend of mine told me you are familiar with Suvikylä's history."

Mrs. Saarikivi relaxed.

"Come on in." She gestured and backed away quickly from Maisa, still facing her.

Maisa walked in and closed the door behind her.

"Quite peculiar that a young woman like yourself is interested in Suvikylä's past," Mrs. Saarikylä said, beckoning her to walk in farther.

She followed her to the living room, where a large chandelier dangled over the coffee table, and more scenic paintings and photographs hung on the walls.

"Sit here, please," Mrs. Saarikivi instructed. Maisa sat in a cushioned armchair. When she took off her jacket, she saw why she had to sit there and nowhere else.

"Is that your husband?" she asked, folding her jacket over the chair's arm.

"Yes," Mrs. Saarikivi said, following Maisa's gaze as if she were surprised. "Those medals are his as well. He was in the war."

"I see. Very impressive. He was a handsome man."

"Indeed," Mrs. Saarikivi said and leaned forward. "And an excellent lover."

Maisa could smell her breath and for whatever reason thought of dentures.

Mrs. Saarikivi allowed her to admire the photographs and framed medals that covered an entire wall. The images appeared to cover the man's entire life, from his early twenties as a soldier in baggy pants—he may have been an officer—until retirement. The rude intensity of his eyes remained the same throughout the years, even when age had made his face sag and features crumple. There was only one picture showing the two of them together, and that's when Maisa noticed their age difference. Anni Saarikivi smiled like a mischievous teenager next to her severe, elderly husband. An excellent lover. She certainly hoped so.

Mrs. Saarikivi decided that the ritual was over and sat across from her. She lifted her feet onto the coffee table. It seemed unsettlingly inappropriate.

"So, about Suvikylä." She sighed and crossed her hands over her belly.

"Yes," Maisa said. "I've heard you lived here before these apartment buildings and stores were built."

"That's right. Since I was a child. I was born about a kilometer from here, in 1931. My old home doesn't exist anymore."

"It must've been sad when all the old houses were torn down and these apartments were built instead."

"How come?"

Maisa didn't know what to say.

"We're better off with those old houses gone. They were absolutely terrible. And all fall and winter long, the yards were pitch-black, no lights. You had to feel your way to the outhouses. These apartments are much, much better."

"I see." Maisa took a moment to collect her thoughts. "Actually, I'm researching stories that people are telling each other in Suvikylä."

"Are you interested in that girl? The one who went missing?"

Maisa jumped. "Excuse me?"

"The one who just recently went missing."

"When was this?" Maisa asked.

"In '87."

Maisa had to let the words sink in, then repeat the year in her mind. This wasn't about Sagal.

"Which girl are you talking about?" she asked.

"The one from America."

In '87. Maisa was sure she knew who it was. Julia. The *beautiful* girl from America. The girl who had hypnotized Samuel. The disgustingly self-assured girl who didn't play fair. The girl who showed off by carrying her video camera everywhere with her. These memories weren't pleasant. Maisa's fingertips tingled. Images of Julia and Sagal mixed in her head like overlapping photographs.

"I knew her," Maisa said. "Was her name Julia?"

"I don't remember the names of kids these days, but I know she came from America."

Kids these days?

"You mentioned that this happened in '87."

"That's right. I remember because my son left that year on a peace-keeping mission to Lebanon."

Maisa hadn't heard anything about Julia's disappearance. She'd locked herself in her house for almost a year when she was fifteen. Then her family had moved away. Her parents had probably decided to move because of her. They never talked about it, but what other reason did they have to sell their townhome and move away from Suvikylä, where their neighbors had been their colleagues and everyone had a good time together at garden parties?

"I didn't know she disappeared," Maisa said.

Her voice rattled, so she had to cough. She apologized.

"Yes, indeed," Mrs. Saarikivi said. "Without a trace."

"Julia lived in that large single-family house over at—"

"Exactly. The last house on the street. Her father still lives there." She leaned forward again. "A complete drunkard these days," she whispered. "Never got over his daughter's disappearance. That hideous woman of his left a long time ago. He lives there all by himself, in that mansion. Curtains drawn day and night."

Maisa had pulled a notepad out of her pocket, her pen poised, but the page remained blank. She couldn't even bring herself to pretend to take notes, to write down that Julia had disappeared. Her memory of Julia was clear at first, but as soon as she tried to bring back details, it became blurry. Like recognizing a person in one situation but not when she passes you on the street. Maisa began to sweat.

"And that wasn't the first time, either," Mrs. Saarikivi said.

"Excuse me?"

"She wasn't the first child who went missing. It happened twice before her, but in those days nobody wanted to raise a fuss about it, unlike today."

"Do tell me," Maisa said.

"After the war," she began, then covered her mouth. Maisa heard a frog-like burp.

"Please excuse me. After the war a boy went missing. Reino Raaska. His family came from the Karelia region. They never found the boy. They claimed he drowned on a fishing trip, because people from Karelia were used to lakes, not the sea, where new groups of rocks form under the surface each year. So he may have hit a rock with his boat, who knows. The result was nevertheless the same: the boy went missing and no one has heard of him since. Then, in the early sixties a teenager, Siiri Vataja, went missing. She was quite a sight with her beautiful, bright-red hair. You just didn't see that around here. She was a little too proud of herself, but we admired her and waited for her to come to Suvikylä from the town by boat. I can't remember the year exactly, but people saw her go back to her boat in the evening, never to be seen again. Even the boat went missing."

Maisa's pen was still frozen in place. An ink spot was slowly spreading under its tip. She was thinking.

"Are these disappearances in any way connected to this thing called the Fairy-Tale Cellar?" she asked. "The stories children tell each other in the bomb shelter?"

Mrs. Saarikivi's eyebrows shot up in confusion.

"How do you know about it?"

Maisa decided to lay the cards on the table.

"I heard how you had once gone there when they were in the middle of—"

"That is correct. What a terrible thing it was. Such a relic from old times, to sit in a circle and tell terrifying stories."

"Did you tell these stories as a child?"

Mrs. Saarikivi shook her head and went quiet.

"Children are telling stories about a strange old lady," Maisa added to fish more out of her.

"They're always making fun of us old people."

"No, I didn't mean they were making fun of the old lady. Their attitude is more like . . . respectful. Fearful, even. They talk about an old lady who murders children with a hatchet."

A faint smile played on Mrs. Saarikivi's lips. The ticking clock on the wall sounded hollow.

"Granny Hatchet," she said, trying too hard to sound mysterious.

Maisa accidentally scrawled a mark across her paper, then stopped.

"You know about that story?" she asked.

"Of course I do. Brats these days and whoever these immigrant kids are still use that term—Granny Hatchet?"

"Looks like it."

The woman threw her head back and laughed heartily. Maisa saw that she'd been right about the dentures: Mrs. Saarikivi's row of teeth tilted slightly in her upper jaw until it clunked back into place.

"You see, I don't pay attention to whatever kids these days talk about, not since that one time I tried to set them straight and it caused such an uproar. I do keep an eye on them from my window sometimes, and it's like watching the Helsinki Olympics. They think they're allowed to do whatever they want."

Her mouth settled back into a thin line.

"But that lady, she was such a monster," she continued.

"Who?"

"Regina von Bondorff."

"She's the source of these stories?"

"We were afraid of her as kids, too. We were also afraid of the stories she told us in the Fairy-Tale Cellar. Nobody dared to say a word about them to their parents. Any child repeating such nonsense would've gotten a smack on the head."

"So, this Regina was telling stories to children?"

"Regina von Bondorff created the Fairy-Tale Cellar. 'To teach children and to civilize the heart,' like she always told parents who weren't convinced their children should be allowed in the cellar. Whether the children lived in the villas or in the farmhouses, they were required to attend every Tuesday evening, every summer. I wouldn't describe her stories as civilized, though."

Maisa recalled the abandoned houses. They had been empty ever since she was a child. Their broken windows and spray-painted walls lined the shore.

"Everyone had to go down to Regina's root cellar, although we were scared out of our wits. And we had to drink that terrible juice. I still haven't to this day tasted anything so nasty. I have no idea what it was, some concoction created by a severely ill woman."

Mrs. Saarikivi shivered.

"It was disgusting. And that smell. Once I threw up on my finest summer dress when I walked out of the cellar into the light. And I wasn't the only one. Many of us got sick, and our tongues were so black we had to use soap to wash our mouths."

Maisa thought about Sagal's recording. About Granny Hatchet, the black tongue, the cellar. Then she decided not to think.

"There was something oddly unsettling about that place. I always had horrible nightmares afterward. Like I said, all of us children were scared, but none of our parents wanted to argue with Regina. She had royal blood in her, and she was married to a wealthy shipbuilder. I do believe Carl von Bondorff was German. He spent his days fishing ever since they lost their only son. He probably drowned, but that's not what Regina claimed had happened."

The woman gave Maisa a meaningful look.

"What did Regina claim?" Maisa saw it was her duty to ask.

"Well, that's a longer story altogether. Longer and more tragic. You see, her husband's past was shrouded in all kinds of intrigue. Bankruptcies, that sort of thing. That's why they settled at the villa permanently. Who knows what sort of goods the man bootlegged. There were rumors at the end of the war that shipments of an unknown poison were delivered to the island from Germany, and that poison was killing all the fish. Something strange had to be going on—you know how the seawater still doesn't freeze around that island? Isn't that peculiar?"

Maisa nodded.

"But that's not all. Mr. von Bondorff's claim to fame was his hunt for the sea monster."

"Sea monster?"

"Yes, just like Captain Ahab. Are you familiar with that old movie?"

"I am," Maisa said, not wanting to point out that it was originally a book.

"Gregory Peck was in it," Mrs. Saarikivi went on. "Mr. von Bondorff wasn't quite as handsome as him, but they were both obsessed in the same way. I used to think the man had gone insane, but then . . . Just a moment, please."

She lifted her feet off the table and pushed herself up from the chair, then walked over to peruse the bookshelf. Her finger flitted past all the Alistair MacLean books and stopped.

"Here it is," she said, leafing back and forth through its pages. "*Confu* . . . Hmph, you read it. You young people know foreign languages."

Mrs. Saarikivi handed the book to Maisa. "You never know; maybe it's a true story."

Maisa looked at a picture book about the World Heritage site in Kvarken, the waters that separate the Gulf of Bothnia from the Bothnian Bay. The page she was on had a small box in the left margin, containing a few sentences with the heading *"Confusarius Maris Baltici."* Just an interesting side note among all the facts. Apparently, a lawyer in Raippaluoto had written a report in the 1700s about a curious sea creature—and he hadn't been the only one. The monster was mentioned by a lighthouse keeper in Norrskär and multiple fishermen. Later, in the 1900s, the sea monster had been reported by Carl von Bondorff, a bankrupt shipbuilder, who had obsessively begun to research and try to locate the mysterious sea creature. Maisa wrote down the Latin name and left her notebook open on the table.

"Fairy tales or not, Mr. von Bondorff went to his grave believing in them," Mrs. Saarikivi said. "Apparently Regina handled his peculiarities just fine, but then they lost their son. Their only child. That must've finally broken her. She wasn't always mad. My mother used to tell me stories about how she chatted with her across the bay before the war. To her, Regina was a sophisticated and friendly woman, who never looked down on people below her stature. She tended to her small field of potatoes and managed to make it bloom in that rocky soil. But that's not the Regina I remember. She looked filthy, and . . ."

Mrs. Saarikivi looked at her hand with soft, unfocused eyes.

"Her arms were always covered in strange, round wounds. In the summer heat, pus leaked out of them, and they smelled. She always waited for us children at the shore with a hatchet in her hand, but she certainly had not used it to work on the potato patch—it was an overgrown mess. Who knows what sort of a devil had gotten into her."

She shrugged. "I suppose sorrow can be a personal devil, when it's heaped on indefinitely. At any rate, Regina believed that the sea monster snatched her son. And . . ."

She shook her head, distressed by a distant memory. "That's what her stories were all about."

"In the Fairy-Tale Cellar?"

Mrs. Saarikivi gave Maisa a quizzical look.

"Is that where she told you about her son?" Maisa asked.

"Yes. And how we were supposed to go see the monster."

Maisa was now confused. "See the monster where?"

Mrs. Saarikivi sighed. "That cellar was a strange place," she said. "It was like a cave that led downward. It's hard to describe."

No need to, Maisa thought, almost saying it out loud. Only the tiny dot of ink from her pen made her focus and control herself. She stared at it on the paper, her neck muscles gradually tightening.

"This sea monster supposedly lived under the island. Regina claimed she had captured it. How absurd. I wonder what she would have done if someone had actually followed her down there. Who knows, she could have whacked them with her hatchet. She was already then so unpredictable. She could be silent and then scream or laugh for no reason. She kept telling us that she watches us sleep at night. That she follows us in the dark when we have to use the outhouse and carries her hatchet with her, and you never know when she is right behind you. I do not understand what sort of sick pleasure she gained from scaring little children."

Mrs. Saarikivi leaned forward to grab the World Heritage–site book off the table. She stared at the pages—the part about *Confusarius Maris Baltici* was Maisa's guess—as if they would unravel the mystery of Regina von Bondorff.

"One day she told us that the monster had escaped. She managed to ruin many beautiful summers for us children for years—nobody wanted to go swimming again. As soon as you did, and if your foot sunk into the mud even a little, it felt as if something were grabbing your ankle. Just think about it: we'd listen to her terrible stories in the cellar, surrounded by disgusting smells and with only an oil lamp for light, and once we climbed out we had to walk along the shore to get home. The only way to get to the tip of the peninsula is to jump from rock to rock over the narrowest part of the bay. As soon as we were at the tip, we'd run fast without looking back."

Maisa thought about Sagal's recording. She imagined the damp smells of the villa's cellar instead of the bomb shelter. And beyond that smell, another stronger stench. The darkness. She had to focus. She had to take her thoughts back further, to the summers decades ago, to children jumping from rock to rock. To distant memories.

"Did anyone write these stories down?" she asked.

"Bah! Who'd want to write nonsense like this? Besides, it all came to an end. You see, Regina went a little too far. She had this idea that the creature underneath the island was actually her soul. And that's why the creature wouldn't leave. She kept on repeating this to us as if she were in a trance. Then one time . . ."

Mrs. Saarikivi lowered her voice again to a whisper.

"One time, when we all arrived, she was wearing nothing but a nightgown. Her mumbling made no sense, and one of her breasts was hanging out. There, in the middle of the day. She was touching herself. 'Masturbating,' if you want to use more sophisticated terminology. Her lips and teeth were all black. Her skin seemed to have aged rapidly. Then came the last time we ever saw her . . ."

Her eyes glazed over. She was looking through Maisa. Then she pulled her feet off the table again and pushed herself up.

"Please wait a moment while I look something up."

She walked to the hallway and opened a door to another room. Maisa could see the foot of a bed and burgundy curtains. There was some clattering, and suddenly she saw Mrs. Saarikivi standing on a chair that creaked dangerously, reaching up and going through boxes that had been put away on shelves out of everyday reach. She heard cardboard boxes shuffling around, accompanied by annoyed muttering and hissing, which Maisa was evidently not supposed to hear.

"That damned bastard shit."

Maisa looked around. No dust on any surface. Even the floorboards were shiny. The bookshelf was not full: the MacLean books nestled together with a row of Kalle Päätalo novels, with *Papillon* at the end of the row like a crown jewel. All most likely left behind by Mrs. Saarikivi's lover.

"My goodness," Maisa heard her say as she stepped off the chair. "It's in the basement. Now I remember."

"What are you looking for?"

Mrs. Saarikivi walked to the foyer. Maisa heard keys jangling.

"Come with me. You'll see."

The apartment door creaked. Maisa grabbed her coat and bag just in case and rushed to the door. Mrs. Saarikivi was already walking down the stairs. Her footsteps echoed in the stairwell. Maisa followed her after she closed the apartment door behind her.

"Did you say you worked for a newspaper?" Mrs. Saarikivi asked over her shoulder as they descended.

"No, I'm a researcher. I'm writing a dissertation."

"I see. What is your field?"

"Religious studies."

The woman stopped and turned to Maisa. She covered her mouth with her hand.

"Oh, dear me," she whispered. "And I've been saying all sorts of rude things to you. To a priest!"

"I'm not . . ." Maisa began, then decided not to get into explaining the difference between religious studies and theology. "You have not said anything rude to me."

"Well. I suppose people aren't quite as inflexible as when I was younger. After all, I didn't even imagine that a young lady like you could be a priest."

"I am not going to become a priest." Maisa decided to clarify. She didn't want Mrs. Saarikivi to start mincing words with her.

"I see." She was visibly calmer. "Why would a priest be interested in the Bondorffs, anyway?"

"Probably wouldn't be."

They kept walking down in silence. Maisa hoped that mentioning religion hadn't turned Mrs. Saarikivi completely mute. Her skin began to tingle as they reached the ground floor and continued past it below-ground. Maisa forced her thoughts back to her research.

The light in the basement hallway turned on with stuttering flashes, accompanying Mrs. Saarikivi's hasty steps down the hallway. Maisa had to catch up with her. The woman stopped in front of the last of the five identical-looking doors. She looked for the right key.

"Mind your step," she said over her shoulder as she opened the door.

Maisa followed. The smell inside the storage area was sweet, as if it were used to store vegetables instead of belongings. The little lamps on the wall buzzed and flashed, about to go off. Flies had managed to wiggle inside the yellowed, stained lampshades, where they lay dead. No one had bothered to clean here. The woman unlocked an exaggeratedly large combination lock to enter her personal storage unit and began to shift boxes until she found what she was looking for.

"Here we are."

She was holding something. Maisa stepped closer. The buzzing noise from the lights annoyed her. She couldn't shut it out of her mind.

Mrs. Saarikivi held a small, red wooden box in her palm. A sailing boat in a storm had been painted on the lid, but the paint had begun to crack. It was covered in dark stains.

"What is it?"

"Open it." Her face jerked into a smile.

Maisa lifted the box between her thumb and forefinger, then placed it on her palm. She opened the lid carefully.

Nausea hit her immediately.

"What is this . . . ?"

Buzzing. A sudden feeling that they weren't alone in the basement. That they'd forgotten about someone who had been with them all this time.

"This is what she sent me," Mrs. Saarikivi said. "To a small child. Her own tooth."

Maisa thought about the letter she'd received and the picture of the teeth. Her first thought was that she was on *Candid Camera*. That was the only way life's little surprises would remain amusing.

"That was so long ago, too," Mrs. Saarikivi said and picked the tooth up.

Maisa thought about bacteria and their lifespan. Mrs. Saarikivi held the tooth between her thumb and forefinger, rotating it as if she were observing a precious jewel. The root of the tooth was yellow. The gum line was still visible. Above it the tooth was dark gray. It was clearly a front tooth. A wide tooth, chipped at one corner. The root didn't branch out. Maisa wanted to ask her to put the tooth away. It belonged to someone else.

"I'm glad I didn't attend the very last Fairy-Tale Cellar," Mrs. Saarikivi said, rolling the tooth between her fingers. The sweet smell of root vegetables grew stronger. Maisa looked at a daddy longlegs stretching his legs behind Mrs. Saarikivi. The spider seemed to be looking for warmth from the lamps.

"I had come down with a fever—apparently I was even delirious. Regina von Bondorff had sent a little wooden box to all the children, even those who couldn't attend. She had collected beautiful boxes from all over the world. I'm sure she got them from her husband, his being a shipbuilder. Eini from next door brought me mine. She told me; I don't remember it myself. I found the box in my hand the next morning. I opened it and even in my feverish state I knew what had happened. It didn't feel so out of place then. I just knew immediately."

"You knew what?"

She shrugged. "Iida and the other girls told me later that Regina had told them her very last fairy tale and then announced that she won't be a human much longer. Then she had brought out a pair of pliers, and . . ."

Maisa felt a shiver between her shoulder blades.

"The girls told me she had pulled them all out, right in front of them. And she hadn't made a peep. Just yanked them out one by one, then placed each in a wooden box. Then she handed every child a box and smiled. She had cried and explained that she didn't need teeth anymore, now that she was going to grow a beak."

"What?"

Mrs. Saarikivi giggled. It reminded Maisa of the smiling girl next to her severe man in the photo. The girl Anni Saarikivi had once been.

"A beak," she said. "Like a parrot's. Just think about it. That's how mad her stories had become."

Maisa stared at the tooth, not knowing what to say.

Mrs. Saarikivi stopped her giggling and suddenly spoke as if she'd never found the story amusing at all.

"Honestly, you can't judge people when you reach my age. We don't get to choose our destiny. Regina was . . . Regina. We all will face the Lord's judgment the way we are."

"What happened to Regina?" Maisa asked.

"Devil only knows," Mrs. Saarikivi said. "Our parents finally found out about all that nonsense and came to the conclusion that she was not quite right in the head, but by that time we all had more important things to think about: all goods were rationed, and men returned from the front with horror stories of their own. But whenever someone went missing in these parts, Regina's name came up. At least when we children talked about the disappearances."

She laid the tooth back on the black pillow in the box, gently, like a memory.

"It's yours now," she said and snapped the lid shut. She wasn't holding back her smile this time. "I don't want it anymore. Can you imagine what people would say if they found this box after I've passed on? They'll think I'm the Boston Strangler or who knows what monstrosity, although I've only killed a few chickens and a litter of kittens."

Maisa looked at the storm-ravaged ship painted on the lid. The ancient fingerprints smeared across the lid in black.

"Thank you," she said, because she couldn't think of anything else to say.

In the corner of her eye, she saw the daddy longlegs settling in the lampshade, his legs still. To Maisa it looked like he'd given in to the restless buzzing of the light and realized that he'd never achieve a more profound peace than this.

The red box weighed more than Maisa would have expected, and she could feel it moving in her coat pocket when she left the building. She sat on a bench outside. She chuckled, then looked for a pack of cigarettes in her pockets, although she hadn't smoked in two years. There was no one else in the yard. The box was heavy in her pocket. It pressed against her thigh and felt hot.

Maisa called Pasi, but reached only his voice mail. She immediately regretted calling him. She just wanted reassurance. What had just happened was amusing in some twisted way, right? It was hard to tell when she was alone.

Maisa drew a long breath and blew it out as if she were smoking. She imagined how the cigarette's calming effect would spread into her limbs until it became reality. She relaxed. She took out her notepad and flipped it open.

The one who went missing. Julia had disappeared. In her teens Maisa had always wished that the cocky American Julia would go away and never come back. The same Julia Samuel was in love with. And now there was Sagal. Maisa wasn't responsible or liable for either. Not at all.

She turned her eyes to the large rock in the middle of the yard. It had been there before there were buildings, and it would still be there when people fled in the wake of a catastrophe. The cold, barren buildings would begin to crumble, like all structures people thought were built to last forever, but the rock would remain.

Maisa had intended to ask Mrs. Saarikivi about Samuel, but she couldn't bring herself to do it. She hadn't talked to anyone about him, and she'd been especially careful not to mention him to Pasi. She couldn't mention the faded newspaper clipping from two years ago, with a picture of a man. That man had once controlled Maisa's every thought. That information belonged to no one else. People had to have amulets, objects containing a secret. People needed tangible benchmarks to organize the random events of life into a meaningful story and clear the way to a recognizable goal.

Maisa realized she was squeezing the box in her pocket. She released her grip and wiped her palm on her pants.

The stairwell door to the neighboring building opened. As soon as he set foot outside, the skinny man began to light his cigarette, not bothering to look around. Maisa was already walking away when she took note of the building. The man hadn't walked out of any old stairwell. Her eyes counted the windows up to the third floor.

That's where Samuel used to live as a teenager. Maisa had looked up at the building's windows thousands of times. Sometimes she had even gone for an evening walk to watch shadows moving inside the apartments—thinking that one of them could be Samuel.

Where are you, shadow? she asked.

It was melodramatic of her, but certainly no one else had asked that question as seriously as Maisa had during the two years Samuel had been missing. Or so she told herself. Samuel's wife wouldn't have asked, nor his faceless children. Maisa could have given birth to them and they'd still be the same little humans. Life took unexpected turns, but there was always that one point marking the beginning of a life when everything else could be possible. Samuel's shadow in the window. That had been her future. Their future.

Maisa forced herself off the bench. When she reached the street she saw the woods surrounding the buildings, and when she looked right, she could see the deck of Julia's house. Behind the house again just woods, like all around the edge of Suvikylä. Then there was the townhome where Maisa had lived, watching Julia's house with smoldering eyes. Her dad had always admired Julia's dad—a success story, a man from Hollywood, an entrepreneurial spirit, a great noncommunist. And there was Maisa, hating even Julia's shadow.

She had never met Julia's dad. She'd only seen him as a face in a taxi flying by, or as a distant figure smoking on the upper balcony of their opulent home. In her imagination Julia's dad lived somewhere beyond the lives of everyday folks and their everyday chores.

A complete drunkard these days.

Maisa took off toward the house with determined steps, but slowed down soon. The air seemed to have become too heavy to breathe, almost liquid. She thought about Julia. The Julia she hated, the Julia who had gone missing. Julia may well be lying somewhere six feet under right now. She'd been disintegrating there for decades. When Maisa had helped carry her couch into a moving van heading to Turku, bacteria may have been eating at the green color of Julia's eyes. When Maisa had opened the blinds at her Turku studio for the first time, Julia's smooth skin had been flaking off her cheekbones like charred paper. And somehow Maisa felt like it was her fault. The fault of her envy and anger.

Typical magical thinking, Maisa tried to convince herself. But what can you do?

Her shoe stopped with a crunch on the asphalt.

Her lungs jerked like a wounded baby bird.

Julia was gone, yet she was everywhere.

That night Maisa couldn't sleep. As soon as she closed her eyes, she saw decomposing skin, vitreous humor oozing out of eyes with shreds of membrane sticking to it. The soil swallowed it all without a single witness.

At three in the morning she got up and drank a glass of juice. The wind made the windows creak. The fall had been surprisingly warm, and the trees struggled in the wind, furious for having to wait for winter this long. The horizon flashed. Maisa drank her juice and thought about the last time she'd seen lightning this time of year.

She tried falling asleep twice more, but failed. She got up again, walked to her coat in the foyer, and took Anni Saarikivi's wooden box out of the pocket. She placed it under her pillow.

The flashes continued behind Maisa's closed eyes.

She thought about Samuel. She squeezed her thighs together, then moved them apart as an afterthought. She allowed her fore- and middle fingers to help her. Her other hand squeezed harder around the box under her pillow.

Once her body relaxed she was finally able to fall asleep.

Samuel dug a grave for Arvid. The soil was mixed with small stones, and it took him three attempts to find a spot where he could dig a deep enough hole. They lifted the dog into it together. Samuel threw a shovelful of soil over Arvid, but it somehow felt wrong. Julia fetched a sheet and placed it gently over him, then nodded. The falling soil began to cover the shining white sheet.

When they came back into the house, they saw Helge at the table, looking out the window. He had collected the papers off the floor into a large pile and held his hand on them, like a paperweight.

Julia went to the sofa and collapsed on it with her dirty shoes on. Samuel sat across from Helge. It was getting brighter outside, and the wet lawn glittered through the wavy glass of the old windows.

"You should never drive a man to the point where he has nothing left to lose," Helge said, still looking out. Maybe he was expecting to see Arvid running in the woods.

"It's not a wise thing to do. Is it, Samuel?"

"I guess not."

"It is not."

Helge grabbed the half-empty bottle of vodka off the table, but then changed his mind.

"Did you know that I always thought I'd kill myself when Arvid died? Isn't that crazy?"

"Yes," Samuel said, avoiding his eyes. "It's just a dog, anyway. Was."

"But I had no one else. Just a dog."

There was nothing Samuel could add to that. He hoped everyone would find out about Arvid's death. Then they would leave Helge alone, or at least they'd become friendly enough to not bully him or show up in the middle of the night to demand booze.

A painfully awkward silence followed, interrupted only by the calm ticking of the grandfather clock.

"The Bondorffs hate me. I always knew it."

"Why would they hate you?" Samuel asked.

"Because they know I'm the last one."

"The last one?"

"There won't be any children. I'm the last in the family. Since my great-grandfather, we've been entwined, us and the Bondorffs. When my father died they started to worry, but my mother convinced them everything was all right. She told them Helge would find his lady eventually, as soon as the right one would come along. Then my mother passed away and I moved in. The final guardian."

"What are you guarding?"

Julia had stood up from the couch. Helge glanced at her, then looked outside again. He let out a joyless little laugh.

"I don't even know. Nobody knows anymore."

He sighed and rubbed his face. His eyes were still hazy from all the alcohol, but his mind was slowly sobering up.

"Maybe I guarded the island."

"Why?" Julia asked.

"You tell me. It was always so mysterious. Come to think of it, my family was full of secrets. Everyone just dropped hints, and I was supposed to know what to do without anyone telling me outright."

They didn't dare to question him further. They just waited.

"The Bondorffs used to be fine folk. People of principle. Real patriots. Then things began to go . . . wrong. They became obsessed, even paranoid. That island of theirs is a curious place: some say there are caverns underneath where water flows throughout the year. The Ice Age moved large boulders in such a way that a labyrinth formed beneath the island, like a termite's nest. You can hide anything under there. Regina von Bondorff began to claim that she had . . ."

Helge laughed again but didn't smile. Samuel looked at his hand and the papers it was weighing down. Old biology tests from school. Writing in the margins in a red pen. Helge hadn't taught for at least the past five years, and yet he was going through his old tests. Samuel paused to think how peculiar this was. It was also strange that the ball lightning hadn't burned any of the papers. It hadn't even charred the edges. Helge removed the tests off the top of the pile to reveal black-and-white pictures and yellowed papers full of scribbling in small letters and strange drawings. Helge tossed a photo to Samuel.

"That's a picture from the coast of Norway from 1954."

The photo wasn't exactly clear: it seemed to depict a man dressed in a long white coat, leaning over a shapeless mass that had been laid out on black fabric or a tarp. Another man stood next to it, wearing horn-rimmed glasses and smoking a pipe. Whoever had taken the picture had perhaps climbed up onto a ladder for the angle to make sure the creature on the ground would be entirely visible.

"What's that?"

"*Architeuthis dux.*"

The reply seemed fittingly strange. Julia was now leaning over to examine the picture.

"Wow," she said. "Gross."

She was still upset over what had happened to Arvid, but there was already a hint of excitement in her voice.

"Almost fifteen meters long. They found it dead on the shore. Back then it made headlines all over the world. People have seen even larger ones. During the war there were stories about the creature picking men off their lifeboats when ships were torpedoed. It's a beast. It holds on to you with its tentacles and pulls you into its mouth, and you can see it . . . Here."

Helge's shaky finger pointed at the photograph.

"Its mouth looks like a parrot's beak. The tongue has tiny teeth in it. It cuts any food it eats into fine bits. The esophagus runs through its brain, so it has to chew on the food carefully."

Julia gagged. A strange expression had come over Helge's face, as if he were proud of what he was telling them. She grabbed the photo, looking mildly alert now.

"You're telling me this thing lives under the island?" she said.

Helge looked through her. An unsettling smile spread across his face. Samuel was sure he wouldn't have recognized Helge from a picture if he had looked like that.

"Are you?" Julia repeated.

Helge was knocked out of his reverie. He blinked a couple of times and began to howl in laughter. It startled both of them.

"Of course not," he said. He took the photo from Julia and placed it on the table, picture side down.

"Well, who lives on that island, then?" Samuel asked.

"I don't know," Helge said. "I don't know if anyone lives there these days. Maybe Raaska is guarding an empty lot. The Bondorffs always stressed how important it was to keep things the way they had been. To them, death didn't change a thing."

The clicking of the grandfather clock. A dead sea monster in the photograph.

*

When they left, Helge grabbed Samuel by the arm.

"Don't go there," he whispered.

Helge never touched anyone. He definitely never squeezed anyone's arm. Julia was already marching across the yard.

"The island may be abandoned, but it's a nasty place," Helge said. "You will be eighteen in three years. Then you can get the hell out of here."

"Come on, we don't plan on going there," Samuel said.

"Some things remain secrets because that's how it's meant to be. You're a young and beautiful boy . . ."

Samuel yanked his arm away.

"Just keep your hands to yourself and sober up," he said.

He regretted his words immediately but didn't turn back to apologize.

Julia was waiting for him at the edge of the woods.

"You know where we're going today, right?" she asked when they were out of Helge's earshot.

Samuel had a pretty good idea. He thought about Helge's warning and looked down at his feet, carefully avoiding each tree root and rock.

"We're going there right now," Julia said. "I'm getting my camera. I don't want to miss another spectacle again, the way I missed that ball lightning."

He was about to tell her that they shouldn't go to the villa when his ears popped. He stopped, then laughed.

"What is it?" Julia asked.

The sounds of the woods flooded his head. Then the smells came. The smell of soil and bark, and the mixture of all green living things and all that was decaying. And Julia stood in the middle of it all.

"Nothing," Samuel said. "Go get the camera."

Pasi called Maisa when she least expected it. She'd actually been certain that the caller was Samuel. What a ludicrous idea. Maisa had begun to carry the newspaper clipping about his disappearance in her pocket. It had only been two years. There was no reason to declare him dead yet. Men under fifty who wanted to take a break from their formulaic lives ran away surprisingly often. There were statistics about this.

Yet there was Pasi's name on the screen. Maisa didn't pick up right away. That gave her two advantages: first, she had time to think about counterarguments; and second, she could create the illusion that she was living a busy life that he was not a part of.

"Hi there," Maisa said.

She pretended to be out of breath and walked out onto her balcony to catch the sounds of life going on around her in the background.

"Do you know what I'm doing right now?" Pasi asked.

She could hear that he was either drunk or high or both.

"I don't know," Maisa said. "Braiding your wife's hair?"

Pasi laughed. "Even better. I'm waiting for you to come here."

"But I'm in Vaasa."

"So am I."

Maisa jumped. "What do you mean?" she asked.

"I'm at Hotel Astor. The town's oldest hotel. Want to come over for a drink?"

Maisa turned to look at the motionless reality of the dark courtyard. *Under no circumstances should you go*, the courtyard seemed to advise her.

"All right," she said. "I'll be there in thirty minutes."

*

Pasi sat alone in the lobby bar. A deer head was mounted on the wall, along with paintings of men posing with shotguns and dogs. How appropriate for Pasi. Maisa sat down.

"Praise the Lord," he said, raising his pint glass.

"What's Herodes doing here in the provinces?" Maisa asked and ordered a coffee.

"What *wouldn't* Herodes be doing in the provinces?" Pasi responded.

He was even more wasted than she'd assumed from the phone call.

"I'm serious. What are you doing here?"

Pasi slurped his beer and shrugged. "My protégé received a bizarre threat while on a job. What else could I have done? I protect my herd."

"Be real with me for once," Maisa said. "Cut the Jesus act."

Pasi pulled out a pack of cigarettes. He clearly wanted to smoke, then remembered that smoking wasn't allowed in bars anymore. He probably hadn't been to a bar since the new law passed, limiting his drinking to appearances at faculty or student parties.

"Fine, no Jesus acts. Carl von Bondorff. Does that name ring a bell?"

Maisa didn't answer. "Go on," she said.

"Quite an influential fellow from your old haunt. From Suvikylä."

"I'm listening."

"A former intelligence officer told me that he was an important figure in the area."

"I see."

The waiter brought Maisa's coffee and lit a candle at the table. She thanked him and resisted the urge to blow it out.

"He had some sort of special status in the community," Pasi continued. "He was allowed to practice"—it was obviously hard for him to swallow his pride—"his religion."

"How interesting," Maisa said. "That doesn't sound like a ghost story at all. Or like the Yakuza. Or the Nivala BB-gun rituals."

"Touché," Pasi said. "Want to go up to my room?"

"What for?"

"To fuck, of course."

Maisa laughed. "Only if I can call your wife and ask for tips on how to work on my abs first."

Pasi calmly looked straight into her eyes.

"You have a good case here," he said. "I'll support you any way possible."

"Only business students, lawyers, and journalists who write sensationalist crap talk about 'cases.'"

"You know what I mean."

"But I don't. This is really important to me—it's not just an anonymous case file. You thought I was making shit up, and you were wrong. Your instincts failed you. And now you're trying to get a slice of my pie."

"Whatever, Maisa, but face it—you need me. Did you know they used the ice-road routes across the sea to bring goods through Sweden? They brought in lead-based poison that would make people go cuckoo. It was entirely against the Geneva Conventions. This Bondorff couple were middlemen in the operation. Top-secret stuff."

"And?"

"And the Bondorffs believed in the mythical idea of the fatherland. The wife was apparently a real Madame Blavatsky. They were cultists, but with an Ostrobothnian flavor thrown into the mix. Children were disciplined without sparing the rod, and anyone snooping around would quickly get their comeuppance. 'Our dear country Finland, O thee,' that sort of thing. Have you ever actually stopped to think about the lyrics to that old 'Citizens' Song'? They talk about 'the wonderland of wonders.' 'Wake up,' a Jehovah's Witness would say."

"You're drunk. I don't think I can listen to you much longer."

Of course Maisa was interested in what Pasi had to say, but she had a headache. Bondorff Island was tangled up in a thick, misty shroud of legends, and it was making her head hurt.

"I did spend a few hours in the restaurant car on the train ride here, but do you see how lucid my thinking is? Anyway, back to that place, Suvikylä."

"What about it?"

"There were all sorts of wild rumors about the place before the suburban neighborhood was built. An overly zealous bishop from Lapua tried to get the Bondorffs excommunicated, but his higher-ups reminded him that only the Pope had the power to decide such matters. He also had to be reminded that the Finns had been Protestants for quite a long time. Have you ever heard of *confusarius maris baltici*?"

Maisa sipped her coffee. "No," she said coolly. "Tell me more."

Pasi smiled and jabbed her with his index finger. "Your eyes betray you. You've heard about this!"

"Just tell me."

"A sea monster," he said. "I had never heard about us Finns having our very own little Nessie. But it's mentioned over a hundred times in official documents spanning multiple years. The latest police report came from—you guessed it—Carl von Bondorff. Apparently some creepy-crawly was splashing around in the waters of Kvarken. And it was a large one, too. Most likely it was a whale that had lost its way, but of course locals were convinced it was the Leviathan, or at least Iku-Turso straight from the myth in the *Kalevala*, sent here to ignite the apocalypse. These folks prayed to the sea. And whatever they preached was inspired by Hermes Trismegistus: the road to holiness could only be obtained either through extreme good or extreme evil. Alms for the poor or human sacrifice, either worked—as long as you took it to the absolute extremes. The locals were rumored to opt for sacrifice rather than put in the effort to organize benefit concerts. They dabbled in animal sacrifice at least, but some children went missing, too. Did you know about this?"

Maisa was sure he could read the answer on her face.

"And all this while secretly under government protection. So are we in this together or not?" Pasi asked.

In this together. It meant that Pasi would take credit. He'd fuck his protégé a couple of times and then remember to mention in passing that she was an assistant.

"I'm only interested in how religions are born in modern times," Maisa lied.

Pasi raised his palm like an umbrella against a flood of bullshit. "Don't fuck with me."

"I'm serious."

"That's exactly what I'm afraid of."

"Be afraid all you want," Maisa said. "Feel free to chase headlines with your stories about 'secretly under government protection.' Conspiracy theories are your field. At least at the university. I'm serious. There's not a dishonest bone in my body."

Pasi shook his head, convulsing with fake laughter. Maisa knew that jab had hit him where it hurt. Behind his pompous demeanor, Pasi was nothing but a forgotten loser in a small and underfunded department; he was the joke that faculty members from other, sexier disciplines laughed at behind his back all year long, and to his face at the university Christmas parties.

"Not a dishonest bone in your body, huh?" Pasi took an unnecessarily long drink from his glass. "But we already know how religions are born," he finally said. "We've known this since the beginning of the last century. Who's interested in researching that anymore?"

"I don't know," Maisa said.

"You don't know what?"

"How religions are born."

"Yes, you do. You've sat through my lectures. Unless you've gone gaga over those Jung quotations. This issue was resolved ages ago, so you're wasting your time dwelling on it. The prehistory of religion involves apes incapable of speech thinking that thunder and earthquakes were living beings. Just like when our computers don't cooperate, we tend to instinctually treat them like living beings that need to be punished by a flood of curse words and a couple of quick smacks at the screen."

Maisa remembered these examples from the first lecture she'd attended as a naïve freshman: if we stub a toe on a door, our first reaction is to protect the toe by holding it in the air or warming it with our hands. The next reaction for the majority of people is to hit the door or aim other hostile actions toward it, as if the door were a conscious being. But if the source of our discomfort is not a door or a crashing computer, but, let's say, a tsunami, we don't react with threats—we react with holy terror. This is completely irrational, but even the most cool-headed of rationalists will follow this route without it ever even registering. "That's the explanation behind all religious behavior in a nutshell," Pasi had said under the admiring gaze of freshman girls. "Only a tiny minority of us is immune to empathetic animism."

Naturally, Pasi counted himself among the minority.

Maisa also recalled her disappointment. She felt like Pasi had cracked open a door that revealed a basic human experience, but had then immediately shut it in her face. He'd even locked the door behind him. Now Maisa felt transported back to that same lecture, except this time she had almost a decade's worth of confidence and stubbornness to back her up.

"Apes would scream in terror during a thunderstorm," Pasi continued. "Throughout the centuries those screams became ritualistic, until at some point they decided that whenever the sky raged, this was how they should scream. That's how thunder got its name. That's how their god got its name. Then the number of gods began to multiply, and someone came up with a theology for them, but that's the long and short of it. Case closed. That's what religious studies is all about. If I could turn back time, I'd go to business school, or the theater academy. Money has little room for interpretation. Same with applause. I would happily walk onto a stage every single night just to hear the applause, and occasionally have someone recognize me on the street. So how about it? Want to fuck?"

Pasi suddenly looked exhausted, his hair streaked with gray. He'd forgotten his wedding ring in the hotel room. The deer head on the wall stared at the two of them with its empty black eyes.

"No," Maisa said. "Can I use your informant?"

He was smirking again. "If you'll go upstairs with me."

"You sound incredibly lewd when you're a stammering drunk. Come on, I'm serious."

"So am I."

They stared at each other. Then Pasi leaned back nonchalantly and glanced at the empty tables around them. A barely audible clink of glass rang from the bar. Neither of them had raised their voices, but their intensity had probably stirred some interest on a quiet night.

"You're so like your apes," Maisa said.

"Why?"

"You say you think about religion, but all you think about is fucking."

They both laughed, for the first time ever simultaneously. Maisa had already brought her coffee cup to her lips, and now managed to sputter it onto her nose and chin. They laughed some more.

"I need to know, though," she said, serious this time, "how my thunder got its name."

Pasi laughed once more, then calmed down. "I understand. Sort of."

"It would be amazing if you could help me. And without any tricks or bargaining, just this once."

He twiddled his thumbs above his belly.

"I already did," he said. "I don't have any informants at the secret police."

Maisa had never believed that part, anyway.

"This ancient professor in Helsinki told me about it. He's originally from around here and tried digging around for more information, but he never found enough evidence of illegal military equipment. He drew his own conclusions and moved on to research something more sensible."

"Thanks. What's his name?"

Pasi stopped moving his thumbs. He frowned theatrically.

"What I'm going to do now is pay for our drinks, then I'll go up to my ten-square-meter suite and drink some more." He clumsily shoved the table as he got up. "And I'll have you know, miss, that the number of Mr. Jack's wonderful room is 405."

Maisa sighed. "It was nice to see you," she said, staring at her coffee.

"Likewise."

Pasi walked to the bar, whistling. Maisa heard a quiet conversation. The waitress laughed and then wished him a good night.

Maisa remained seated, pondering her self-worth and the overall insanity of her actions. Even the animal on the wall appeared to shake its head at her.

She finished her coffee and got up. She didn't even look at the front desk as she rang the elevator up to the fourth floor. The small lobby behind her was completely quiet. Perhaps all of the staff was asleep, except for the waitress.

The elevator was claustrophobic and dimly lit. The car jerked with a screech as it began its ascent.

Maisa was overcome with panic before she realized what was happening. Her thoughts were still with Pasi and the thunder and the hotel lobby. Her body, however, was in full fight-or-flight mode.

The dim light flickered.

If you're not a good girl . . .

The car shook. Maisa held on to the walls.

Your heart will be dug out . . .

The invisible pulleys in the machinery groaned softly just at the edge of her hearing. It reminded her of other sounds, of darkness emitting a strange rumbling.

Maisa pressed her palms against the walls. She was prepared for the floor to cave in at any moment. When she got to the fourth floor, she lunged at the door. It didn't open. The car had stopped, but the door remained shut. Some metallic latch was keeping it shut. Maisa pushed against the door again, sweat beading on her forehead. When it finally swung open she fell out and landed on her elbows on the hallway carpet.

She struggled to get up. The panic attack subsided enough for her to think, *I hope Pasi didn't see that, please, anything else, but don't let Pasi see that.*

The hallway was empty. Completely silent. Rows of doors lined up neatly behind her and in front of her. None of them opened.

She looked for the stairs and walked down them carefully. A person in distress could easily fall over. Just take it easy, one step at a time.

As soon as she was outside, Maisa focused all her thoughts on the calming waves of fresh air in and out of her lungs. There were things too immense to remember. Or to forget.

Maisa looked at the rain and the dark clouds. She thought about the roiling storm front inside her and shivered.

Maisa called Pasi as soon as she was back at her apartment.

"Just listen to me and don't say a word, all right?" she said when Pasi answered the phone. "I'm going to tell you something."

"All right," he said after a long silence.

"When I was fifteen, I went to a place where we weren't supposed to go. I had a crush on a boy, who . . . Well, it doesn't matter now. It was teenager stuff."

Maisa closed her eyes, but the darkness felt debilitating. She opened her eyes, staring at the teacup in front of her and the steam rising from it.

"It was a large, old villa. It was on an island, but the ground was high enough for us kids to hop across the water on rocks. I went there with my dog, Nippu. I got to the villa and threw a stick for her, and I wondered why on earth we'd always been told not to go there and why the villa was supposedly so scary. It was in the middle of the day. The sun was shining. I made a huge ruckus on purpose, called out for Nippu, and whistled. I was not afraid at all."

The hand holding her cell phone had begun to tremble. Her cuticles hurt as if they were on fire.

"Then someone was suddenly behind me. I didn't hear or see anything, except the figure's shadow in front of me. Whoever it was pulled a burlap sack over my head and led me into a cellar. They locked me there. It all happened so quickly, I didn't even have time to be scared."

She could hear only the white noise of a phone line.

"OK," Pasi said, then, seriously, "That's . . . terrible."

Maisa nodded, although nobody saw it. "I was in that cellar for almost two days. I screamed. I beat at the door. You can just imagine."

"Were you forced to do anything? Like . . . was that person some sort of a . . . you know."

"No. They just kept me there."

"All right, good," Pasi said, sounding almost inappropriately relieved—as if Maisa had avoided the worst possible outcome by having remained physically intact.

Silence.

"What about the dog?" he then asked. "Didn't your dog defend you . . . or bark, or—"

"Nippu didn't bark. She didn't make a sound. I don't know what happened to her. I never saw her again."

"Who did this to you?"

"I don't know that, either."

"What do you mean, you don't know? Surely the police—"

"No police. No adults. Nobody ever found out. I lied to my parents about needing to pee really badly and how I went into the cellar of an abandoned house and the door got stuck. There were a lot of abandoned buildings in Suvikylä then, so it wasn't implausible. I lied about Nippu, too, and told my parents she had run off while I was in the cellar. Mom and Dad were in shock. Dad wrote a letter to the local newspaper's editor, demanding that the abandoned buildings be torn down."

"That's a hell of a story. Must've been traumatic."

"Yes, it was," Maisa said. "It is."

"But luckily nothing happened to you."

Maisa gritted her teeth, barely containing herself. She heard shuffling on the other end of the line. Pasi was most likely balancing the phone between his shoulder and his cheek to pour another drink. Or maybe he was settling into a more comfortable position before he asked something he thought would make Maisa uncomfortable. She was already regretting her decision to have told him anything. It seemed that he was treating this story like a slightly more inconvenient occurrence than locking yourself out on the balcony in the winter or getting lost while picking berries.

"So . . . why are you telling me this?" Pasi asked. "Now, don't get me wrong. I'm happy to be a shoulder to lean on."

Bullshit.

"But your calling me at this hour, although we just—"

"There was someone there."

Her hand began to tremble again. She tried to focus on the teacup and the wisp of steam.

"Where?"

"In that cellar."

"What do you mean?"

"I mean exactly what I'm saying."

The nauseating stench flooded back. The splashing from deep in the cavern, as if something had climbed out of the water and was pulling itself along the rocks. But that wasn't the worst part.

"Someone spoke to me."

The voice came back to her immediately. Maisa had been blocking it from her memory through sheer willpower. But her confession broke down all the barriers and dams inside her mind. Her hands now shook so violently that she had to put the phone down on the table and turn on speakerphone. Pasi's breathing sounded like he was in a small matchbox.

"What did the thing say?"

Maisa moved the tips of her fingers like the restless legs of a spider. She leaned over the phone.

"It told me that I had to be a good girl. That I could never tell anyone. And if I'm not a good girl, my heart will be dug out of my chest with a hatchet—"

"And buried in the potato patch," Pasi said on cue, as though he didn't realize he was speaking out loud.

Maisa nodded again to her invisible audience. "And that my heart would remain there until it was thoroughly black. And the rest of the story you know."

A gust of wind made the window rattle. Maisa jumped and turned to look. She stared at the dark window and finally allowed herself to recognize the truth.

Of course she knew where Sagal was.

The storm left a calm world in its wake. The wind had died out, and the rows of reeds stood still in the water. Dry leaves crunched loudly underfoot in the absence of crashing waves.

"I can't see anything," Julia said.

She stood on the first rock leading up to the Bondorff villa, the video camera on her shoulder. The rocks ran across the bay, like a path that had been tiled for that purpose. Julia took the first step. Her sneaker couldn't get traction, and for a moment it looked like she would fall into the sea, camera and all. Samuel managed to grab her.

"Give me that camera," he said. "I'll go first."

Julia gave it up reluctantly. As always. Samuel had occasionally been allowed to film, but it was clear who had the privilege of watching the world through the lens. Julia would be fine in front of the camera for a moment, but would soon demand to be behind it again.

The jump from the first rock to the next was the worst. The island looked just as abandoned as Julia had said. The rocks were already dry after the storm. The sun was shining in a cloudless sky. As Samuel reached the last rock, his fears were completely pushed aside. He hopped onto the Bondorff lawn like a brave moonwalker and looked around. Julia was right behind him.

Samuel didn't offer to give the camera back, nor did he ask if he was allowed to film. He simply lifted the camera over his eye and pressed the "Record" button. He wanted to see the world the same way Julia did, through a lens. It was important that they saw the world the same way. Julia didn't protest.

The villa first appeared on film as a hazy blob, then it came into sharper focus. The trees around it were nearly as still as the house itself. Samuel followed Julia, who marched toward it. Grass had grown on the lawn up to their knees. He thought about adders hiding in the grass and how they should've worn rubber boots. A blade of grass tickled him between the straps of his sandal, which felt like a warning. He was happy that Julia had worn sneakers. He could die happy knowing that she'd been saved. What a strange thought. Samuel was so mesmerized by it that at first he didn't register the nausea that had made him slow down.

Then Julia stopped and turned to the camera.

"Ew, what stinks?"

She looked pale. For the first time Samuel realized Julia could be scared. He continued filming in silence. The smell was earthy and nauseating, overwhelming. His dad had once asked him to find out what reeked in the kitchen, and Samuel had discovered a herring that had fallen between the stove and the cupboard. This stench was a hundred times worse, and more insidious, too. He first felt it in his thoughts, and only then in the pit of his stomach.

"This is . . ." Julia began, but her sentence was interrupted by mute gagging. She pressed her arm against her nose and mouth.

Samuel tried to focus the camera on her, but he couldn't because now he had to gag, too. He tried to focus on the buzzing insects all around. On the little dots flitting across the screen.

"This is so gross," Julia said.

He paused the film. "Wait," he said and ran back to the shore. His vomit splashed onto the rocks in three waves.

"Sorry," he said between retching.

Julia laughed, but not for long. Samuel wiped his mouth and thought about competitive sports and throwing darts and anything at all where he had to concentrate really hard although everyone was gawking and yelling at him. He raised the camera over his eye.

"All right," he said and started to record.

Julia looked sick on film. She still held her arm over her face.

"What's that sound?" she asked.

They heard a shriek among the rustling of the trees and the buzzing insects. Like someone screaming inside a bottle.

"It's coming from over there," Julia said, pointing at the building. Samuel turned to look. "Come on."

She walked up the stairs to the porch. She let her hand fall onto the door handle, pressing down with her palm and letting go as soon as the door opened. She walked in. Samuel followed her.

The voice was now louder.

"It's coming from the cellar," Julia said and pointed at the stairs leading down. "Come on."

Samuel was right behind her. The sound became clearer. It was a human screaming.

They stopped at the cellar door. Julia turned to look at him, as if he had any answers to any of this. The door had been barred shut, but either one of them could lift the latch. Samuel's hands were full with the camera.

"What are you doing here?"

The voice came from behind them. From the yard. A woman's voice.

The stench became unbearable, as if the woman's breath reeked all the way into the cellar. Julia's face told Samuel that she was thinking the exact same thing. His hand began to shake, and the camera shook with it.

"Let's get the fuck out of here," Julia said.

They ran up the stairs and out the front door. He stopped shooting, sure that someone would grab his shirt before he'd make it outside. The smell alone was so revoltingly thick, it could turn at any moment into a sticky membrane that would trap them and pull them back into the villa.

Samuel bumped into Julia on the porch.

She lost her footing for a moment, but didn't move.

There was a human figure standing in the yard. It took a moment for Samuel to recognize it was a woman.

"What are you doing here?"

Inside the house the question had sounded threatening, shrill. Now the voice was playful. It could've even been happily surprised, but the words came out muffled. Samuel's first thought was that the woman was drunk, or mentally disabled.

"We just . . . heard some voices."

The woman was a curious sight. Her skin was white as a sheet, and the skin around her eyes had collapsed into craters. Yet she didn't appear old. She was maybe the same age as Samuel's mom, if she'd still been alive. She wore a dark dress. The lace around the collar and the sleeves reminded him of photos in his history textbooks. Her unkempt hair was unnaturally red.

"Do you live here?" Julia asked, jumping down one step casually, as if nothing weird was going on.

Samuel followed slightly more cautiously.

The woman grinned. "I do believe so."

Her lips were dark. She was missing at least two teeth.

"Aren't you sure?" Julia laughed.

Another light-hearted jump and she was safely on the grass.

The woman's smile waned. She turned her head to one side, as if to contemplate this question, as if it had never occurred to her before.

"Of course I'm sure," she then said.

They heard screaming from the cellar again. It was drowned out by chirping birds. The sun was blazing hot and so suffocating that Samuel was tempted to ignore the screams. The bay remained calm. He stole glances at his surroundings. It wasn't too late to run away.

"Surely you know where you live," Julia said, "or are you kept here as a prisoner?"

The woman grinned again.

Such a grotesque sight. Samuel wanted to film her, but he didn't dare. He hid the camera behind his back.

"What's it like nowadays?" the woman stammered.

"What's what like?"

"The mainland."

Julia didn't know what to say. "I don't know," she started. "There's . . . all sorts of things."

The woman glanced over her shoulder and took a few quick steps toward them.

Samuel stepped back. Julia remained standing, but she squeezed her hands slowly into fists.

"I tried to go there," the woman whispered.

She really reeked. Her eyes were askew and hollow.

"This was the only thing I had time to take with me," she said.

She shoved her hand within the layers of her dress. She then held out a small white rock in her palm.

"All right," Julia said. "That's . . . nice."

Samuel saw what was wrong with the woman's eyes. One of the pupils was enlarged like on a frightened cat. The other was a minuscule dot.

"You could come with us," he suggested. He was surprised at how serious he sounded. Apparently Julia was surprised, too, because she jerked her head toward him. "There's someone in the cellar. Let's take whoever's down there with us, too."

The woman's stare made Samuel's skin crawl.

"Ha!" the woman shrieked. Then she began to laugh hysterically.

Her tongue was dark. She seemed to have something in her mouth that shouldn't be there. Samuel caught a glint of metal before her lips closed shut.

"Really?" Julia said. She had apparently noticed the glint, too, because her voice was tinged with distress.

The woman began to walk in jerking motions. They moved out of her way too quickly to be considered polite. She walked next to the front steps of the house, lifted up her skirt, and squatted.

"I'm taking a piss," she said over her shoulder.

"All right," Julia said, glancing quickly at Samuel. "Go ahead."

Their eye contact was brief, but it was enough to dissipate their fears. He saw how Julia was trying hard not to laugh. This would make a great story once they were back on the mainland, where there were people and mopeds and cars.

"But does it want to leave?"

The woman spoke to the side of the house while peeing. The screams had stopped.

"I think it does," Samuel responded.

The woman turned her head toward him deliberately.

"Don't know about that," she said. "It's been so . . . peaceful."

So it seems, he thought. Like in a Jehovah's Witness's paradise.

"Let's go ask," Julia suggested. "Then we'll find out."

The woman stood up and absentmindedly straightened her dress.

"Are we allowed to do that?" she asked, looking first at one of them, then at the other.

"Of course," Julia said. Samuel could hear she was still about to laugh.

The woman thought about it for a moment, then walked up the stairs and didn't say another word.

"Come on," Julia whispered and followed the woman.

Samuel looked one last time at their escape route and followed her. He'd already gotten used to the smell, but as they walked into the villa, it became stronger again. The woman stood at the bottom of the stairs, looking up at them.

"I don't want to open it," she said.

"Samuel can open it," Julia suggested. "Can't you, Samuel?"

"Of course," he said and handed the camera to her. The faster they'd get this done, the better. He reluctantly descended the stairs until he was close enough to the woman for their clothes to touch. That's when Samuel was no longer amused. They touched for a split second, but even that slight brush electrified his skin. He concentrated on holding the dry heaves back. Someone screamed behind the door again. It was a hoarse voice that couldn't scream anymore. But now he could distinguish a single word.

"Please."

Samuel yanked at the latch, but it was stuck. He pulled harder. The latch popped up and the door screeched open. The stench was now so overwhelming, he gagged and fell over on his back. An unrecognizable lump rushed out at him from the darkness. All he saw was a dirty face and a gaping mouth.

"Take me away from here . . ."

The lump held on to Samuel so tight that his ligaments cracked. The stone stairs pressed into his vertebrae. He was sure he was going to pass out.

"Take it easy. We'll get you out of here."

Julia's voice. She had appeared next to Samuel.

"You're Maisa, right?" she asked. "You're going to be all right."

The name brought Samuel back from his stupor. He looked at the dirty face and the wide, wild eyes.

Maisa.

Speaking the name out loud made her loosen her grip. He pushed Maisa off him and looked around nervously. The woman had disappeared. The hallway was narrow, so it didn't make sense that she would've just vanished.

"Where did she go?" Samuel asked, leaning against the wall. "Where the hell did she go?"

He thought about that brief touch and was suddenly afraid that she was right behind him, ready to attack.

Julia didn't hear him. She held Maisa by her wrists and tried to calm her down. The girl shook and sniffled in a monotonous tone. The crotch of her light-blue shorts was wet. Her white T-shirt was covered in black stains, as if she'd been pulled through a chimney.

"We're leaving now," Julia said and began to pull her up the stairs. Samuel gladly agreed. Maisa's feet were unsteady, so he pushed her in front of him. Julia stopped.

"The camera," she said down the stairs to him.

"What about it?" he asked in a desperate voice.

"I put it down."

Julia's eyes grew wide in panic. Samuel could see the horror on her face, more serious than her response to anything they'd experienced on Bondorff Island so far.

There were no other options. He cursed and turned around. He walked down two steps and looked for the camera. Not a trace.

"Find it," she demanded. "I'll walk Maisa out of here."

"I'm not fucking staying here," Samuel mumbled, but Julia was already on her way out with Maisa.

He turned to look at the open door that led into the cellar.

He felt the air wafting up from the cellar. It was like the worst possible morning breath, and all he saw was pitch-blackness—except one small red dot. Samuel had to squint to make sure he really saw it. In the commotion the camera had been kicked into the cellar, and it was still running. Julia could watch the tape later. It would show either a determined hero marching toward it or a coward trembling at the cellar door. Samuel forced his legs to move. He rushed toward the darkness and its morning breath, his arm extended to grab the camera.

"Hey, boy."

He stopped so abruptly his sneakers slipped on the floor. He almost fell over. He peered into the darkness where the voice had come from.

"My name is Siiri."

"All right," Samuel responded.

The ensuing silence tingled along his spine. He realized he was thinking about how the stench of the cellar would stick to his clothes and skin and couldn't be removed with regular detergent. He'd smell it even when he'd be back at school, and then he'd have to sit at the front of the bus alone, where none of the cool kids ever sat.

"I'm Samuel," he whispered into the darkness.

The camera was so close. It would record everything. He thought he saw a figure behind the camera, but his eyes may have been playing tricks on him.

"Siiri used to be a beautiful woman," the voice said.

It still stammered, but now it was more excited, hurried. The moist *s*'s hissed. It reminded Samuel of how he and Harri had tried to pronounce song titles from the band Celtic Frost with mouths full of chocolate.

He didn't know what to say. So he blurted, "You're still . . . really beautiful."

He thought about the woman squatting next to the stairs outside. The dark, wrinkly skin around her eyes.

I'm taking a piss.

"You're a nice boy," the woman said. "But I'm no longer beautiful. Can you imagine—my hair used to be completely red."

But her hair was still red. Hadn't she looked at herself in the mirror lately?

"That does not matter anymore, because I've seen something so beautiful that everything else has become meaningless."

"I see."

"Wouldn't you like to see it, too?"

"See what?"

"My soul."

Now Samuel could clearly discern a pale shape in the darkness. An outstretched arm.

"Some other time, thanks," he said. "I have to go. My . . ."

Girlfriend?

". . . friend is waiting."

He slowly moved his hand over the camera. Its plastic shell was warm and clammy.

"I'm sure you'd love to see it," the woman said.

"I'm sorry, I just don't have the time—"

"It changes color when it's angry or afraid. Can you imagine that?"

Samuel could not.

"Do you know what it's called?"

He shook his head. His hand was on the camera. The escape route was wide open behind him.

"Its name is the Ever-Devouring Night," the woman said. "I made it up myself."

Samuel picked up the camera and flipped the screen closed. He made sure that its light was off. Julia was always careful about conserving battery. The woman didn't seem to care that he was slowly backing out of the cellar. The outstretched arm remained where it was. It would not grab him.

The Ever-Devouring Night. Samuel realized he was tasting the words in his mouth. The way the woman said it, the sounds were mixed up, the words melting into each other.

Theevadevahrahnigh.

But it was familiar.

"'So I see you eye-to-eye,'" Samuel said, "'the Ever-Devouring Night.'"

Silence. Then a question.

"You know that one?"

"It's from a poem by Koskenniemi," he said. "I know it."

Another step backward. The outstretched arm floated without a body in the darkness.

"People still read them?" she asked.

"What, poems?"

"Yes, Koskenniemi poems."

"I read . . . all sorts of things."

The arm remained unnaturally still. Samuel couldn't help but think it was bait. The darkness pretended to be human and held that arm out like a lure, and he was the fish mesmerized by it.

"We had to memorize poems at school," she said.

Muhmuriz.

Samuel was still walking backward. He tried to recall what the woman looked like. Maybe she wasn't such a monster after all. First impressions had merely done her disservice. She was just a lonely woman who read poetry. And her name was Siiri. Samuel had never known anyone called Siiri.

"I was good at it," she added. "At memorizing. I only needed to read a passage once and I remembered it, and I read everything I got my hands on. But it wasn't until down here that I truly understood the words I'd read. That the Ever-Devouring Night exists, that there is a place where a full moon glows over stalks of wheat, that there is a homeland of poetry and truth, where we swim on the surface of the cold eyes of gods forever, and . . ."

Shuffling. A thick fabric was pulled across the rocks. The outline of the arm became clearer.

It was obvious he should've run. He should've taken off and laughed about an old lady squatting and pissing. He should've laughed so hard he cried, but something stopped Samuel in his tracks. Something told him that the door behind him would always remain open, that he didn't need to hurry to go through it, that it would always be there, that those boys on the mainland would always fix their mopeds or ride their buses and think about whether to go to trade school or high school, and of course they'd go to trade school and then order a pizza and see the new Bond movie.

The hand reached closer.

"Your friend could join us, too. We'll be one big family—"

Her sentence was cut off. Samuel heard heavy sloshing in the darkness. Like deep sighs. The clattering of rocks.

The hand stopped near his face. Then it pulled back quickly, into the darkness. He jumped and backed away.

He hadn't seen the woman, but he knew she had turned to look deeper into the cellar.

Then he had an alarming thought: how far did the cellar go? The floor under his sneakers didn't feel like any ordinary floor. The cellar at his grandmother's house hadn't sloped downward, and its floor hadn't been uneven or covered in sharp rocks. Samuel recalled Helge's stories about caves under the island, like a nest of termites. The pictures of a slimy creature stranded on the coast of Norway, observed by a man coolly smoking a pipe.

Then another thought. The most ludicrous of them all.

Could it all be *real?*

Was he actually smelling the odor emanating from some creature in its death throes that had woken up from its slumber, moving its limbs only to realize it was still trapped in an unknown hole?

"Did you hear what I said?" the woman asked.

"Yeah," Samuel replied. "But I have to go now."

"Why?"

"I have to take a piss," he said and turned to clamber up the stairs to the front door. He had taken only two steps when his shirt tightened around his neck and he fell backward. He tried to grab ahold of the wall, but he fell all the way to the floor. He landed on a sharp rock, hitting the back of his neck and between his shoulder blades.

"Stay," the woman said into his ear. "Nobody will come looking for you, and we'll always be—"

Samuel yanked so hard he tore his shirt. Then he pushed himself up, which was not easy because the ground was slanted and slippery under his sneakers. But he got up and ran up the stairs. The door grew larger and larger until Samuel was outside. In the still, damp air. His stomach was cramping. His entire body jackknifed as he threw up. His ears were ringing. He had a hard time focusing his eyes. But he saw a boat on the shore. A man had gotten out of the boat. He had a fishing reel over his shoulder. He stopped.

"Hey, boy."

Samuel took off running. He sprinted so fast he couldn't feel his legs. At the shore he didn't jump from rock to rock, but instead rushed splashing into the sea. His sneakers got stuck in the mud, but he waded onward with the camera above his head, the leaves of the reeds making small cuts in his arms. As soon as he had crossed the water, he took off running again, down the path through the woods, past the garages. He didn't stop until he reached the yard at home. He fell onto his knees at the sandbox, then onto all fours. He panted like a sick dog.

Granny Huhtala came over to ask what was wrong.

Samuel pushed her hand away. It was too similar to the touch he'd felt in the cellar.

"You smell like an old person, young man," she said, insulted by his rudeness, and walked away.

If Granny Huhtala said so, then you really did stink. Any other time Samuel would've been worried about who would see him and who would smell him. Now there was no time for that.

He looked at the sandbox and the crumbled sand castles, and thought about how they existed in the same world as whatever he had just seen and heard only moments ago.

"Young man stinks of old shit!"

Granny Huhtala's shouting in the distance would have been embarrassing at any other time, but now it was meaningless. The sun was shining. An unrecognizable bird sang in the trees. A trash can lid fell with a boom somewhere. An unknown woman's voice told some children to stop whatever they were doing. Music was playing near the garages. It was some mindless pop tune.

"Let me, darling, let me come right next to you . . ."

Samuel looked at his shadow. It was a panting stowaway that had followed him from the cellar. A rotting sea creature had transformed itself into darkness, corrupting sunlight and sand castles in its wake. Their crumbling walls and wind-whipped rounded edges appeared sadder and larger under his cast shadow, creating their own private world. A desert town at night, consumed by time.

We'll swim forever on the surface of the cold eyes of gods.

Samuel thought about living among the sand-castle ruins: they had enough life in them to create a world. He and Julia would walk past that toppled steeple and look up to see the moronically smiling moon.

"Is everything all right?"

He stared at the sand castle and muttered an answer. The camera was yanked out of his hands. Samuel couldn't hold on to it, even if he had wanted to.

"You hear me?"

A smack on the head. He turned to look at Julia.

"Or do you want to play in the sand?"

Julia's smile was wider than ever. She had a small cut above her right eye. Probably from a reed.

"Wasn't that fucking great?" she asked.

"Yes," he said.

"Say it once more. To the camera."

Samuel looked at the red dot, although he should've looked into the lens.

"It was fucking great."

Only then did he turn his gaze to the lens. He observed the convex figure reflected back at him. It could've been human, or a hand reaching out in the darkness.

"You smell a little," Julia said and held out her hand. It was a hand Samuel wasn't afraid to hold.

As the night fell they walked to the cape to look at Bondorff Island.

"Where is that man now?" Julia asked. It wasn't actually a question. Neither of them could've known.

There was no point in asking about the woman.

Lights moved within the villa: glowing flames of candles, then a colder, silver flickering.

Samuel wrapped his arms around Julia. They both knew it was the woman pacing inside the villa. She walked the empty rooms, performing strange rituals. Maybe she pissed indoors, talked to shadows, didn't remember the visitors earlier that day.

"How's Maisa?" he asked. He'd thought about her all day but had not wanted to ask.

Julia just shrugged.

And that was that.

The lights continued to wander within the Bondorff villa.

The moon above was pale and partially consumed.

Maisa woke up to her cell phone ringing. She turned over, annoyed that she'd forgotten to mute the damned thing. Her knuckles brushed against the wooden box under the pillow.

Her eyes flew open. Maisa grunted and pushed herself out of bed. It was three thirty in the morning. Her steps were unsteady as she navigated toward the glowing phone somewhere in the living room. It was Pasi. Of course it was.

"What?" she mumbled.

"Guess where I am?"

His voice was just a stammering whisper. Maisa heard wind in the background. It made the line rustle as if Pasi were stomping on cardboard boxes while talking on the phone.

"Downstairs at the front door, where else?" she said. "Go back to the hotel. I'm not letting you in."

"Wrong answer."

"Come on, not at this hour," Maisa begged.

"Here's a hint," Pasi whispered.

A pause.

"Madame Blavatsky was here."

Maisa shook her head, annoyed. She grew even more annoyed when she realized she was waking up. She wouldn't be able to fall back asleep again before her alarm went off.

"Come on, stop it," she said.

She stared at the tree trunks waving in the wind outside her window and tried to grasp at her thoughts. Thoughts about what drunk people would usually do in the wee hours of the morning. About what drunken university professors in their forties would do. And finally, what Pasi would do.

"And just so you know," he said, still whispering, "someone's home."

A large maple leaf smashed into Maisa's window. It slid down the glass like a starfish. For a moment it wasn't such a far-fetched idea that the apocalypse had begun and that the sea had begun to send out its dead.

"You're not telling me you're—"

"You have a fucking great case here."

Pasi hung up.

Maisa watched the starfish shivering on the window, until the wind whipped it away to join the mad carnival the world had hosted while she'd slumbered.

KILLS CHILDREN

"Let's go somewhere together," Pasi said to the phone. "Let's leave all this behind."

He'd found Maisa's number and held the cell phone to his ear, but he hadn't yet pressed the call button. Maybe he wasn't drunk enough. Maybe he didn't have news shocking enough. He'd call when he'd reached the Bondorff villa.

"My life is full of shit," Pasi muttered into the silent phone. "Let's steal a yacht from . . . some millionaire and sail into the sunset like pirates."

The taxi driver glanced at him in the rearview mirror but made no comments. Pasi set the phone down.

"Just talking to myself here," he said, holding the phone so that the driver could see. "I didn't call yet."

The driver let out a barely audible grunt. He'd protested at the beginning of the drive, but Pasi had managed to convince him to go along with all his demands once they'd agreed on a price. The driver had walked into a dark townhome—perhaps his own—to fetch rubber boots, size forty-two or forty-three. He called his colleagues to find out where the Bondorff villa was exactly. He didn't turn the meter on. Still, the man was tense and didn't speak much. His hands wrapped around the steering wheel too tightly. He sighed and complained under his breath.

When they arrived at poorly lit Patteriniemi Road, the driver pointed into the woods and gave vague instructions on how to find the villa.

"Wait for me here," Pasi said as he was about to get out of the car.

"How about you pay for the trip so far," the man said, "and call another taxi once you're done. I should be getting back home."

"What about these boots?"

"Keep them."

Pasi held the door open for a moment, then closed it, still sitting in the car.

"My, aren't we skittish." He laughed and looked for his wallet. He'd spent all his cash, so he paid with a credit card.

"Charge a little extra. Buy something nice for yourself. Like a new pair of poison-green rubber boots."

The man said nothing. He shoved the card reader over his shoulder, staring ahead. Pasi typed his PIN and removed the card. He didn't request a copy of the receipt.

"Have a good evening," the driver said, but Pasi had already slammed the door.

The taxi dug into the gravel as it sped away. Pasi stood alone in the parking lot with rubber boots dangling in his hands. He looked up at the apartment buildings: only one window had a light on. The wind hissed so loudly he couldn't hear any other sounds.

Pasi took a swig out of a small Chivas Regal bottle, then leaned against a garage to put on the rubber boots. He left his shoes on top of the trash can and began to walk in the direction the taxi driver had pointed. The woods were dark. He could see only the waving tops of trees against the night sky.

"I love you, Maisa Riipinen," Pasi said out loud and began to second-guess himself. With crystal clarity he realized he was doing this only because he was drunk—which was precisely why he had to do it.

Many of his best decisions were made under heavy influence. Like right now.

"Comfortably wasted," Pasi muttered and staggered onward.

After he'd walked a few steps, he began to hum a tune. He wasn't exactly afraid of walking in unknown territory in the early morning darkness. Instead, it made him feel lonely and melancholy, so he had to fill the void with something. Pasi used his cell phone as a flashlight, and it worked well, as long as he didn't light the path right in front of his toes—that made him lose his balance.

He found the shore. The taxi driver had told him he could walk to the island. He used the cell-phone light to look for the rocks and began his slow, unbalanced tightrope act. He whistled Michael Jackson's "Thriller" all the way. Occasionally he'd stop and listen, thinking he'd heard a swishing sound nearby. Drunken paranoia, he decided, and managed to reach the island with dry feet. He jumped onto even ground and searched for his bottle as he walked determinedly ahead. Then he heard it again.

Pasi stopped and listened. A swish. Accompanied by a quick clink. Then silence again. He looked around. Darkness waved in the wind.

"Whatever," he mumbled, turning his cell-phone light left and right.

His mind was playing tricks on him, interpreting some neutral nature sounds as highly meaningful. He had to keep his cool, even when he was drunk. Pasi realized he often dreamed within a dream, and when he was drunk he realized he was drunk, which put things into perspective.

The outline of the villa began to appear in the darkness. The wind joined in on the drunken hum in Pasi's ears, building his confidence. The light from his phone wasn't quite enough to illuminate its walls, so he turned it off. Besides, his eyes were already adjusted to the darkness. The steps leading onto the porch gave a hollow boom under his boots as he marched on without hesitation.

Pasi knocked on the door's window. There was no point in it, but hey—he couldn't disregard good manners, even if he was in the middle of nowhere. He stood there, staring at his dark silhouette reflected in the glass. He thought he heard sounds from inside, footsteps stomping toward the door, but it was just his imagination. When you knock on a door, you expect to hear steps. Touching the door handle, Pasi was just about to push it down when someone spoke.

He wasn't startled. He recognized a momentary tingling on his skin, but it was like one of those nightmares where you realize you're awake. He slowly lifted his hand off the door handle and turned toward the voice.

There was a chair on the porch. Something was on it. Maybe a human being, maybe an object covered in fabric.

"Is someone there?" Pasi asked, realizing how much he was slurring his speech.

No reply.

He must've heard wrong. When you knock on a door, you expect someone to appear. He was keeping his cool, yet supposedly that person was sitting right there now.

"It's locked," the voice said.

A woman's voice.

Pasi chuckled.

The figure on the chair was now clearly human. Not a pile of black fabric. A real human being. A woman who had slumped in the chair. Her arms were hanging off to the sides. Her fingertips almost touched the porch, her head tilted. But her voice wasn't drowsy. It was excited, happy.

"I didn't see you there," Pasi said. "I'm terribly sorry, intruding like this. I don't mean any harm, I'm . . ."

He didn't quite know where to go with that sentence. At least he'd stopped slurring. He had a talent for shutting out drunkenness when he needed to.

"That door is locked for you," she replied, as if she had not heard him.

For you?

The tilted head and the arms slung to the sides weren't moving. It reminded Pasi of a ventriloquist doll. He barely suppressed his giggles.

"All right. Of course, of course."

For a moment Pasi stood there in the midst of howling wind and uncertainty, which made him realize he needed to take a piss, and badly.

"Sit down," the woman said.

Pasi looked for a place to sit. There was another chair to the left of the door.

"Why not," he said.

He sat down, thinking about possible reasons why a woman would sit alone on the porch of a dark house in the early hours of the morning, but he decided not to dwell on it. It was more important to come up with an excuse to take a leak and convince the woman he had a good reason to be sneaking around on her porch at this time of night. Luckily the woman didn't seem too concerned about him. He leaned his head back against the cool siding.

Pasi couldn't see all the way out to the sea in the darkness. He only heard it murmuring somewhere under the moonlit clouds. He was sure he'd imagined the faint white foam on the waves, just like he'd imagined the footsteps after his knock.

He took out his small bottle of Chivas Regal and took a swig. He turned to the woman and offered the bottle to her.

"Want some?"

"No, thank you," she said.

A slumped head. Hands loosely hanging off to the sides. What a goddamned bore.

"All right, then," Pasi said and finished the bottle, then put it back into his breast pocket.

They listened to the waves in silence. He wanted to take out his cell phone to illuminate his partner on the porch, but it felt somewhat inappropriate. Her voice didn't betray her age, but Pasi came to the conclusion that she wasn't very old. Maybe around his age. Ten years older than him wouldn't have been too alarming, either. Life was constructed from experiences. Nobody needed to know.

"Why here?" the voice said.

Pasi looked at the woman and pondered this question, then turned his gaze back to the sea.

"You mean, why am I here?" he said.

There was no reply, so he continued.

"Well . . . I heard about this place and thought I'd check it out."

"It piqued your curiosity?"

"Yes. Sort of."

"A boring old place like this?" the woman said.

No rebuttal came to mind, so Pasi laughed instead. The woman laughed, too, and for a moment they laughed together. It cleared the air. He liked her laugh. It was scratchy in a perfect way, not like some suburban Miss Sings-Karaoke-and-Smokes-Too-Much, but like a woman who didn't care about keeping up appearances. He was sad the whiskey had run out. He stopped laughing when he heard the swishing sound again.

This time it was followed by a knock. A clink. Then another sound. A tapping on wood. It came from somewhere really close. Pasi turned toward the noise.

All he saw was meaningless darkness. He wanted to ask the woman about the noise.

"This is not a boring place," the woman said.

"I'm sure it's not," he said, still trying to locate the sound.

"When nothing changes, all sorts of things just accumulate."

Pasi's gaze still rested on the darkness beyond the porch. It took a few seconds for his drunken confusion to make sense of her words.

"Nothing changes . . ." he repeated.

He looked back at the woman.

She was no longer slumped. Her arms weren't lifelessly hanging to the sides. She had sat up straight. Her face was still shrouded in darkness, but she was clearly looking at Pasi.

"Is your last name Bondorff?" Pasi asked.

"I don't know," she said.

"Surely you know your own name."

"Of course I do."

Pasi snorted. "My, aren't you mysterious."

He was about to ask her name again when a new sound emerged. A clatter from inside the house, followed by a muffled mutter.

"Do you live alone?"

The figure shrugged. Pasi recognized the gesture clearly. His eyes had now adjusted to the darkness perfectly. He had cat eyes.

"It's hard to be alone here."

"I see," he said. "But you're still doing all right?"

"Of course."

They began to laugh again. The woman leaned forward, her entire body convulsing. She was no doll—just a nice, drunk woman with a lovely, hoarse voice. Pasi glanced at the way he had come. Darkness had swallowed the woods and the path lined with reeds, but farther beyond he could see little lights. The streetlights of Patteriniemi Road. He wasn't out in the boonies. Maisa would admire him until the end of time. Lovely Maisa.

"What do you say we go inside, and you'll get us something from your bar? Anything," Pasi suggested.

"From the bar?"

"I'm sure a house as grand as this has a bar."

"And anything?"

"*Any*thing."

The woman burst out laughing.

"Anything at all," Pasi said. "We'll drink it up and then you'll take your clothes off and we'll see what happens. How about it?"

Silence. The wind and the waves. The hum of perfect intoxication.

"You're insane," the woman responded. "You have no idea what . . . what people usually . . . which is . . ."

Pasi waited for her to finish, but she just laughed again.

"You can't come inside," she then said.

"Why not?"

"You just can't."

He weighed his options. He wanted to go in, drink some more, lick a little pussy, have sex numbed by his drunkenness and a condom, and then he would let the lady sleep while he rummaged through the house and called Maisa to tell her whatever evidence he'd find about the disturbed Bondorff family or the lack thereof. But Pasi was also a logical thinker, who would know in his dreams if he were dreaming.

"Let's drink out here instead," he suggested.

"But I'll be cold," the woman said, "if I'm naked."

"Well, well—we'll have to drink first and see about that part later."

The woman was about to die laughing.

"You're really something," she said.

She jumped out of the chair. Her face was suddenly right in front of him. It happened disturbingly quickly. His drunken gaze didn't have time to refocus on the woman.

"Wait here," she said.

Her breath smelled sweet, reminding Pasi of his childhood and rowanberry candy and Arctic-bramble liqueur. And something else. Something nauseating. Then the face was gone.

"Wait," she said. She walked to the door and yanked it open.

Pasi stared at the empty space where the face had been. The dark eyes . . . But everything would look dark in the darkness. Her pale face . . . But everything except black would appear pale in the darkness. And so on.

That mouth.

He heard booming footsteps inside the villa, wandering the rooms, walking away, then returning toward the door. Pasi looked up at the moon and touched the cell phone inside his pocket. He rehearsed what he'd tell Maisa. Then he called her.

He waited for her to answer as he looked at the little lights shining on Patteriniemi Road, the little votives of safe everyday life telling him everything was all right. Maisa answered.

"Guess where I am?" Pasi said.

She sounded clearly excited. He answered her questions as best as he could, which was difficult because he had to listen to the footsteps inside the villa.

"You have a fucking great case here," Pasi whispered when the footsteps got closer. He was about to tell Maisa something else, too, but what could he do.

The door blasted open just as he shoved the phone back into his pocket. The woman stood in front of him with a bottle in hand. Naked.

"Wow," he said.

"Isn't this what you wanted?" she said, lifting the bottle.

"I guess so," Pasi said.

He was supposed to feel exalted. Her age was still a mystery, but she definitely hadn't shaved down there. She looked just like in the porn magazines Pasi had sneaked a peek at as a kid. She was no trimmed neurotic who had grown up bingeing on *Cosmopolitan*. She was naturally naked, and she just stood there, in this cold weather, with a wide smile across her face. A bit too wide, actually.

"Sit on my lap," Pasi said. "So you won't freeze."

She walked over and sat down. They both laughed, but more nervously now. The bottle had no label on it, but the liquid in it was dark. It looked like red wine.

"Should we kiss now?" the woman asked.

"Not just yet," Pasi said, stroking her back. Her goose bumps tickled his fingertips, as if he were reading Braille.

He just couldn't get over the way her mouth looked. Pasi hadn't been scared when the woman spoke for the first time, nor did he feel threatened at any point after that. But that smile. It reminded Pasi of a hospital waiting room when he had broken his thumb playing baseball, and his father had taken him to the doctor. A woman had sat in the waiting room. She had been sent straight from the dentist's office to the ER. The dentist's drill had torn the side of her mouth, but she hadn't felt a thing under anesthesia. His father had talked with her, but Pasi had just stared at her face where the corner of her mouth stretched slightly too far into her cheek. He had thought of an illustrator falling asleep in the middle of drawing a face, letting his pen wander off by itself on the paper.

He was about to drift further into this unpleasant memory when the woman pressed her lips against his. Her eyes were right in front of his. First Pasi resisted, then relaxed. It was just an ordinary mouth. Cold lips and a tongue rough like a kitten's.

"Are you sure we can't go in?" Pasi asked when she pulled away.

The woman nodded.

"I'm sure. Want some?" she asked and lifted the bottle in front of her face. Its cold surface tapped Pasi on the nose.

"Sure, why not. What is it?"

"It does terrible things," she said. "Only to be used in emergencies. If the bad folks come, we mix it into the caviar."

"Mix it into the caviar?" Pasi knew when he shouldn't laugh, even when he was drunk.

"Yes."

"What does it do?" he asked.

"It makes you happy," she declared.

"Is that so?"

"Yes. It makes you too happy."

Pasi thought for a moment. Then he said, "I want to be too happy."

"Of course you do," the woman said. "Everyone wants to. We called it Project Berserkir. Have you heard of it?"

"Berserkir, you said?"

"Yes. I'm sure everyone knows about it now that all the Russkies are gone!"

Now Pasi couldn't contain himself. He burst out laughing. *Now that all the Russkies are gone?*

"So it's a genuine Viking drink? In case the Russkies come?"

She didn't reply. She just smiled with the bottle in her hand. Pasi evaluated the situation. He'd been in this situation once before, at a kitchen table in a dorm room where lightbulbs and small crystals looking like sea salt were laid out in front of him, while young fools who pretended to be shamans surrounded him. That evening had ended up being quite nice.

"In that case I must try it," he said, "but ladies first."

Pasi was no idiot—he was just a hedonistic realist.

The woman brought the bottle to her lips and knocked her head back.

She gagged.

"Looks like it doesn't taste all that great," Pasi said.

"No," she said. "But soon I'll *feel* great. The stars grow so bright that everything else loses its meaning. Now close your eyes and open wide."

The liquid ran down her chin in gray streams. The right corner of her mouth was darker than the left. Pasi squinted his drunken eyes and thought about calling Maisa. He should tell her to get here right away. Or no, don't come, for Chrissake, call the police. That would be so like her. She'd panic and think that the stupidest possible thing to do was to drink anything this crazy naked woman offered him.

He took another moment to assess the situation, but just for a few more seconds. The memory of her skin was still on his palms and fingertips. Her stretchy, wrinkly skin. Like an old person's skin. Nonsense. Stop worrying. Pasi closed his eyes and opened his mouth.

He felt the cold bottle on his lower lip, and a couple of beats later, liquid began to flow onto his tongue. It tasted peculiar. It wasn't wine nor straight-up alcohol. It wasn't beer, either. He swallowed obediently although it tasted sickeningly bad.

Pasi opened his eyes.

He heard the woman whisper. Not to him—away from him.

"Close your eyes," she commanded and removed the bottle from his lips.

He didn't recognize the flavor. He didn't know this woman. He looked around. There was no one else here. Who was she whispering to?

And more importantly: who the fuck cared?

"Let it flow," Pasi said and closed his eyes again.

The memory of the cold bottle against his lower lip lingered, but no liquid flowed into his mouth. He assumed the woman took her time to drink her share.

"Hey, leave some for me," he said.

The woman lifted her weight off his thighs. Pasi tried to open his eyes, but a clammy hand was pressed over his eyelids.

"What are you doing?"

"Keep your mouth open."

The voice was no longer pleasantly scratchy. It was still scratchy, though.

Pasi thought about it. "All right."

He opened his mouth.

A swish. A clink.

Completely harmless, delightful sounds among the wind and the waves. He really should've called Maisa earlier.

I love you.

The cold penetrating his throat felt like liquid at first. She must've been pouring more for him.

Then Pasi tried to swallow. His throat muscles constricted.

Pain.

This probably would've registered as much more significant if he hadn't been so drunk. Now the sensation was just an unpleasant object in his throat. Excruciating pain, but nothing he couldn't get rid of.

Pasi opened his eyes. Coughed. Then gagged. There was actually something in his throat. Not a problem. He gagged again. The pain became unbearable.

He looked around.

The woman was gone.

He tried to speak, but his throat had stopped cooperating. His entire pharynx had stopped cooperating. The darkness hummed in all the colors of the world.

The pain began to wash over his wall of numbness. There was no negotiating with it any longer. Instinctually Pasi shoved his fingers into his mouth, as if to fish out a strand of hair he'd accidentally swallowed. His fingers located a slippery string that led down to the back of his tongue and then deeper, much too deep to do anything. His hand tried to grab at the strange, taut shape that led a shivering sliver of light out of his mouth into the darkness beyond the porch, where the waves whispered under the moonlit clouds.

Pasi tried to speak again, but by now his tongue had been rendered useless from the swelling. It was still his tongue, although it felt like an unfamiliar, sick slug in his mouth.

He gagged again.

What a mistake.

The hooks dug deeper into the soft tissues of his pharynx. He felt liquid flowing slowly down into his stomach and only remotely realized that it had to be his blood.

"Now nobody can help you."

The woman spoke right into his ear.

He heard another swish.

The string escaped Pasi's fingers and was pulled taut like a bow. It shivered in his field of vision, like a spiderweb. He now recognized it as fishing line. Heavy-duty fishing line. The kind used for a big catch.

His pain crossed an unknown limit.

First it electrified him, then turned into fog. Pasi followed the thin line with his eyes, slowly realizing he had to follow its every movement. He stumbled off the porch, walked down the steps on all fours, and crawled across the lawn. He could see the woman's bare feet in the corner of his eyes; he could hear her laugh. Her feet had walked this path before. Then something swung next to her legs. The rusty blade of a tool. The woman said something, but Pasi was no longer listening. A male voice responded to her from the darkness.

Pasi was no longer interested in their words. He howled and crawled like an animal.

As the waves hit his knuckles, he understood. He was a small pike, pulled toward his death by a fisherman. He wasn't being pulled out of the water, but from the air into the water, with the same hollow inevitability. What a pitiful little drama.

Then his consciousness exploded.

These colors.

These shapes.

Russkies are no more.

The things you could see within the sea foam of the waves. Entire worlds as the bubbles were born and burst and everything in between.

Pasi turned his head to look up toward the moon and began to scream. Not because of the pain, but because of an unknown feeling he felt pounding beyond the pain. The pain had died and been reborn as music that welled and welled and welled, and even flowers awoke in bloom to this music. Pasi kept on screaming at the old mute moon he had never really seen before. He screamed at its pale beauty and dark-blue craters, as if in a dream he could not wake up from, because it was the first and deepest dream of all times that had dreamt everything else in this world.

He felt a whack between his shoulder blades, but it felt inconsequential, like a disturbance on a distant planet. The woman turned him on his back and brought her face too close to his. Her tongue stuck out and the eyes shivered with some raw emotion Pasi had never seen before. The corner of her mouth did indeed stretch out too far into the cheek, but who cared about a careless dentist now that he was flying into the stratosphere.

As the seawater pulled one of his rubber boots off and flooded in through the sleeves of his jacket, Pasi felt for his face and its numb cavities and realized he was a moon.

"I should make a phone call," Pasi tried to say, but his throat and its muscles were already like moss, their petrification almost complete.

Water rushed into his ears and the world turned silent.

One phone call.

The hatchet hurtled down and sank into the mute dust of the moon.

VIDEO TAPE

VIDEO TAPE

Samuel and Julia agreed to meet every day at ten in the small park between the single-family houses and the townhomes. They hadn't verbally agreed to not ring each other's doorbells, but he was still shocked to see her at his door.

He heard the doorbell through the noise from his Walkman but didn't move. Who else could it be? Aki's bratty friends coming over to make a mess and ask stupid questions about Samuel's records and books and then brag about finding a broken cigarette on the street or that they'd seen this or that neighbor drunk somewhere? Harri had come by the previous night to drop off a cassette tape through the mail slot in the door: he had copied a demo he'd gotten from his older brother in Germany. He'd written a note in all caps, *SABBATH: FRAGMENTS OF A FAITH FORGOTTEN. LISTEN TO IT!* Samuel had listened to the demo all morning, deep in thought, but he hadn't bothered to look up the word "fragment" in the English-Finnish dictionary to find out what it meant.

Then suddenly his dad was at the door, looking slightly embarrassed. Samuel removed his headphones.

"There's a girl," he said.

"Oh, yeah?"

"Looks like she got her ass beat. She's crying."

"I'll take care of it," Samuel said, jumping out of bed.

I'll take care of it? What did that even mean? That everything was all right, and his dad should take a hike before he came up with a sarcastic comment? Samuel wasn't truly worried until he reached the front door.

"Hey," Julia said.

She had a scar on her cheek. Sure, it was a small, maybe a centimeter long, line of coagulated blood, but the skin around it was maroon red and puffy like a balloon.

"Does she need any help?" his dad called behind him.

Julia shook her head.

"No, we're fine," Samuel said without turning away from her. Why, why did his dad have to open the door wearing houndstooth-patterned underwear, now of all times? He quickly pushed his embarrassment to the back of his mind. He couldn't take his eyes off the wound.

"I can take her to the doctor," his dad called again. "Or if you'll tell me who did that to her, I can walk over and—"

"We really don't need any help," Samuel repeated, then walked into the stairwell and closed the door behind him.

"He's completely mental," Julia said. "I can't go home."

She really had been crying.

"I've got my bags downstairs. I packed whatever I managed to grab."

A faint pink scratch trailed from the wound to the corner of her eye. Julia had probably wiped her cheek with the back of her hand before it began to scar.

"Where are you thinking of going?" Samuel asked.

She shrugged, then looked at him with puppy-dog eyes. He got it.

"I'll think of something," he said and hugged her. The gesture was stiff at best, as he couldn't shake off the image of his dad standing behind the door in his patterned underwear.

"Wait here," he said.

He went back in and got dressed quickly.

"It wasn't that Jape and his gang who did that to her, was it?" his dad asked from the living room. Even Aki had appeared to gape at the scene.

"It's none of your business," Samuel said and grabbed the keys hanging off the hook in the hallway.

"It is my business. Just tell me a name. And the girl can stay with us if she needs to."

Samuel didn't reply. He ran out and slammed the door behind him. Julia and his dad eating breakfast together? No way. He would die of embarrassment. She would run away after the first morning. But where else could she go and hide?

He carried Julia's bag out from under the stairwell on the bottom floor and weighed his options. There weren't many.

"He'll come looking for me," Julia said when he walked back to her. "He's gone nuts and he has a gun."

Samuel remembered Julia's dad's quick, languid movements and his clipped, nervous way of speaking. He didn't have a hard time imagining the hands he'd seen flipping burgers strangling someone's neck or pulling a trigger.

Then he had an idea.

"Follow me."

When Samuel and Aki were younger, they wanted to spend a night inside their little storage unit up in the building's attic. It was a little hut made out of a wooden frame and chicken wire, and back then it had been the most exciting place ever to them. All the other buildings had storage units in the basement, which made them scary and oppressive. Attics, however, always felt like places ripe for adventures. Samuel and Aki had built a little nest for themselves between an old drawer and a box full of Christmas ornaments, and they carried stacks of comics and piles of toy soldiers to their new home. Their mom was still alive and had been against it, so she did her best to scare the kids with stories about mice and rats and ginormous daddy longlegs that would creep into their mouths when they slept. Samuel and Aki had cried themselves to sleep from sheer disappointment.

He showed Julia the way to the attic.

When the door closed behind them, the hum of the wind made Samuel stop.

"Wait, you can't stay here," he then said. He thought about his dad's suggestion. It was an idiotic option, but what else could they do? His dad would fart at breakfast and talk about the magnificent tractors built in the Soviet Union.

"Yes, I can," Julia said.

She walked along the corridor lined with chicken wire and let her fingers trail across the wire.

"This place is amazing."

Her exhausted voice had a glimmer of familiar fearlessness, the kind that sounded much too large to fit into a small person like her.

"Really?" Samuel asked.

"I've never been anywhere like this."

When she turned back and smiled, her swollen cheek partially covered her eye.

"You look like an Eskimo," Samuel said.

"Why do you say that?"

"Half-Eskimo, half-Californian."

Julia attacked him, tickling his armpits.

That was the old, familiar Julia. Not the one who had been beaten up to form a half-Eskimo.

They rolled on the floor for a while, then slowed down to kiss each other, then rushed to tear each other's clothes off. Samuel managed to control himself long enough to open their storage unit and pull out his mom's old curtains to use as drapes over the doorway for privacy. Neither of them cared enough to worry about condoms. Some things just happened within larger waves. The time for worrying came once the wave had pulled away, and they were left panting helplessly on the shore.

"Everything's even more fucked now," Julia said.

"You're right."

They looked at the ceiling and squeezed each other's hands.

"Can I stay here?" she asked.

"Of course. Let's both stay here."

They took some time to rearrange boxes and shelves so that it would be impossible to tell by glancing from the doorway that someone was living up in the attic. The boxes formed a comfortable, small cave in the back, where they could easily forget about the world outside. An old mattress fit on the floor of the cave, and Samuel used a laundry bag filled with his and Aki's old baby clothes as a pillow. A perfect nest for two. They would have to leave only to shower or pee in the public washrooms in the basement, but that was not a big deal.

"I have just one wish," Julia said when they sat down to rest.

She pulled something out of her bag. It was a small videotape.

"My final message to that asshole."

Samuel took the tape.

"Drop it in the mailbox. Early in the morning would be best. He won't wake up until eleven."

"What's on it?"

"Revenge," Julia whispered and smiled so hard her right eye was almost completely shut.

Of course Samuel would perform this favor, although the mere thought of walking up to Julia's dad's house was absolutely horrifying. But he'd do anything to protect their cave, their home.

"Some man has called you three times," his dad said when Samuel got back from the store. It had been Aki's turn to go, but he'd pretended to have the flu, in the middle of summer of all times.

Samuel dropped the shopping bag on the floor and kicked his shoes off.

"Who?" he asked, fearing the worst.

"He didn't say, but he said he was your friend's—"

The phone rang.

"Sheesh, must be something really important," his dad said and went to the living room.

Samuel stared at the phone and didn't move.

"Pick it up already!" his dad yelled and turned the radio up. In the other room Aki was overcome by a flurry of fake coughs.

He picked up the receiver and stated his name.

"I saw that tape," a man said. "Your dick's in it."

The radio was so loud in the background, Samuel wasn't sure if he'd heard him right.

"I don't know about any videotape," he said.

"Don't lie to me, you little runt. I'm watching it right now. It shows you messing around with a condom wrapper like a fucking *retard*. It's shot in some slum, which I assume is your home, and my . . ."

A wavering sigh.

"My little girl's in it."

Julia's dad's words were like glowing embers in Samuel's mind, burning each time he touched them.

"And you look so fucking ridiculous, so ridiculous in fact that I would've laughed myself sick if Julia hadn't been on that tape. And you know what? I'm going to share my enjoyment with as many people as I can think of. I have the best business plan ever. Now listen carefully."

Samuel heard rattling. Mike was probably shoving the receiver closer to his mouth.

"I've got editing equipment, the works. I'll turn this into a hit movie, and it'll be so popular you won't even believe it. I'll make ten copies. You understand me? Ten."

He stared at his reflection in the mirror. A fragile creature looked back at him. A defenseless creature waiting to be crushed completely.

"Nine of them will go to porn producers all over the world. Yeah, I know people like that, too. I'll make you a star, I guarantee it. The tenth copy will be delivered to a very special address. Can you guess where?"

Samuel didn't speak.

"One day, when you're least expecting it, I'll be at your parents' door and hand it over personally."

My mom's dead, Samuel wanted to correct him. *My mom's dead.*

"I won't drop it off through the mail slot, so don't think about waiting at the door. I'll hand it to them personally. Got it? I'll tell them that it's a fucking special delivery, and that the tape contains something about their son they should know. And I'll tell them that the girl on that tape, forced to perform all sorts of things, is my . . ."

His voice broke at the last word.

"Is my little girl. Get it, *loverman?*"

"Don't do it," Samuel whispered hoarsely. "Please."

"Oh, you're begging now? Where's your spine, son? I'll tell you what will happen now. You'll bring Julia to me within the next hour. If you'll do it I might . . . I just might not do what I told you."

Mike hung up.

Samuel begged the phone once more, "Please don't do it."

He set the receiver down slowly. His ears were ringing. Now the reflection looking back at him was a jumbled expression of vulnerable skin, startled eyes, and stupid clothes. His dad asked who called, but Samuel didn't hear him. He slipped into his shoes and walked out to the stairwell. As he raced up the stairs, a stupid tune invaded his mind.

Maisa, Maisa, will you let Samuel fuck ya . . .

The world was a sinister machine, and its only purpose was to crush one Samuel Autio. It would all be over in a second, because the world would do it at full force. Yet the world would barely feel a thing. It would chew Samuel up in its cogs and then go on existing like it always had. His shame would be instantly revealed to anyone he passed by. His dad and Aki. His grandma. Even his mother would see it, although she was dead. He'd be forced to stand naked in front of people, like in his worst nightmares. And they'd laugh, and he'd know nothing would ever make them forget. Game over.

And it was all because of Julia. Out of all the people in the world, it had been Julia.

Samuel opened the attic door and marched to the storage unit. Julia's flashlight shone faintly through the drapes. He'd been stupid to think of it as their nest. It was just a cage made out of unfinished wood and metal wire. If the Big Bad Wolf marched over and huffed and puffed, it would collapse instantly.

"Samuel?" Julia said. "Is that you?"

He'd told her to turn the flashlight off if she heard the door open. He stressed how important it was to never say anything. He opened the little door and walked in. Julia's smile died on her face.

"What's wrong?" she asked.

Samuel told her.

He spoke like an automaton sent to play back Julia's dad's words from the recording inside his brain. He remembered each detail and turn of phrase.

"Why did you do it?"

Julia didn't speak. Her chin began to twitch.

"Why did you film it?"

"I film everything."

"But why?"

"Because of Dad," she said. "He told me to. After Mom died he's made me film all the people I ever hang out with."

"Has he watched everything we've filmed?"

"No. Not everything. Or . . ."

Julia lowered her eyes.

"Now he has."

They both stared at a spot on the storage floor, a tiny dent in the concrete, like a tiny cave burrowed by a small animal. *A rat,* Samuel thought. Maybe there were rats in the attic, although his dad said Mom had just tried to scare them.

"I'm sorry," Julia said. "I hated him so much that I . . . I wasn't thinking straight."

Samuel shook his head slowly.

"What do we do now?" she asked. "I can't go home."

That was a good question. A scary question. Where would they find a place where the crushing machine that the world had become would not find them? Where all the bullies with their songs and evil eyes and Julia's dad's gun wouldn't reach them? A place where shame and fear would slowly die with the years, and the wound would stop bleeding like the cut on Julia's cheek. Samuel still stared at the dent in the floor until he lost a sense of perspective. The dent became a sinkhole in the desert. Or maybe on the moon. The moon's left eye.

What a scary question.

"We have no other choice," Samuel mumbled.

There was one place.

In one pocket Maisa carried a box, its cover depicting a ship struggling in a raging storm. In the other she carried a newspaper clipping.

She strode past the beech whose branches looked like petrified tentacles. She brushed hastily through the reeds, much more clumsily than that first time so long ago, although her dog had been pulling her forward. The leaves had been green then, and their sharp edges cut her skin. But now, in the glow of the flashlight, she saw only faded yellows waving on both sides of the path, like rustling papyrus paper.

The shore was unchanged except for the rocks. Each of them was now clearly visible above the sea level. The ground around the Bondorff villa was slowly rising, and eventually the island would connect with the mainland. It was an unpleasant thought.

Maisa shone her light on the three rocks nearest to her and estimated how slippery they'd be. As a teenager she'd had to get her shoes wet. It was here where she had let go of Nippu's leash. The dog had rushed into the sea straight away, swimming furiously toward the shore with loud splashes.

"Stay," Maisa said quietly. She reached out with her right hand as if to touch an animal right next to her. At first she thought her fingertips touched something, like the smooth hair of a dog. She pulled her hand away and turned to see what it was.

But Nippu wasn't there. Nobody knew where Nippu had gone, but by now she would've died of old age, even if she had run away and found someone else to take care of her.

Madame Blavatsky was here.

Maisa reached out her hand, trying to steady the shaking. She was no longer a child. She was an adult, and she was in control of things that back then had felt like earthquakes. The waves licking at the toes of her shoes looked tiny and pathetic. They had no power over her. The adult Maisa had seen it all. In the Mediterranean she had let huge waves slam her onto the beach so hard that she'd lost the top of her bikini. She had swum in waters so clear that she thought she was flying high above the ground, able to see all the way down to the bottom of the ocean. It had made her feel like an inconsequential speck in the rushing rapids. These puny waves were nothing.

The waves that slowly soaked her shoes didn't care. They were like northern animals who kept on surviving, sure about their importance in the world because they didn't know any better.

Maisa jumped from rock to rock until she reached Bondorff Island's shore.

The villa hadn't changed. The paint was slightly stripped on the side where the bay winds hit it the hardest. She didn't see anyone around. She only heard a sudden rustling, which made her turn and shine her flashlight toward the sound. She saw a flash of shiny, wet fur. A dog. Once her hand steadied she realized the knee-high brush rustled in the wind like an animal's footsteps.

Maisa pulled her cell phone out and tried to call Pasi once more. No answer. She put the phone away and turned off the flashlight. Darkness closed in around her. The lack of light made her more conscious of the freezing-cold wind, as if it had suddenly turned into a tangible substance. She smelled the muddy waves lapping in from the north, as they roared toward her face. The darkness was subsiding quickly, and Maisa saw the horizon behind the trees already turning from black to light gray. The sun would eventually rise. The Bondorff villa wouldn't be able to hide anything from the piercing fall-morning light.

But it had been light when she was here the last time. It had been a sunny summer day, and what consolation had that light offered then? The sun could be taken away at any time. Just pull a bag over your head.

Maisa turned the flashlight on again to get a better look at the yard before walking determinedly toward the house. No one had mowed the lawn. The tall grass hissed against her legs, but despite it all this was still just an ordinary old house, with an ordinary yard, and an ordinary wind howling in the woods. Her footsteps became lighter as she felt her body become more fragile. She felt like a stubborn animal that had to be properly hidden away from curious eyes. Maisa forced herself back into adult mode to face the imposing villa with defiance.

The villa's windows reflected the fall night sky and the waves of the sea. Maisa held on to the railing and took the first step. The planks creaked under her shoe. She stopped.

"Pasi?" she said, first with a whisper, then louder.

Nothing. The door wasn't thrown open. Nobody grabbed her hands.

And why would anyone grab her? Couldn't an adult, a researcher who had enough money and was in good health and quite charming for her age, just walk into an abandoned building out of sheer curiosity without someone attacking her?

She opened the door. She wasn't surprised to find it unlocked. She stepped into the familiar smells of the house. Familiar, yet without its former edge, like the reeds outside.

Maisa shone the light on the walls and the hallways, still calling Pasi's name.

Silence. Then a response in the dark.

She tilted her head, trying to figure out where it came from.

"Pasi, where are you?"

She heard the voice again. Not deeper within the house, not from upstairs. From below. Maisa turned the flashlight toward the stairs.

The cellar. Of course. Pasi would've headed down there straight away because Maisa had told him about it. He wanted to prove he was a fearless pioneer who'd storm a place like this and wave his hand dismissively at his or other people's traumas.

The way to the cellar was clear in the light. *Welcome*, Maisa thought. Whatever she'd find down there wouldn't be able to destroy her. She talked herself into moving forward—there were no other options. Decades had smoothed and rounded the stone steps, so she had to be careful her shoes wouldn't slip. That was the only thing to worry about.

"I'm coming down," Maisa said.

She descended easily. No slipping, no fear. The cellar door was locked.

That's when she lost her cool. The disgusting wave that reeked of mud was rearing its head again, slowly oozing into the house toward her from behind the closed door.

Maisa yanked at the door twice.

"It's locked," she said, then realized she sounded like she was about to cry. Pasi didn't need to hear that.

"Let me out."

The words came from right behind the door. It wasn't Pasi's voice.

"What did you say?" Maisa asked, just to hear the voice again.

"Let. Me. Out."

A girl. Sagal. Maisa pulled her fingers off the door handle. She swore her fingertips were on fire. They tingled and ached as if blood were trying to force her fingernails to grow through the skin.

"Let me—"

Maisa noticed a large plank blocking the door. The most primitive lock in the world, the easiest in the world to open.

But did she have the guts to face Sagal? After all the worry and guilt, Maisa wasn't so sure anymore. How would it feel to comfort a girl who had been captive in the darkness, surrounded by muttering voices, where she scratched at the door and slowly turned into a tortured animal? Maisa wasn't sure she could do it.

"Let me out," Sagal whispered.

How could she control her voice that well? Maisa squeezed the flashlight so hard, the beam of light shivered and made the small space seem even more claustrophobic. Did Sagal even deserve to be let out if she hadn't lost her voice from profound fear? If someone else survived the cellar's darkness without mentally collapsing, it would make Maisa a special case, a weak human being.

"Everything's all right," she said.

Her voice sounded unfamiliar to her ears. It belonged to the adult Maisa, the one who thought that this sort of nonsense and panic had become unbearably boring a long time ago.

The plank screeched as she lifted it up. She tossed it onto the stone floor with a loud clang. Yet the door remained closed. No human wreckage rushed out into Maisa's arms, smelling of piss and fear.

She opened the door.

Her light beam found Sagal huddled on the floor. Her eyes were round. Her scarf was covered in black stains.

The marks of an invisible hand, Maisa thought. A hand that felt you all over to estimate whether you fit the part or not, like testing out a slave or cattle.

She had no idea what her next move should be. Everything was wrong. Pasi wasn't here. Instead Sagal was there, not even moving, screaming, or tearfully thanking Maisa for overcoming her greatest fear and opening the cellar door.

"How long have you been—"

Sagal interrupted Maisa by sharply lifting a finger to her lips. The finger trembled. Her shoulders heaved silently.

Maisa listened.

Footsteps. High above them on the second floor. Then they descended the stairs to the main floor. It had to be Pasi.

Maisa started to say, "Oh, that's just my friend who—"

Sagal shook her head furiously. She pressed her finger tighter against her lips.

The footsteps were approaching. They were coming right toward Sagal and Maisa.

Sagal slowly let her hand fall. She reached out to Maisa, gesturing for her to come inside the cellar.

"No," Maisa whispered. "Let's go—"

The footsteps had almost reached them.

Sagal's hand now motioned faster, demanding. The fear in her eyes was on the edge of rage. Maisa couldn't say no to it.

She stepped through the doorway and pulled the door closed silently behind her, although her fingers had gone numb and warmth began to spread down her thighs, as if she'd already peed herself. Sagal grabbed her hand, which still held on to the flashlight. Maisa looked at Sagal's panicked gesturing and realized the light had to be turned off. Maisa did as she was told.

Now they were in complete darkness. The old familiar darkness. The kind of darkness where she could hear and feel anything.

The footsteps had reached the stairwell leading down to the cellar. They came to a halt.

Maisa heard a mumbling voice. A man's voice.

She concentrated on the voice because everything else was unbearable to think about.

Whatever horrible things the man had done to Sagal, it couldn't have been worse than this darkness.

It sounded like the man was talking to himself. There were no replies or pauses.

Then a thought came to Maisa, and it made her fears subside temporarily. The voice didn't belong to Pasi, but it was familiar. She leaned toward the door, cocked her head, and listened.

The voice stopped talking. Had the man noticed that the plank blocking the door was gone? The thought should've terrified her, but instead she remained still and breathed calmly. This man was no unknown force of nature who had been sent to crush them and tear them apart. Maisa would recognize his face. She could talk to him. Maisa almost *wanted* to talk. She wanted to hear the voice again.

She was just about to open the door when she heard the footsteps again. They were walking away. They returned to the first floor, then clumsily disappeared into the rooms on the second floor.

Maisa tried to hold on to the man's voice, repeating it like a secret code, but the memory was already disappearing into the surrounding darkness. She realized her breathing was still stable. Her fingertips had regained sensation. The darkness no longer swallowed her. It just was.

She'd forgotten about Sagal until she heard a sob somewhere behind her. The girl had disappeared deeper into the cellar. Maisa was the braver of the two, after all, the one who had seen this before. It was her duty to calm the girl down and comfort her.

"Hey," Maisa said and crawled toward the voice. "Everything will be fine."

She felt around in the darkness until her fingers found fabric. The sobbing was jerky, panicked. The girl would hyperventilate if Maisa couldn't calm her down. She hugged Sagal and reached into a stock of comforting words that she blurted out in a confusing litany while she stroked the girl's head.

"We're getting out of here right now," she promised. "There's nothing to worry about anymore."

Sagal's body heaved in her arms. For the first time in her life, she felt motherly love and wanted to protect this fragile girl at all cost. She pressed her face into Sagal's hair, although it reeked of the damp cellar.

Maisa decided she'd get pregnant as soon as she could. It was a ridiculous thought to have in a dark cellar, but that's what occurred to her. Fear had completely left her, no longer in her neck or veins or marrow. She was ready to live again.

"I'm here," Sagal said.

"That's right," Maisa replied, hugging her harder. "I found you."

"I'm over here."

Momentary confusion.

Maisa must've heard wrong. The cellar walls echoed oddly, so who knows where the voice came from. She stroked the matted hair in her lap.

That's what was wrong.

There was no scarf. Just dry, matted hair that was sticking to Maisa's fingers.

"I'm over here," Sagal repeated.

The girl's voice trembled in fear.

It came from the door. Behind Maisa. What sort of trickery was this?

Maisa felt with her hands and touched a piece of fabric riddled with holes. A heaving body. The sobbing against her shoulder. She slowly loosened her grip. The head was still resting on her shoulder.

"Then who is—?" she asked the darkness.

Sobbing.

Movement.

Whoever it was, it was in tears. Who cares if it had once been a hysterical teenage girl. But something was wrong. The tears were held back, as if someone were trying hard not to cry.

Or laugh.

The darkness shuffled. Changed.

The muddy wave was gathering in force.

"Over here," Sagal whispered, far away.

Then someone laughing. Laughing so hard that spittle fell on Maisa's hand. It was slightly warm.

Maisa struggled to get free, stumbled away, and turned the flashlight back on.

Sagal screamed. It filled the entire cellar, and for a moment it sounded like the walls and rocks themselves were howling. Maisa peed herself but was unable to make a sound. She just stared at the shaking beam of light that revealed a grimacing face in the corner. She gasped for breath, because darkness had turned into water and was slowly blocking her airways, disregarding the protective glow of the light.

The figure stood up. Metal scraped against rock.

When Maisa regained her voice she shrieked.

"Run!"

Seeing Sagal listen to her was barely a comfort. Maisa herself stood paralyzed like prey, the cocksure idiot who had returned to the place where children were killed.

Maybe she had never grown up.

They arrived on Bondorff Island out of breath and scared, carrying a single bag for Julia. Samuel promised he'd go back for his stuff later, including the money he'd saved up in a tin box. The wind was tossing the trees on the island, but the villa and the yard were just as immobile as before.

Julia fell down on the grass first. Samuel gave up and did the same.

"We can't stay here," she said, sitting on the grass. "This is no place for people to live."

"But that woman lives here," he said, looking at the house. The front door was ajar.

"She told me we could always come back," he continued. "To live here."

Julia followed his gaze.

"Shit," she said and buried her face in her hands. "Why was I ever born?"

Samuel had felt the same way ever since Julia's dad had called him. Why was he born? Why did he exist? Why did he have to stand at the edge of a deep oblong hole, watching his mother's coffin descend into the ground and seeing one of the pallbearers accidentally toss the strap into the grave? And after all that, why was he granted a promise of great happiness in the form of Julia just to lose it? How could anyone live to be thirty or older if shit like this was all you got?

The evening was turning into night. Yet they just sat there.

"Oh, no," Julia whispered and pointed.

Samuel looked toward the rocks they had just used to cross the bay. A human figure wobbled on the opposite shore. It stumbled back and forth, seemingly drunk, and punched at the reeds in its way. Its incomprehensible mewling carried across the bay, but they couldn't distinguish any words. Until one word rang clear.

"Julia."

The voice broke, either from panic or rage, or both.

"Dad," Julia whispered.

They looked at each other with wide eyes.

"Come on," Samuel said and pulled her up by her hand. They crouched and ran toward the villa, then up the stairs, all the way into the stench of the still air inside. He glanced around, the whites of his eyes shining in the darkness, but didn't see anyone or hear anything. He almost wished the woman would appear. Anything would have been better than what waited for them outside.

"He saw us," Julia said, peeking out the window in the door.

Samuel walked up to her. The window was broken, warped, and dirty, but he could easily see Julia's dad approaching. He stepped clumsily from one rock to another, then jumped into the water and waded the rest of the way in mud, looking like his legs were tied down with iron shackles.

"Julia . . ."

It was the voice of a madman. They could tell no amount of reasoning would get through to him. Now the man was climbing up the shore, almost on all fours. Then he straightened himself.

"Oh, no," Julia said again. "He has a gun."

Samuel saw it now, too. He'd never seen anyone brandish a pistol, except on TV or at the starting line of a race. Julia's dad stood in the middle of the yard, looking toward the door. A stumble, a step to steady himself, more mewling.

"What do we do now?" Julia whispered.

Her dad began to walk toward the door.

"Into the cellar, now," Samuel said and pulled her with him. They staggered down the stairs.

"He'll find us here," Julia protested.

"No, he won't," he said, lifting the wooden plank away from the door. "Tunnels. Remember what Helge told us? The island is full of tunnels."

Julia didn't seem impressed.

"It stinks," she said, as if that mattered.

They heard footsteps thumping on the steps outside.

"Let's go already," Samuel hissed and pulled Julia into the cellar, closing the door behind them.

They crouched in the darkness right next to each other.

The front door opened.

"Julia?"

There was a moment of silence. Then the steps proceeded farther into the house.

"We could run—"

Samuel covered Julia's mouth with his hand.

The footsteps boomed back and forth until it was hard to say where they were coming from. Samuel stared at the slit of light above the cellar door, waiting for Mike's shadow to cover it. When the conversation began, he thought he was hallucinating.

First Julia's dad said something. Then a woman.

"Are you hearing this?" Samuel whispered.

Julia nodded.

Mike's voice grew louder. They couldn't tell individual words apart, but the tone was crystal clear: he was swearing up a storm—"fucking retard," probably. Samuel's memory filled in the gaps.

The woman responded with her monotonous, unexcited mumbling. The same way she had recited the Koskenniemi poem.

A gunshot silenced her.

The sound startled them both. They leaned into each other even more. Then it was quiet again. No footsteps, no talking. The darkness enveloped them in cold black ice.

Then that sound.

It at first reminded Samuel of a cat in heat, but as it grew louder it turned into an unrecognizable howling. It made his skin crawl. He thought that if the ball lightning that had crashed into Helge's cabin had been blessed with the ability to speak, it would've sounded exactly like this.

Chaotic footsteps followed, then stumbling, then clanking. Another voice rang out. Julia's dad was screaming. Cursing. Footsteps boomed now closer to them. The front door flew open and then wind blew in. Footsteps stomped on the stairs outside and then softly on the lawn.

"He's gone," Julia whispered.

They stayed hunched over for a while, until Samuel stood up and told her to stay there. He cracked the cellar door open. Nobody there. He didn't hear a peep. He saw the front door swinging slowly back and forth.

"Wait here," he whispered into the darkness behind him.

Samuel walked up the stairs. He stopped whenever his shoes made even the slightest creaking noise. At the top of the stairs he turned to look outside.

Julia's dad was up to his thighs in seawater, wading back to the opposite shore. He was holding his right hand. Samuel didn't see whether he still had his gun.

Suddenly he detected a thick smoky smell emanating from the house. He followed it deeper into the rooms. The floorboards creaked.

He came to a room full of dusty, old furniture. The walls were covered in paintings in which grave-looking men and women posed in fancy clothes. The wallpaper had peeled off and rolled down where the walls met the ceiling, revealing dark wood beneath.

There was blood on the floor. Bloody handprints. And a hatchet.

Samuel jumped and turned around. He went to check the front door to make sure that Mike wasn't coming back. He saw a bloodstain in the doorway.

He went back down to the cellar and opened the door.

"He's gone," he said.

Julia turned the flashlight on and crouched in the harsh light that illuminated her swollen face.

"He's too scared to come here," Samuel said. "We're safe."

"How do you know?" she asked. "What happened up there?"

"I'm telling you, we're safe. I'll go get some food and my stuff from home. You wait here."

"The fuck I will!" Julia yelled.

"Your dad won't be coming back."

"But that woman is here."

"She won't hurt you. She saved you."

She shook her head. "Take me to Helge's cabin," she said. "This is much worse than any—"

"Your dad will find you there."

"I don't care, but I know I can't stay here."

"All you need to do is—"

Julia began to scream.

Samuel did what he had to do.

"You can't leave me here!" she yelled.

He pushed Julia back into the cellar and shut the door. He dropped the wooden latch back into its groove.

"I'll be back in fifteen minutes," he said, his lips touching the rough surface of the door.

He could still hear her screaming when he took off running. The scream became shrieking howls, but in his heart Samuel knew Julia would eventually forgive him. Everything would be fine when he got back.

Samuel sprinted until he was past the rocks and the path. He slowed down when the thought of Julia's dad waiting in ambush popped into his head. He also realized how suspicious his running looked. He thought all kinds of things, yet he kept running.

The gravel near the garages crunched under his shoes. That July night smelled of grass and asphalt that was slowly cooling down. Samuel registered headlights in the corner of his eye as he crossed the street, but he didn't react. For whatever reason people liked speeding and circling the buildings in their cars at night. Samuel had never cared for cars or understood why he'd need to. This was especially true now, when they had nothing to do with Julia or his plans. Cars belonged to the people he intended to leave behind.

First the world swayed, then it rolled over. Samuel tried to grab ahold of the slick windshield with his palm, but the impact was too sudden and immediate. He had never experienced anything like it, not even when he'd ridden a bike down a hill and crashed, or when he had jumped off the tallest of the diving boards at the swimming pool. He rolled onto the car roof and tumbled down.

As he lay in the street, Samuel expected to feel pain. He wished it would be so intense that the darkness he saw approaching the edge of his vision would be kept at bay. He knew right away that this darkness was like the thunder. It would suffocate him underneath it and cast its shadow on everything, and then something irreversible would happen and nothing that came before would mean anything ever again. His pain would be an anchor, and he'd hold on to its rope until the storm had passed.

Instead he only felt numb. He heard the bass thumping from the car stereo when the doors opened. It was Popeda and their song "Long, Hot Summer." How fitting.

When the first people to arrive at the scene leaned over Samuel, blocking the sky from his view and asking stupid questions, he wanted to tell them to step aside. He wanted to see the moon and its moronic smile, its left eye. He needed to remember why he was lying there.

Julia is still there, Samuel screamed in his head. *I can't leave Julia—*

His scream took over his world, but outside of it his tongue and lips only twitched mutely, as if tiny electric shocks had been routed through them.

There was no pain. Only darkness.

NOBODY TALKS

Sagal ran down the path surrounded by waving reeds and didn't look back once. She didn't know whether it was morning or evening, but the light shed by the sun felt odd, cold, and cruel—as if she were on Mars. She wheezed as if her lungs resisted the air she breathed.

Sagal fell over. Her hands sank into the cold, wet mud.

Her father had been right. This wasn't home. This was a frozen, unfamiliar planet.

She panted and listened.

Nobody was following her. She saw the path curve ahead of her, but the large beech was not yet visible. They'd carried her past it to the island. Sagal had not actually seen it, but she'd grabbed ahold of the tree's crooked branches with both hands before someone had loosened her grip one finger at a time. Someone had bit her on the thumb, huffing and growling like an animal. Sagal had not had enough time to figure out where they were taking her before she'd had to let go. Only later in the darkness, once her panic had subsided, did she remember the shape of the branches in her hands. The Bondorff villa. The missing children.

She tried to clear her head. She'd been able to do it in the cellar, so why couldn't she do it now? She was sure someone was waiting for her at the end of the path. They had more pranks up their sleeves.

Sagal stood up and rushed into the reeds. The leaves cut her hands and cheeks, but she was not going to be predictable. She was not going to run straight into their arms. They had probably planned everything. And now they were just listening for her footsteps. Sagal slowed down, moving in the knee-high water and crackling reeds as quietly as she could.

After wading for a while, she stopped.

She should've felt the shore under her shoes already. The reed panicles waved in the dim light. Sagal looked around and listened. She heard only dry rustling, like candy wrappers rubbing against each other, the calm lapping of the waves, and the screams of the seagulls.

And a voice. A whispering girl's voice.

"Sagal," it said.

She turned her head left and right, trying to locate the source. But what if there was none? In the pitch-black cellar she'd heard so many whispers and murmurs and rustling of clothes and giggling that she couldn't trust her ears anymore. Sagal had even heard the voices of her father and mother and brother while she was down there, but she always knew they'd come when she was about to fall asleep and hallucinated.

Yet this whisper was now clearer.

Sagal wrapped her fingers around the reeds next to her to keep them still, as if it would stop them from rustling.

"Over here," the voice said.

She stared right in front of her, listening, until she realized that the day had gotten lighter. So it was morning after all. Relief washed over her. The light would grow, and nothing could hide in the shadows. She just needed to get to the shore. There she could shout as loud as she could, and someone on their way to work would hear her. The smartest thing would be to not walk toward the whisper, because that's where they waited for her.

Suddenly the wind picked up, and Sagal jumped. She looked at the reeds around her, now waving furiously in the wind, the panicles twirling in little vortices. She thought how Mira and the others were behind this all. They had powers over natural forces on this bizarre planet. It was a ludicrous thought, because she knew only God could command the wind. Sagal waited to hear the whisper again to make sure which way not to go.

The dry, crackling rustle of the reeds grew louder behind her until she heard a tearing, crunching sound. Sagal turned around and held her breath.

Something was moving behind the frantically waving reeds. First Sagal thought it was them—they'd seen where she'd run and simply followed the path of crushed stalks.

But this sound was different. There were no sloshing footsteps. The sound came in waves. She heard the roar of the roiling waters. The tops of the reeds suddenly dropped out of view, as if someone were tugging a large boat through them with forceful jerks.

Sagal faced the sound, frozen in fear. The dawn light had now stripped the reeds of their golden hue, turning them grayish blue.

"Hey!" she yelled. "Who's there?"

She had to speak to the rumbling sound. She had to do something—anything but just stand there, waiting to see who would appear among the endless bed of reeds.

The sound grew louder as the panicles closer to her were slashed down. The water bubbled and swirled. The waves began to hit Sagal up to her thighs.

"Who's there?" she whispered.

Her stomach had become a cold pit, radiating its iciness all through her body, her fingers, her toes.

She finally saw movement in the stalks. A dark figure that Sagal couldn't even describe. There was no boat. No people. For whatever reason she thought of the wind, and how it had transformed into a clumsy beast. Then she thought of the large beech. How someone must've cut it down and was now dragging it through the reeds. That was yet another stupid thought. She had to clear her head.

Then she saw something round. A perfect yellow round shape. Another circle was within it, completely black. She saw this for only a split second, but the image burned in her mind clear and bright like an ember in the darkness, as if a voice much older than Sagal's had spoken to her: "This I'll remember. This is important. This is serious. Forget everything else."

Run.

Sagal screamed, not knowing why. She turned around and began to struggle toward the shore through the reeds. Her legs knew exactly where the sounds were coming from, and it was perfectly fine for them to run toward the commotion. The higher the waves were behind her, the faster she ran.

When she reached the shore she leaped over rocks and fallen tree trunks without looking back. Her vision was blurred by exhaustion, but she could see a human-like figure ahead of her. It didn't matter who it was. Just let it be anything but whatever was behind her.

Her legs caved in. Sagal fell over in mid-run. Her wrist ached, but the pain registered from a distance. She saw legs in front of her.

Mira's legs. Sagal had always envied those shoes.

She tried to spit on them, but only managed to drool on her chin. Her spit slowly reached the ground. She tried to stand up, but her wrist couldn't take her weight. Mira reached over to help her. Sagal slapped her hand away. When she finally stood up and leaned against a tree, she screamed all the possible curse words she knew in Finnish and Somali at Mira.

Mira just stood there, facing the sea and listening to her. Sagal jumped and turned around. The reeds waved wildly. Something had to be walking through them.

"What is it?" Sagal yelled and began to retreat.

"I don't know," Mira replied.

She sounded tired, beaten. Not like the Mira Sagal knew.

"I really don't know."

Mira looked pale. Or perhaps not paler than usual, but the dark blue under her eyes made her skin look ashen. Sagal looked toward the sea again. Seeing Mira's face helped to make sense of the world again. Nothing was approaching them. It was just the wind rustling in the reeds and creating waves.

"I don't know what it is," Mira repeated.

"What is what?" Sagal asked, because she couldn't see anything.

Mira raised her hand. She pointed at Bondorff Island. They saw the roof of the villa behind the waving reeds. Sagal had to turn her gaze away. She walked up to Mira and looked into her eyes, closer than ever before—so close that she could see Mira's tiny blood vessels, that fragile, light-red conjunctiva leading into her light-blue eyes, making them glow in ways that a thousand years before the cellar would have made Sagal squeeze a blanket between her knees at night.

"It was your fault!" she yelled. "Do you have any idea what it was like?"

Don't cry, don't cry, don't—

"My mom and dad must have called the cops, and I'm going to tell them everything!"

Mira's face remained expressionless.

"It's taken care of," she said. "The police aren't looking for you."

"I'm sure they are, and then you'll have to tell them about your little gang and you'll all go to—"

"I told your mom that you were staying with me."

Mira's face was still void of any emotions. It was frozen ash.

"I told them you were pregnant and that we'd take care of it."

Sagal forgot to breathe. Her ears began to ring with a high-pitched whine.

"She understood right away. She called the cops and said they found you, and promised to come up with a story for your dad and brother."

Sagal opened her mouth but didn't know what to say. She realized she hadn't completely shed the darkness of the cellar. It would follow her and lock the doors for her without asking her opinion.

"And because she didn't kill you, you get to go home."

For a second Sagal thought Mira meant her dad.

"Kill me?" she shrieked.

How could Mira be so calm? She was clearly horrified and torn to pieces, yet looked like an emotionless insect or a martyr or a snake in hibernation.

"Who didn't kill me?" Sagal asked hoarsely and more politely than she meant to.

Mira was still in hibernation, immobile. Then she nodded. A minuscule movement toward the Bondorff villa.

"What is she?" Sagal asked.

The memory of the lump in the cellar stirred, just a short glimpse in the beam of the flashlight. Yet it made Sagal's skin crawl, and her shoulders shot up to her ears. She had to press her fists into her chest. She wanted to curl into a ball.

Mira shrugged. "Nobody knows," she said. "She kills children. But she spared you."

The wind pushed the reeds down to the ground, revealing the villa on the island behind them, and Sagal thought about Mira and the countless, faceless others and how they controlled the wind. She saw a dim light in the second-floor window. And shadows, pacing the room. Figures scurrying around like moths stuck inside a lampshade. For the first time since she escaped, Sagal remembered the woman who had saved her.

"There was this one—"

"She had to go there," Mira interrupted her. "I led her there, but that's none of my business."

Sagal repeated these words silently, trying to comprehend the contradiction.

"You say you led her there," she said, "but it's none of your business?"

"That's right," Mira said.

Sagal looked her straight in the eye. Mira looked back in a haze of cigarette smoke and blood vessels that contained hundreds of planets and new worlds beyond them. It was the expression of the terrifying and wondrous core of her secret, slimy cruelty.

"But it is your business," Mira said.

Sagal realized Mira had lifted her hand toward her. She had something between her fingers, obviously meant for her. An envelope. The paper looked bumpy and damp. Mira's long, beautiful fingers trembled. Her entire arm shook—the same arm that had always calmly lifted a cigarette or a joint or a bottle of cider, even when a fistfight broke out around her and blood had stained all their picnic napkins.

"What's that supposed to be?" Sagal asked.

She was shivering. The morning light was no longer warm.

"None of my business," Mira said.

She pointed over Sagal's shoulder.

"The envelope was over there."

Sagal looked and saw the large beech, the Octopus Tree. Exactly where it was supposed to be, not in the reeds.

"It's your business now."

Sagal didn't know what she meant, the tree or the envelope. Maybe both. She didn't want either. She didn't want to touch the envelope. It smelled of the cellar. Its damp surface was disgusting. In some bizarre way it reminded Sagal of old skin, powdery and fragile.

Mira spread her fingers and let the envelope fall on the ground.

Sagal watched as she walked away. She was suddenly overcome with sorrow. She was no longer afraid, just sad.

The envelope rested on the moss. It had been opened. Maybe Mira had read it. It might give Sagal some meaning or provide instructions on how to operate this stupid planet where she had been left alone to survive.

She leaned over and picked up the envelope.

The treetops behind her rustled and waved.

Thunder boomed in the distance.

ANTS DEVOUR THE MOON

Ants were slowly devouring the moon.

This image was crystal clear and remained so, although all other thoughts meandered, died, or repeated a memory like on a broken tape. The memory of the girl's hair in the low rays of the summer sun. Her hand slowly reaching to push strands of hair behind her ear. The memory of sand castles crumbling down and how the woods smelled after a thunderstorm.

The ants swarmed inside the moon's craters. They gnawed at its core. They worked nonstop while the world kept turning.

They worked slowly, because the ants were so tiny you could only see them as a shivering swarm where the surface of the moon was slowly corroding. At first it looked like the ants would take forever, or at least for so long that anyone witnessing it at that moment wouldn't stick around for the outcome.

Then suddenly, one of the moon's eyes was gone. Its mouth was gone. Only thin shreds were left behind, like a shattered wasp's nest.

Restlessness was settling in. First to go were the memories. If the moon disappeared as well, what would remain?

*

Samuel opened his eyes in an unfamiliar room. He tried to push himself into a sitting position, but something resisted. A light yet determined touch pressed on his chest.

"Just rest now," his dad said.

Samuel relaxed and fell back on the bed. Aki sat next to their dad, who wore the same smile he'd seen on his mom's face in her final days.

"Where am I?" he asked.

"At the hospital."

"What happened?"

His dad took his time answering.

"Jape from next door hit you with his car," he finally said. "He was drunk. He had no license, either. As soon as you're feeling better, we'll go and have a little chat with him."

"Are my legs all right?" Samuel asked and lifted his head. "Am I going to be in a wheelchair?"

"No." His dad laughed. "You will need crutches for a while. But most of the time you'll get to take it easy and lie in bed and listen to that shrieking you call music. Aki and I will bring you food."

Samuel calmed down. He looked up at the ceiling and listened to the sounds of the hospital. Beyond them he heard a white hum that he could hear only if he really paid attention to it. It reminded him of television screens and their snowfall of static. He pulled his hand from under the blanket and touched his head. He could feel the gauze, but only faintly. His fingertips felt numb.

"Just a little bump on the head," his dad said. "Nothing serious."

Samuel let his hand fall to his lap. He looked at his little brother.

"Aki, you must be so bored right now," he said. "You didn't have to come."

"I'm fine," Aki said, absentmindedly playing with a rubber band he'd wrapped around the metal rungs of the bed.

An awkward silence hung in the air for a while. His dad straightened his back. Then he crossed his arms. Then he uncrossed them and cleared his throat.

"About that girl."

He crossed his hands, then pulled them apart as if he were caught praying.

"They want to ask you more about her."

Samuel looked at him. The last shreds of the consumed moon flashed in his mind. Maybe it was a face, after all.

"What girl?" he asked.

There had been eyes and a smile.

But that was data, not a memory. The memory had been gnawed away.

*

Samuel lived the good life.

He started high school and finally had some room to breathe—Jape and his gang of idiots were gone. He had always known that somewhere out there was a world brimming with freedom and better people. After high school he wanted to move out and didn't care where. The cubes of the Patteriniemi buildings were his prison, and the wind that blew from the sea still smelled of mud. Even their neighbor, old Grandma Huhtala, passed away. It was a world in its death throes.

Samuel moved out as soon as he turned eighteen. He wasn't accepted into a university, so instead he studied at a nursing school and graduated with a specialization in geriatrics. He had to do something to get away.

Others said it was his calling. Samuel knew how to interact with old people. He knew exactly what to tell them and how to exude kindness in those thirty seconds he could spare to chat in the corridors on frantically busy days. As the years turned into decades and beyond, he occasionally thought of his dad. They sometimes talked on the phone, but Samuel didn't go back home to see him. He held old people by the hand, people who had once laughed in the low glow of a summer night without giving death a single thought, and now Samuel was there to lead them from the unbearable pain into the unknown. He was there making amends.

The good life.

He met Krista at Harri's bachelor party, which had none of that gender-segregated bullshit or stupid, embarrassing stunts. They sat on the seashore late at night, Samuel demanding her phone number. He saw his dad at his own wedding for the first time in ages. He looked visibly older, confused and desperate to make up with Samuel. *What did I do to you?* his face seemed to ask, but that could've just been Samuel's guilt talking. When he hugged him, he tried to will the darkness that had developed between them to disappear, but instead it just grew. The darkness disgusted him. He could smell the sea in it. The mud mixed with clay that rose to the surface on those slow, gray, cloudy days whenever he'd gone for a swim in Suvikylä.

Then Aada was born. Samuel's world quaked as he held the small, wrapped creature who smelled of milky vomit in his arms. Then there was Iines. Now there was a family he had to take care of, people whose needs came before his, even if he sometimes made mistakes. Those rare hungover mornings were nothing compared to the inevitability of taking care of those who were helpless.

The good life.

Samuel watched his life through glass, as if he were peering into an incubator. He touched the cold, smooth surface where he hoped to find skin and warmth. Every night he woke up to make sure he had locked the door—sometimes two or three times during difficult times. Krista was a light sleeper and complained. Samuel claimed he didn't remember getting up. It felt good to say that, although he remembered his movements in the dark house the way people remember an inconsequential detail. He forced himself to remember the image of the moon from his window, along with the relief he'd felt when he could walk around without a care in the world, back when he had no responsibilities. The feeling that he didn't need to decide which was more important: making sure that the door didn't let anyone in, or that it would not let him out.

The good life meant that locks would never break.

But then that phone call came.

"Dad is—"

On the surface everything remained the same. The calendar on the break-room wall, with the Christmas party already marked down although the season was three months away. Someone in the ward asking him to call an elevator. His computer hummed. He needed to pee. The absentminded worry that the ache in his left eye was an onset of Horton's syndrome. The illusion of a parking garage where something irreversible would happen.

The locks opened.

Behind the door were approaching headlights. Like two moons.

LUCKY GIRL

The Inspector already saw from afar that he'd come too late. A police car was parked between the garages. A few natives circled it, sneaking glances toward the woods.

The Inspector parked away from the scene, took his briefcase from the trunk, and lit a cigarette. He took his time finishing the cigarette before he made the phone call.

"I'm here," he said. "A bit late."

He heard an unhappy huff from the other end of the line.

"Folks from the criminal-investigation unit or just some baggy pants?" the voice asked.

"The car belongs to baggy pants," the Inspector said. "Nobody else is here."

"Good. I'll call the Vaasa office—you just get those guys the hell away from there."

The Inspector hung up and crushed the cigarette under his heel. He took the long way round to the shore to avoid the relentless gaze of the natives. When he got to the foundation of the burned house, he stopped and signed a cross over his chest. He hadn't ever really enjoyed any of his assignments, but burning that man inside his little cabin had been exceptionally nasty. The Inspector stopped again at a small grave, where a little cross made out of old window siding read "Arvid" in cursive. The Inspector placed his hand on the mound, then continued on. As he pulled his wading boots on, he looked toward the island where two police officers loitered in their baggy blue coveralls. What a pity that the police these days looked like underdressed sewage workers. The Inspector's wading boots were lined with cashmere.

"Find anything?" the Inspector hollered as he approached the shore.

His boots didn't even get wet as he hopped from one rock to another.

A policewoman with a long ponytail turned to look at him. The other officer, a man, apparently hadn't heard the question. He continued to crouch in the reeds.

"And who are you?" the woman asked.

The male officer lifted his head above the reeds.

"One of you folks," the Inspector said and clambered onto the shore.

He knew his outfit would impress them. A tie and wading boots. A contradiction like that usually did the trick.

"What do you mean, 'one of you'?" the male officer asked.

He was now standing up. He waved his arms around like a boxer looking for action.

"I just came to tell you that this guy has been sighted elsewhere," the Inspector said.

The officers looked at each other.

"Where?" the woman asked.

"On the ferry to Sweden."

The Inspector lit another cigarette.

It was evident that his response wasn't satisfactory. He also noticed that the female officer dangled a rubber boot in her hand. That would cause some problems.

"Is this sighting confirmed?" she asked.

"Absolutely."

The officers looked at each other again. The cute little Sherlocks and Watsons of mundane crime. They were putting two and two together within the limits of their knowledge, pondering questions that were

beyond the reach of their consciousness, which was already too preoc-
cupied by questions like what to eat for breakfast and who should pick
the kids up from daycare. The Inspector wished they at least had the
balls to smoke cigarettes or get into fistfights at hot-dog stands outside
bars instead of hopping onto stationary bikes.

"But we were tipped off about this place," the male officer said.

"A taxi driver confirmed that he dropped the man off here," the
woman continued. "The driver had given him rubber boots."

Here we go. The hand holding on to the rubber boot shot up.

"Did he take off for the ferry without his left boot?"

A good question. This is probably how they managed to solve
crossword puzzles, too.

"He must've taken off in a hurry with one wet sock," the Inspector
said. "Hope he doesn't catch a cold. Anyway, the sighting was confirmed on Swedish waters, so we can wrap it up here."

Immediate resistance in their glaring faces. This used to be so easy.
Everyone just fell onto their knees like in some Shakespearean play.
There were no women back then, either. Just men in berets and pink
shirts too tight around their bellies. They were often hungover with
blood pressure through the roof, but at least they wore ties. This new
breed in their coveralls was unfamiliar.

"Apparently other people have recently gone missing around here,"
the woman said. "Last week they were looking for a teenage girl. And
before that . . ."

My, she had memorized a list.

"Is that so?" the Inspector said when the woman was done. "We
have a goddamned Bermuda Triangle here. But didn't that girl turn
up? And this man has now been seen elsewhere. He's singing ABBA
in a northern Swedish bar while we are here, racking our brains over a
single rubber boot."

The officers weren't budging. The setup was straight out of an old Western. Everyone waited to see who'd draw first. The Inspector turned to look at the villa.

He saw a woman standing in the upstairs window.

"What was your name again?" the male officer asked him.

The Inspector laughed and quickly looked away from the villa.

"Feel free to call your superiors if you don't believe me," he said.

"Who are you?" the female officer repeated.

"Just make that goddamned call so we can get this pissing contest over with."

Actually, they sometimes organized such contests in the days of berets and ties.

The Inspector relied on his stern gaze, trained to communicate years of experience. The situation was getting on his nerves, and the feeling was apparently mutual. He didn't dare to check whether the woman was gone from the window. After a long, silent debate, the female police officer dug a cell phone from one of her pockets and made the call. The Inspector took his wading boots off while he listened. Only the soles had gotten wet.

"What did they tell you?" he asked when she hung up.

No reply. Well, that was a reply, too.

"So it's all sorted, then," the Inspector said. "It was a pleasure meeting you."

Yet they still stood there glaring at each other, thinking about the rubber boots and other issues in their tiny worlds.

"Why are you here if he was seen in Sweden?" the woman asked.

"I'm only a messenger. I came to make sure your valuable time isn't wasted here."

The male officer's phone rang. Great timing. The Inspector snuffed the cigarette butt on the lawn with his heel. The caller's message appeared to be unambiguous, because the officer's only words were "Understood, understood."

After the phone call the female officer raised the rubber boot.

"What are we supposed to do with this?" she asked.

"Gosh, I don't know," the Inspector said. "Try hollering inside it. Who knows who'll holler back at you."

The male officer cursed, shoved the phone back into his pocket, and yanked the boot out of the woman's hand. It flew in a beautiful arc across the yard and landed crashing in the reeds.

The female officer was quiet, but her opinion on the matter was obvious on her face. They parted. Surely this incident would come up with their colleagues over a glass of beer or with their spouses. Let them have the pleasure. People would talk, but in the end they trusted that the officials always knew what they were doing. And they were correct. They knew what they were doing with the Bondorff family.

When the baggy pants had leapt their way across the bay toward new adventures, the Inspector turned back to the villa window. The woman was gone. He dialed a number. The phone was picked up immediately.

"There's someone else here," the Inspector said.

"Tell me."

"I saw a woman in the window."

Silence.

"Maybe it was that—"

"No," the Inspector interrupted. "They don't screw around during the daytime, especially if there are people around. You know that."

A longer silence.

"Go see what she's about," the other end of the line said. "I'll send the boys to the shore. They'll be there in thirty minutes."

The Inspector hung up and watched the empty window on the second floor. He lit another cigarette.

They weren't even sure of all the things that lay under the island, but they were sure whatever it was had to stay there. Special instructions for dealing with Bondorff Island were passed on from one retiring

Inspector to the next. The envelope had appeared on his desk twenty-three years ago. It was an easy area to patrol with good pay. Before this he hadn't been on an assignment where he had to obey so many prohibitions instead of taking action. Don't meddle. Be careful. We are not officially a part of this. So on and so forth.

The Inspector put out the cigarette, walked to the villa's door, and opened it. He listened for a second before stepping in. He saw only one way out from upstairs, so he decided to take his time downstairs first. He walked into the large living room, where he saw a movie projector and a box of film reels. Some were on the floor, but otherwise everything appeared normal. He checked the other rooms. Photo albums and diaries were lined up neatly on the shelves, exactly where they were supposed to be. The Inspector had sometimes browsed through the unsettling stories they contained. *Whoever wrote them was insane,* he thought, but you'd better not tell a black widow how to spin a web, his predecessor had told him.

The Inspector climbed the stairs to the second floor. He saw an open door and walked up to it.

"Hello," the Inspector said and knocked on the door frame.

A woman stood in the corner. She looked pretty nasty, and judging by the stains she'd been in the cellar. Not good.

"What are you doing here?" the Inspector asked and lowered his briefcase onto the floor.

The woman stared at him. Her hands appeared to be cramping. She squeezed her fingers one at a time.

"This is private property," he said.

The woman responded, but he couldn't tell what she said.

"Excuse me?"

"They didn't want me," she said.

The Inspector tried to come up with an appropriate answer.

"I see," he said.

"I knew them," the woman continued. "And they knew me. But they didn't even remember me."

What a loon. He walked closer.

"Anyway, you need to go now. Does anyone know you're here?"

The woman shook her head, staring into the distance.

"Have you called anyone?"

She didn't react, so the Inspector pulled on his rubber gloves and walked one step closer. The woman didn't resist when he felt through her coat pockets. She barely even noticed when the Inspector took her cell phone.

"All right," he said, bagged the phone, and placed it in his pocket. "We should be going now."

He led the woman by her arm down the stairs. That was the easy part. She didn't fight until they reached the front door. She kicked and struggled in his arms and tried to steal glances toward the cellar. The reception committee was already waiting at the shore when they walked out. Two men dressed for the outdoors, looking like friends or a gay couple on their morning run. One of them held a canvas bag. The Inspector greeted them and was glad to hand the woman off.

"I'm going back to make sure the place is clear," he said. "I should find one stiff, unless they took care of it themselves."

"All right," said the man crouching over the canvas bag. He tore open a packet that contained a syringe. The other man was talking to the woman in a calm voice while he felt around in her mouth with his rubber-gloved hands, and asked her to stick her tongue out.

The Inspector saw a third man beyond the reeds on the other shore. He loitered, nonchalantly observing his surroundings. But he touched his earbud constantly—the Inspector had to remember to talk to him about that.

"Everything is all right," the man inspecting the woman's mouth said and pulled the gloves off.

"She said they didn't want her," the Inspector said.

"Lucky girl."

When the woman had received her shot, the same man took his time splashing them both with a disinfectant.

"All clear," he then said.

The Inspector turned around and walked back into the house. He fetched his briefcase from upstairs and on his way out stopped at the stairs that led down to the cellar. He sighed. He looked over his shoulder toward the shore. Everyone else was already gone. That was quick, just like it was supposed to be.

He really did not want to take a single step toward the cellar, but this was an exceptional situation. He had to inspect what was down below. He announced his presence three times, then opened his briefcase and took out a gas mask, which he pulled over his head. He checked the fit and walked down the stairs. He opened the door and stopped before stepping through the doorway.

"Is everything all right down here?" he asked the darkness.

No answer. That was no surprise. The purpose of the question was to alert anyone hiding in the cellar to his arrival.

The Inspector waited for a moment before repeating the question.

He heard clothes rustle against the rocks.

"Good," he said then. "So everything is all right. It looks like the new Fisherman has settled in, and so on."

Shuffling in the darkness. Whispering. Then a man's voice.

"My name is Samuel."

"No names, please," the Inspector said. "We don't use names here." Special instructions, section four.

The gas-mask lenses had begun to fog up at the bottom. An old piece of crap the Inspector had been carrying in his briefcase without bothering to check its condition.

"Feel free to carry on—you won't be bothered anymore. Any questions?"

The darkness remained mute.

"Good. I'll be going then—"

"Have you seen it?"

The Inspector turned back toward the darkness.

"The Ever-Devourer."

Special instructions, section four: only ask what you need to know. Don't answer any questions.

"Just carry on as you have," the Inspector said. "Until next time."

Which hopefully would never come. He'd retire in five years. He'd throw a party where his guests would praise President Kekkonen's era and the golden days of the Soviet embassy on Tehdas Street and how things were so much better then.

"It's like a soul. It changes color when it's startled."

The Inspector didn't respond. He turned away from the voice and began to climb the stairs.

"Or when it gets mad."

That was a woman's voice. And it didn't come from behind him. It came from above. The Inspector looked up.

The light from outside had been blocked by a wavering shadow. His fogged lenses revealed a dark figure ahead. Matted hair, like a crow's nest. The strap of her dress had slipped off her right shoulder. He saw light through the holes in her hem. A tool hung from her hand. The Inspector had heard about it.

Special instructions, section two: always keep a distance of at least three meters, especially from the woman.

He slowly reached into his pocket for his stun gun. The woman was now descending the stairs. He held out the gun, but before he could react it was knocked out of his hands. Judging by the pain, his knuckles had been shattered with the blow. The Inspector grunted, more in disappointment than in pain. Another blow hit his shoulder. Now the Inspector howled in agony. His legs gave in. He fell backward and slid down the stairs. He tried to grab ahold of the door frame, but his fingers couldn't find the cellar door. He rolled through the doorway down into the darkness.

His consciousness became hazy.

Special instructions, section one: under no circumstances should you go into the cellar.

The Inspector tried to hold on to his gas mask as someone tried to yank it off his face. He didn't succeed. He swiped at the darkness, trying to find anything to hold on to, but his fingers didn't obey. He was dragged over sharp rocks somewhere deeper.

"You need to see it."

It was the man's voice this time, but the woman was there, too. The hatchet blade clattered along the rocks.

The Inspector could hear sloshing. The smell of the sea began to mix with something thick, something chemical.

Under no circumstances—

His palm touched a metal surface. Under any other circumstances the Inspector would not have touched the barrels, but now he felt for them with his fingers. But he couldn't hold on. He heard a metallic boom drifting away from him as a barrel teetered but did not fall over. His head hit a rock. The Inspector passed out.

*

"Look at it."

The woman's voice was right next to his ear. The Inspector realized he was sitting. He was propped up, the woman and the man holding him by his arms. His eyes were open, but all he saw was black.

Can they see in the dark? he wondered.

Pure black. Sloshing water. Nauseating stench.

Then he detected flickering colors. They were first barely visible, but they slowly formed a purple glow that began to form an unrecognizable shape as the color turned brighter.

When the Inspector realized that something large was coming at him, his lungs let out a sound he didn't recognize. The sight was incomparable to anything he'd ever seen before. He wasn't sure whether he should forget about his retirement party. There'd been no special instructions for this.

THE BLACK TONGUE

Maisa opened her eyes gradually.

A blue, cloudless sky. The scent from the sea. Not the muddy and stuffy smell of her childhood, but the scent of an open ocean. A genuine sea.

Maisa stretched her limbs. A gentle wind caressed her bare arms. She playfully blocked the sun with her palms, but its light was irresistible, breaking through her fingers. She gave up, yawned, stretched some more, and sat up.

The sea around her was pleasantly calm. She saw lazy, slow waves that only rarely turned foamy white. She leaned back past her towel, touching the hot fiberglass.

She saw an island ahead. It was overwhelmingly verdant, and the green slowly transformed into a sandy beach at its shore. Maisa smiled.

"Is that . . ." she started to say and looked over her shoulder.

The man behind the wheel stood at the edge of her vision. A figure waving in the wind.

"Bora-Bora," the man replied.

Maisa turned back toward the island and thought about the people hiding in its lush vegetation. She was privileged. There weren't many who could experience this. To wake up in the morning to this sight, to smell a real ocean around you, to feel a warm wind on your bare skin, and to look at a mysterious lushness, thoughts brimming with excited anticipation. Everyone should be allowed to feel this way, Maisa decided. Instead of making wrong choices, being born into the wrong family, into a stuffy apartment building where people spin evil stories in a bomb shelter like a spider's web.

Maisa kept her eyes on the mesmerizing shades of green, until they seemed to flow into her, an endless green light.

A man stood on the shore. She shaded her eyes and tried to focus.

He stood in the water and waved his arms in large arcs. He occasionally stopped waving and put his hands around his mouth. He appeared to shout into the wind.

"Are you seeing this?" Maisa asked and pointed at the man.

There was no reply. She turned around to ask again but didn't see anyone there. The wheel turned from left to right on its own.

How irresponsible. She should've shouted and told the man off, but it wasn't easy when she didn't know the captain's name. Maisa hooked her bikini top, jumped up, and struggled to find her balance for a second on the waves. They had indeed grown stronger. Or maybe the boat had already reached shallow waters, which made the waves feel worse. She wobbled over to the wheel and past it, to the stairs leading down to the cabin.

The stairs were hewn of stone. Why would a boat have stone stairs and a door made of rotten wood?

Maisa called out to the nameless man and descended the stairs. Her feet, warm from the sun, soaked in the icy coldness of the stone.

She opened the door.

A stuffy cellar. A man lying down in a fetal position. An almost bloodless purple appendage stuck out of his mouth, but it appeared to be too long to be a tongue. It looked more like an organ that had been vomited out.

Maisa shut the door and ran back onto the deck. She grabbed the wheel and tried to steer, but the waves kept on sending the boat toward the shore in an increasingly frantic motion.

The man waving at her from the shore had given up. He just stood there, observing the approaching boat. The sandy beach was gone. The lush greenery was gone. Only a rocky island remained, and a ransacked villa stood on its tallest hill like a shipwreck that had drifted ashore.

And the figure wasn't a man. It was a woman.

Clouds blocked the sun.

The wind picked up.

The woman's black dress billowed like a rag wrapped around a scarecrow. Its tatters spread around her, twisting in the wind.

The waves and the wind drowned her cackling, but there was no use hearing it, anyway. The woman tugged the boat toward the rocks like a raft made of reeds.

*

Maisa woke up without a start. She had grown numb to her nightmares.

She sat up on the edge of her bed and let her comforter fall to the floor.

"What is it now?" she asked her empty apartment.

It responded with the ringing of her cell phone.

Maisa groaned and looked at her watch. Ten thirty in the evening. Her medication had turned a night owl into an early sleeper. She'd be knocked out at nine, whether she liked it or not. And it was good. She was usually the first to arrive at the office now, often even before flextime began; so she had to remember to get up from her desk and sign herself in, then record the hours she'd already been at the office on a separate timesheet.

Maisa looked at the unknown number on the screen and answered.

"Hello?"

Static.

The hollow growl of the wind on the other end, like someone tearing into damp cardboard.

"Help."

Then silence.

Maisa waited for another phone call, but it never came. She looked at the clock and decided to go to work.

The next call came during business hours.

Maisa asked her client to wait a moment. She walked into the hallway and stood there in the air conditioner's hum. She pressed her ear to the phone. Fluorescent lights reflected off the floor.

"Hello?"

The torn roar of the wind. Then a voice.

"When will you be home?"

Maisa said the time.

"When will you be alone?"

She wasn't sure if the voice had been the same one that had asked for help, so she didn't say.

The caller hung up.

*

On her way home Maisa saw a reflection of herself in the optician's window. Her coat was puffed up by the wind. Her face looked like a white mask. The wind had released her hair from her hairpins, so it waved like black flames around a white core. She thought she looked like she was smiling, although her face didn't feel like it was.

The psychiatrist had asked her to not pay any attention. Many psychosis symptoms went away if patients just carried on with their lives. You just had to choose which observations you could trust and which you couldn't. Life made sense. But occasionally it could exhibit nonsensical things, too. Maisa should talk about the sensible things and scoff at nonsense. Only a psychiatrist should hear the latter.

The psychiatrist had asked her to describe the sensation that didn't allow her to sleep. It had been difficult, but she always tried.

"When I close my eyes, it's as if I start hearing voices immediately."

"What sort of voices?"

"It's hard to describe."

"Do you hear words?"

"Maybe."

"What kind of words?"

"I can't understand them. It's like listening to something in a foreign tongue."

The psychiatrist had asked her to give the sensation a name. Maisa had thought about it for a good while. Or rather, she had pretended to, because the answer had come to her immediately. It just felt so stupid.

"The black tongue."

The psychiatrist had been pleased.

"Let that language be whatever it is," the psychiatrist had said. "An unknown mother tongue that you do not even need to understand."

And Maisa let it be. One day it was easy. She was happy to realize that people were meant to sleep.

*

Maisa went to the store and bought oranges, which was unusual—she hated peeling fruit and the smell of citrus on her fingers.

As soon as she got home the phone rang. A voice on the other end said, "I'm here right now."

She didn't walk downstairs.

She turned the TV on and watched insects that seemed to be moving in ecstasy, although they were simply performing their everyday tasks without question. She could tell by the quick movements of their joints. They weren't working on a dissertation. Even these insects had learned that the dissertation should be left alone. Never even start working on one.

What she should do is sleep and stamp her time card.

Maisa fell asleep early.

The doorbell rang.

She looked toward the foyer and turned the TV down. She listened. The room was suddenly alive, full of objects and lights and shadows she'd never seen before.

The mail slot clinked.

"Are you alone?"

A whisper.

Maisa slowly, deliberately, got up from the couch and silently placed the remote control onto the coffee table. The hallway leading to the front door appeared longer than normal, like a tunnel. She waited for a beat, then walked up to the peephole. She decided to look through it, although all of her nerve endings were on fire and a flame burned in her belly.

She leaned forward.

You'll see a police officer through the peephole, but when you open the door there she'll be—

The mail-slot flap clinked again.

Maisa yelped. She knew the person on the other side of the door wasn't the one who had called for help. The thing standing behind the door was a psychosis and too much stress and twenty-four hours she'd mysteriously lost and a sick leave.

She backed away from the door, turned off all the lights, and did not sleep.

She went to work earlier than ever before.

*

What's wrong with me? Maisa wondered.

She wanted a degree and a husband and a child and a dog to show her father she could do it, then abandon it all.

Why did it have to be so difficult?

That night Maisa woke up from a dream and uttered a name.

"Sagal."

She wasn't supposed to think about her dissertation, but now Sagal had popped into her mind. Her face and her broken thumbnail.

She called the number that had placed the call for help.

It was picked up immediately.

They agreed to meet.

Easy.

*

Maisa arrived at the restaurant early. It was attached to the boating club, appropriately tucked away and rarely full. Still, she had begun to second-guess whether the place was suitable for a teenage girl. It was too adult. She hung around the front door and looked out through the old, wavy windows. She saw sailboats waltzing in the wind and felt their loneliness.

Then finally, Sagal was there.

Maisa opened the door and let the girl in. Her blue scarf was wet, and Maisa wanted to dry it immediately. She showed her to their table, fussing over her like an overprotective mother. She ordered their food and made sure there was no pork in it. Sagal smiled and snapped a picture of Maisa with her phone. The waiter joked about the table's condition: they'd had to put a piece of cardboard under a leg to keep it from tilting. When the waiter was gone Maisa apologized to Sagal.

"Why?" She smiled.

"Because I offended you. I wasn't well," Maisa said.

Sagal shrugged and smiled again.

Maisa got up and hugged Sagal, who didn't resist. She truly felt like a mother. They hugged for a while. The waiter probably saw them and didn't dare to bring their food out until she had returned to her seat. With the food in front of them, Sagal confessed that she'd never been to a restaurant before. Her mom had always cooked all their meals.

As they were leaving Sagal thanked Maisa outside the restaurant. She said that it had been the best day of her life but she had to go. Before Maisa could offer the girl a ride, Sagal was already running toward the bus stop. Maisa walked back to her car, happy. She started the car and decided to pick her up from the bus stop and give her a ride after all.

But when she drove past the bus stop, Sagal wasn't there. No one was there.

She stopped and called for the girl through the rolled-down window.

No reply.

Maisa turned the engine off and yelled louder.

That was when she woke up.

The doorbell.

Maisa wiped tears from her eyes, sat up on the edge of the sofa, and turned the TV off. She walked to the foyer and checked herself in the mirror. She thought about her job and logical things. Then she looked through the peephole. She could only see a sliver of a figure, twisted by the convex glass. Some blue fabric that made Maisa think about the police. She opened the door.

Sagal stood in the stairwell. She wore a dark-blue scarf and a green coat.

"How . . . nice to see you," Maisa managed to say.

She had already shaken off any drowsiness by the end of her sentence. What a surprise. Life was so set in its tracks these days.

"What time is it?"

Sagal just shrugged and smiled shyly.

"It doesn't matter," Maisa said. "I've just had a hard time and . . ."

She began to talk. She let her words flow, against her psychiatrist's advice to be careful what she told people. She didn't make any sense, but she didn't care. She was telling Sagal how she knew what it was like to be her age, although of course she didn't understand her cultural background and all the problems attached to it. She talked about responsibility and the guilt she'd been carrying, and how she never actually grew up, and how she was still the same teenage girl who in the '80s had cried watching movies or when her favorite band broke up, but now of course movies and music were different, and oh, my, what was she babbling on about because Sagal had also had a hard time. How was she doing?

The girl remained quiet and smiled.

The stairwell echoed with sudden rustling. Like sand crushed under a shoe.

"Did you bring a friend with you?" Maisa asked.

Sagal kept on smiling silently.

Maisa cracked the door open wider. It stopped before reaching the wall. She heard a metallic clang against the wooden door. She heard fabric shuffling on the floor. Or gasps. Like someone holding back tears.

"Who's there?" Maisa asked.

Or laughter.

Sagal shrugged.

The stairwell hummed. A familiar place. Things that made sense. Her dizziness was caused by her medication. A rocking movement, as if she were standing on a boat deck.

"Come on in," Maisa said.

The girl stood still. Or swayed. Surrounded by waves.

Just before the lights turned off and darkness filled the stairwell and all sensible things in it, Sagal Yusuf opened her mouth.

She stuck her tongue out.

ABOUT THE AUTHOR

Photo © 2011 Mikko Lehtimäki

Marko Hautala's unique blend of psychological thriller and realism has attracted readers of all genres, earning him a reputation as the Finnish Stephen King. His first novel, *Itsevalaisevat* (*The Self-Illuminated Ones*), received the Tiiliskivi Prize, and *Käärinliinat* (*Shrouds*) received the Kalevi Jäntti Literary Prize for young authors in 2010. *Unikoira* (*Seeing Eyes*) was nominated for the Young Aleksis Kivi Prize in 2013.

ABOUT THE TRANSLATOR

Photo © Kochun Hu

Jenni Salmi is a translator and localizer living in Seattle. She was born and raised in eastern Finland near the Russian border, where she learned English, Swedish, German, and Russian. After mostly forgetting the other languages, she earned her master's degree in English literature at the University of Eastern Finland in Joensuu. She's been putting the degree to good use ever since.